MW01491592

CAT DREAMING
A Story of Friendships and Second Chances

Stephanie
Schorow

Small Town Girl Publishing

Cover Design by: Alexios Saskalidis
www.facebook.com/187designz

Library of Congress Control Number: 2023948082
No part of this book may be reproduced or transmitted in any
form or by any means without written permission from the publisher.
For information please contact:
Small Town Girl Publishing
www.smalltowngirlpublishing.com
ISBN: 978-1-960226-09-9 Paperback
ISBN: 978-1-960226-11-2 Ebook

For my mother.

CHAPTER ONE

The Hospital
June 1989

Tina always told everyone the incident at the hospital was really Elektra's doing, even if she inwardly reasoned she might be somewhat responsible. They did drive there in Tina's battered Volkswagen bug, which chugged and wheezed as if it, too, wanted to be admitted, but it was Elektra who charged without hesitation through the revolving door into a swarm of starched coats and wrinkled scrubs. Tina followed, bracing for the smell of disinfectant as annoyingly insistent as those perfumed advertisement cards stuck into *Cosmopolitan*.

As usual, Elektra kept talking, her words running in meandering rivulets. Tina hardly listened; she was wondering what would happen if they were caught.

"This will work, Tina. I know it will work," Elektra said, huffing as they climbed the stairs to the third floor in an effort to avoid the elevator. "You just wait and see. Like this article I read in *People* or maybe *Time*. No, *People*."

"Yes, yes, you told me," Tina said, also breathing hard.

She wished Maureen was with them. Maureen, their editor at the *Stamford Gazette*, was their czarina of reality, whose Filofax schedule had been law for the past five years. Maureen, with her frizzy mane of hair, her hawk eyes, and nails like crimson talons, would have a better plan. But Elektra insisted they act immediately while Maureen was on deadline editing the next day's feature section.

Tina also wished Elektra hadn't dressed as if she was off to one of her celebrity feature interviews, with a baby-blue dress with flounces like icing on layer cake, a rhinestone choker, and navy pumps. Her aqua eye shadow glowed as if powered by neon. The worn strap of the bulging bag at her side plowed a furrow into her shoulder pad. Tina, by contrast, had carefully picked out black jeans and a dark T-shirt from a Bangles concert. Her Mets cap, pulled down over her forehead, hid a line of pimples that marched into formation at her temples, triggered by stress. Or guilt.

Elektra slowly opened the door to the third floor, peeked in, and then strode past the nursing station with Tina following. Elektra was reaching for the door handle to room 312, when an enraged yowl emerged from the bag and ricocheted through the hallway.

"Excuse me," a nurse called out from the station. At least, Tina thought this was a nurse. When she visited her grandmother in the hospital years ago, the nurses had worn little white hats. This one wore what looked like lime-green pajamas.

"What is in the bag there?" the nurse asked in a tone as crisp as over-baked cookies.

"Nothing," Elektra sang out. "We're just visiting our friend Sarah here."

Another yowl erupted.

"Excuse me," said the nurse walking toward them, a clipboard clutched to her chest like a breastplate. "You can't bring animals in here."

"Animals?" Elektra said. "Animals? We are trying to save a life."

"I'm sorry. You will have to take that out," said the nurse.

"You're sorry?" Elektra's tone was only slightly lower than the yowl. "We are trying to save our friend's life. What kind of a place is this? You're supposed to fix people here."

"Ma'am, I am going to have to ask you to leave with that

bag."

"This is a matter of life and death." Elektra's declaration triggered another piercing yowl. Tina tugged at Elektra's sleeve. "Fine, fine, fine. I'm going to drop this back in the car. Tina, give me the keys. I will meet you in the room."

Snatching the keys from Tina's toss, Elektra headed toward the elevator, muttering loudly, "I'm gonna talk to the doctor. I'm gonna to talk to the hospital president. And I'm gonna sue. I'm gonna sue a hospital that doesn't want its patients to get well." She jammed a middle finger on the elevator's down button, the door opened, and she stepped in. A muffled yowl marked her departure.

Tina turned to the nurse, who was watching the now empty hallway as if Elektra might materialize out of the air.

"I'm so sorry. Please understand, we're all upset about our friend," Tina said.

"That's no excuse for yelling at me," the nurse said, as she turned her focus on Tina.

"I know. I'm so, so sorry," Tina said. "We're here to see Sarah Gold. How is she doing?"

"She is in Room 312."

"No change?"

The nurse looked down at her clipboard and turned away. "You can go in. No animals allowed." Tina meekly turned and walked into the room.

Next to Sarah's bed, the roses in the vase of flowers had already faded to the color of a bruise while the lone sunflower dropped its head as if exhausted. The cuts on Sarah's face were fainter, but her eyes were still closed, her narrow face pallid and her short red hair like matted straw on the pillow. Yesterday, when they rushed to the hospital after the doctors said they could visit, Tina, Elektra, and Maureen took turns talking to Sarah, holding her hand, stroking her forehead. They couldn't get more than a flicker of an eyelash, and a sigh.

Tina wasn't sure what to do now. Should she start talking? Tell Sarah what she thought about Maddie and David in the *Moonlighting* finale? Or how terribly sorry she was that she hadn't realized something was wrong? When they met some weeks ago for a long-postponed run, Sarah looked gaunt and her usually trim hair resembled an overgrown lawn. But Sarah insisted she was really over the breakup. She was just exhausted from overnight shifts at the Associated Press. "I'm fine," she said, dabbing her eyes with the sleeve of her jersey. "Just tired."

Tina now thought she should have pressed Sarah for more details – had she heard from Cole at all? Wasn't it time to move on? Hadn't Sarah often remarked Cole was "just another cowboy?"

In the hospital room, Tina watched the rise and fall of Sarah's chest under the sheets, the silence punctuated only by electronic beeps. She jumped when Maureen marched in, clad in her Donna Karan power-suit with Nike running shoes, the florid scent of Giorgio wafting alongside her.

"Hey," said Maureen, looking around as she slung her briefcase on the floor. "Where's Elektra?"

"Oh, well, she got kicked out."

Maureen did not seem surprised. "What happened?"

"She, ah, read this article about a boy who was in a coma. One day his parents brought in the family dog and the boy woke up. So Elektra thought this might work with a cat."

"Let me guess – she brought Carrington."

"Uh huh. We almost made it, but the nurse caught us."

Tina waited for Maureen to explode. But Maureen just shrugged. "It's not a bad idea. I'd want my Hercules next to me if I were sick."

"I can't sleep without the cats beside me," Tina said, relieved Maureen was not upset about the scheme.

"That's what I don't get," said Maureen. "She wouldn't want to leave Carrington like this, right? It had to be an accident. I can't believe she drove into that, whadda you call it, abutment, on purpose? It was an accident, right? She was getting over Cole. She was okay. Right?"

"I think so," Tina said, cautiously. Maureen rarely asked for confirmation. "She wouldn't do this to us."

"No, she wouldn't. No. I don't think so."

"I got the cop reporter to get me the accident report. It was pretty vague: Victim exiting Merritt Parkway about 4 a.m., lost control, struck an abutment broadside. No alcohol or drugs. Something like that. But it doesn't make any sense. What was she doing on the Merritt in the middle of the night?"

"I don't know," said Tina. "I don't get it. Unless..." Tina paused, but Maureen didn't notice.

"She looks like she's just asleep," Maureen went on, turning to look at Sarah. "She always had this theory about cats and why they sleep so much. She said they don't really sleep. They are in another state of reality. She called it cat dreaming."

Tina knew about cat dreaming. Sarah told her about it years ago when they were midway through a bottle of chardonnay and a carton of General Gau's chicken.

"When I got Carrington, actually she was a stray who adopted me, I couldn't believe how much she slept," Sarah said, gesturing with chopsticks in one hand, and a wine glass in the other. "I had to call Maureen to ask if this was normal. I decided she wasn't asleep; she was cat dreaming."

Cat dreaming, Sarah had explained, was a state between consciousness and sleep, both lucid and hazy. In cat dreaming, cats chase mice, birds, fish or leaves endlessly and effortlessly. Yarn hangs from the sky, feathers drift from the ceiling, tiny rubber balls never escape under the dresser out of reach. Cats can prowl along mossy trails, across alleys, through bushes and closets and screen doors. That's why cats sleep so much. They weren't sleeping; they were cat dreaming. "Isn't that right, Carrie?" Sarah said, turning to the tortoiseshell cat perched nearby.

"Cat dreaming crosses between human and feline," Sarah continued, half closing her eyes and setting down her wine glass. "Sometimes, when Carrington is curled up beside me at night, I find myself dreaming of running through alleys and streets, chasing something always a bit out of reach. Yet I am somewhere where everything is as it should be, a calm place filled with possibilities. Sometimes, I catch a flash of black and gold. Something furry is prowling the shadowy landscape of my sleep. 'Carrington,' I call. 'Carrie, come here. Come back.'"

"Does she obey?" Tina had asked, downing the last of her wine.

Sarah just grinned and reached for the wine bottle. "As much as she ever does."

Now, as Maureen perused the chart hanging on Sarah's bed, Tina began to say something more about cat dreaming when from outside the hospital room came a voice singing "Amazing Grace" off-key.

With a clatter of heels, Elektra tripped in, her coat flung over her arm. "'… and now I'm found…' Here we are. Oh hello, Mo. Oh my God, this is such a riot. You wouldn't believe what I had to go through. I had to sing all the way."

"You didn't," Maureen said.

"I did, I did, I did."

From under her coat, she produced a squirming cat.

"Oh my God," Tina said. "Carrington!"

"Let's get her on the bed. Quick!" said Elektra, her voice ecstatic.

Carrington had other ideas. She leaped to the floor and darted under the bed. The three women dropped to their knees to peer under it.

"This might not be a good idea," Tina said.

"It's a great idea," Elektra snapped. "She's just scared."

"No. I would say she's terrified," Maureen snapped back.

"Let's just get her on the bed," said Elektra.

"But the nurse, someone, might come in," said Tina, trying to reach under the bed. "Here, Carrie, kitty, kitty, kitty."

"Forget the nurse. This will work."

They could hear footsteps. "Start singing," Elektra hissed. They all leapt to their feet. "Amazing Grace, how sweet the sound …"

The nurse stuck her head in, clipboard at her hip. "Everything all right?" she said, her eyes sweeping over the room, and making a hard pause on Elektra.

"We're just singing hymns for our friend," Maureen said, using her editor's voice, a commanding tone dreaded by writers who filed their copy past the deadline.

"Sarah sings in our church choir," Tina added. "We thought this might help wake her up."

"Well, okay, but please keep your voices down."

"Yes ma'am," said Tina, nodding vigorously, as the nurse withdrew.

"Oh yeah," said Maureen. "Sarah Gold was the frigging star of the Baptist church choir."

"It just came to me," Tina said.

"It was brilliant," said Elektra. She knelt down again, crawled halfway under the bed and managed to pull out a hissing cat. "Carrie, don't be scared. Here you go." She set Carrington on the bed. Carrington immediately made a break for the floor. This time Tina caught her before she could get away. Lifting her gently, she set her next to Sarah and stroked her back. Carrington flattened herself on the bed, her tail lashing the sheets, staring with hard yellow eyes at the three women. As the women watched and Tina stroked her, Carrington's tail stopped moving. She dropped her head to rest on her paws.

"Now what?" said Maureen.

"Now we wait," said Elektra, starting to hum again.

Tina and Maureen remained on alert. Elektra sang softly, "…that saved a wench like me."

"It's 'wretch like me,'" Maureen said. "Let's go over this again. Sarah was really getting over the breakup, right?"

"Oh yes," Elektra said. "It's been a long time."

"She was doing fine, I mean, she was still sad but she was okay," Tina said, thinking maybe Sarah had really not been okay. "She said she was taking it day by day, you know. Like quitting cigarettes or drinking. She told me she just said she would not call him today. And the next day, not today. That is what she said. And she didn't. At least, I don't think so. She would have told us, right?"

"I should have done something," Maureen said. "I really should have done something more." Tina saw a shadow of fear or guilt pass over her editor's face.

"She loved that bastard," Elektra said.

"Maybe," said Maureen. "Not sure it was love. He didn't treat her right; he was never there for her. I tried to tell her."

"He told Sarah he didn't want to get married again, twice was enough," Tina said. "And there was his son. That was always the issue."

"But she did break it off," said Elektra. "She did. Finally."

"So this is just an accident, right?" Maureen asked.

Tina shook her head. Elektra shrugged.

The women were silent, watching Sarah and keeping an eye on Carrington.

"I don't know if Sarah is coming back," Tina murmured. "I don't know where she is. She has to want to come back."

"She will, she will. Carrington will bring her back," Elektra said.

"I just don't know," said Maureen, her voice breaking. "I don't know what else to do." Tina looked up in alarm – why did Maureen's voice sound so guilty?

"Just wait. Carrington can do this," Elektra said and started humming again.

Maybe Elektra is right, Tina thought. The cat was still, her yellow eyes moving from Tina to Elektra to Maureen. She picked up her head, sniffed, and shifted to press herself against Sarah's side. As Elektra hummed and Maureen leafed through her Filofax, Tina leaned over the bed and said, as softly as she could, "Come back." She looked at Sarah's face. Was that a ghost of a smile? A flutter of the eyelids? No. There was nothing. She is lost, Tina thought. She is lost to us, lost in cat dreaming.

CHAPTER TWO

The World's Best Fake News Writer of 1984

WORDS WIELD AN uncanny power. Tina learned this before the incident at the hospital and even long before she met Maureen, Sarah, and Elektra and became a reporter. Words had authority. A spoken word was more than a puff of air exiting the mouth. Words shaped reality. Her given name might be Christiana Delores Montgomery but she was always called Tina. That sound, like a tinkling bell or a trickle of cool water, shaped her life growing up in a sleepy Ohio town.

As a child, Tina believed that the naming of fearful things brought them under control. She named the monster in the closet Brugger and the one under her bed Bagger. When she thought of them as Brugger and Bagger, they were not as scary. When she prepared to go to bed, she would say, "Brugger! Bagger! Begone!" What she could name, she could face. What she could speak, she could handle. Like her complexion.

Beginning in her teens, Tina started each morning by drawing upon an inventory of the names she concocted to ease the anxiety of the mirror. She assembled a full complement of labels ready to use like silverware in a drawer. She would lock the bathroom door, turn to her reflection, and evaluate her face with steely military detachment. It might be (oh lucky day) just a bouquet of Pimplets in the crescent around the nostril. Or one or two classic Nubbies peeking out from under her bangs, snakes in the grass. Niblets just above her upper lip could be disguised with Cover Girl Peony Blush lipstick. There might be a Thunder Dome, huge, and volatile but with the right pressure, deflated, a slash of irritation easily covered with foundation. Worst of the worst were Sweat Bombs, gradually rising pods, hard as dried peas, which did not yield to pressure until they cast shadows over the rest of her face. They were dangerous; apply pressure too soon and the formation turned an angry red, its height difficult to cover up. They would heal to a thin, furious line, which would only disappear slowly. Tina lived in dread of Sweat Bombs.

Her mother said her complexion would clear up eventually and bought every kind of acne treatment on the market. "Darling, too much makeup just makes it worse. You have to trust me. Your face will clear up. No, you don't need plastic surgery. All your blemishes heal without scars. You should be glad you're blessed with oily skin. Maybe you could just try to stay away from French fries and chocolate."

Staying away from French fries in her hometown, where McDonald's was a twice weekly dining experience, was impossible. So while she waited for her mother's words to come true, Tina conducted daily inventory. She'd say softly to herself, as she applied astringent, there are just two Pimplets and just one healing Nubbie, no Sweat Bombs, no Thunder Domes today. Each eruption required its own form of attack, its own tactical maneuver, from a caress of Noxzema to swabs of astringent to potshots of Clearasil. Tina saw herself as a general of her face, even if a hapless soldier in life.

Tina remembered key events by the state of her complexion. On the day she graduated from high school, she had a Sweat Bomb; she kept one hand on her chin during the ceremony. When she pledged Tri Delta in her freshman year, she had two Nubbies and a Pimplet slathered over with foundation. On her first date with Greg, she had one lone Niblet and she didn't notice when Greg kissed away the lipstick covering it. Not then. Not ever.

Acne was one of the two demons pursuing Tina. When Tina reached sixth grade, she became plump, not exactly fat, but rounded. Even as pimples sprouted like evil mushrooms on her forehead, her body inflated like two beach balls balanced atop each other. Mortified by her complexion and her girth, she found it easy to slip into the role of a quiet fat girl who tagged along with the cadre of more popular girls. She was the chubby one in the rear who added harmony to the gossip chorus. The other girls liked having her as backup. "I'm everyone's best buddy" is what she told herself in the mirror during inventory.

In college she was accepted at the Tri Delta sorority and became everyone's "confidant," a more refined, elegant expression. She listened as her sisters poured out stories of conquest and woe with the guys in their life, wishing she had something to add but glad to be included in the conversation.

Then in her junior year she met Greg.

Greg had chestnut hair which fell restlessly across his murky eyes. He was not tall, only about five-foot-eight, but he loomed over Tina who topped five-foot-two. He seemed constantly in motion even when sitting, his feet tapping out a code, his fingers curling and uncurling around his cigarette.

He singled Tina out at a dorm party and enthralled her with his talk of Strindberg, Ibsen and Beckett. Words, he said as she vigorously nodded, were tools and weapons, arrows and darts, not pretty little pastels in a bowl to be admired. He, like Tina, was an English major, but he also took acting classes and was frequently in college productions, usually playing the hero's sidekick or the villain.

They began to meet for pizza and beer on Friday and Saturday nights, often in a group of theater students. After a night of numerous beers, Tina woke up in his dorm room; her roommate congratulated her on losing her virginity and took her to the campus health center for birth control pills. Greg told her sex would improve her complexion; even Tina knew that could not be true, but the cure became increasingly attractive. In Greg's bed, with the lights off, Tina found herself in another country with her face in darkness and hands that stroked her belly and breasts, approving of her soft flesh. Tina sat in the front row for all of Greg's productions and accompanied him to cast parties where she watched in awe as he kept a crowd in stitches with his dead-on imitations of fellow actors. He would catch her eye every now and then as if to say, "Isn't this fun?" She would wink back.

He was, she believed, the only one who would ever love a fat, pimply girl like her. He was going to be a famous playwright and she was going to be his muse. She would edit his plays (as she sometimes typed his papers) and listen to him practice dialogue. He would work as a waiter and she would work as a secretary while they waited for Broadway or Hollywood to call. He was a bright comet and he would take her on his trip around the sun.

When he graduated a year before Tina, Greg insisted she finish her senior year while he moved to Los Angeles to pitch a screenplay he was writing. They went to Los Angeles together to help him find an apartment and found a cheap place, small but filled with light. At night while he slept, she would sit by the window bathed in the hot air and think of how she had finally left small-town Ohio and how she was ready for an exotic adventure with the man she loved.

When she went back to college in the fall, she and Greg talked every week by phone and wrote weekly. Tina wrote long letters and treasured the postcards Greg sent, a view of Hollywood or of Sunset Boulevard, with a pithy observation scrawled on the back. And even when she couldn't reach him by phone, he would have an amusing story when she did finally reach him. Tales of near misses with celebrities and the agent who eventually agreed to meet him. She made plans to visit him during Thanksgiving break her senior year, dreaming of driving with him along palm-lined highways and waking up in a bedroom with turquoise and coral walls.

On a Saturday in early November, Tina stepped away from the mirror, pleased with the morning complexion review. With a rush of joy, she saw she would have a pimple-free day. Just then one of her sorority sisters called out to tell her Greg was on the hall phone. She was delighted. They would make arrangements for her trip.

"We have to talk," he said. He talked, while Tina was silent. It was time they went their separate ways, he said. His life was going in other directions. They would always be friends. She would always have a special place in his heart. He just needed his space.

"What happened?" Tina could barely speak. "What did I do? What can I do?"

Greg cleared his throat. "We will always be friends."

"Did you meet someone?"

"We will always be friends."

Tina hung up the phone and returned to the mirror. Tears were soaking her shirt and something was wrong with her face. Her skin was clear, but there was something else. Her eyes were hollow as a cave. "Brugger! Bagger! Begone," she whispered. Her reflection stayed distorted, both blurred and sharp as a needle. She needed to find a word. "Broken," she breathed. "I am broken."

She turned away and quit eating. It was not a conscious decision and she never felt famished or satiated. Life was on hold, from hunger to sleep, classes, and friendship. Tina simply shrank. Her sorority sisters first applauded her willpower, then she began to hear them whispering in hushed tones around her. Finally one took her aside in the bathroom and made her look at herself in the mirror. "You are way too thin. Greg was a jerk." Tina now had another word: Jerk. Greg was a jerk. She learned through classmates he was dating an actress. When she looked into the mirror, past her hollow face, she imagined she saw Greg's actress, a tall, thin, raven-haired goddess with perfect skin and a smug smile. "Jealousy," she said and felt a pang of hunger.

Even when she started to nibble food, it seemed something remained broken inside her, and her body held on to the damage for the rest of her senior year. Her sorority sisters told her she was a slender slip of a woman with pale blue eyes and corn-silk blonde hair. They said men turned to look at her in the street. They told her she was still oh so thin. But in the mirror, Tina saw a little fat girl with bad skin.

Tina majored in English with the idea of "writing" some-day perhaps like Greg but not, of course, at his level. She wrote A+ level English papers and dutifully kept a journal that she threw away after Greg used it as a plate for a slice of pizza and the grease thoroughly soaked it. She had always read a lot, even books Greg hadn't recommended. She hadn't put much thought into a career, after all she was going to move to California or New York to be the muse of a famous writer.

She graduated college in borrowed clothes, as nothing fit her anymore. Her mother, usually reassuring and cheerful, told her she was still too thin and begged her to come back home. Tina, however, decided she would move to New York City, be-cause that's where writers lived. At her mom's insistence, she moved to Stamford, a city just across the New York border. Her mother had an old friend who lived with her husband in an apartment in a large complex just blocks from downtown and the train station. The couple was traveling abroad for a year and were happy to help out. Tina didn't have to buy furniture, not even bed sheets. Instead she bought a used Volkswagen and drove East.

Stamford first awed Tina. The grandiose office buildings lining the main boulevard declared this suburb could grapple with the Big Apple for power and prestige. A large mall dominated the downtown, the red brick exterior encapsulating storefronts glittering with promise. Tina began to notice, however, Stamford's streets had few pedestrians and at night the city turned gloomy and menacing. Passersby rushed to find safety in the mall or in the few restaurants fronting the main streets. One was Mahoney's Pub, which breathed out the scent of grease and beer every time someone opened the door. Tina began to see how the lower floors of those grand granite buildings lacked windows as if the structures were fortresses designed to ward off barbarians in the streets. Inside, the mall promised retail paradise, but from the outside it offered a great brick blob. The real promise of Stamford, Tina soon decided, was New York City was only an hour train ride away.

Tina wasn't quite sure where to start her writing career, so she found a job as waitress at Mahoney's Pub, where she took orders for Buds and burgers from men in ragged jeans and for white wine and broiled chicken from well-dressed couples – her boss called them yuppies. She worked mostly nights and hung out in the Stamford library where she could read all the region's papers in a well-lit room with worn leather chairs. She found a new word, a new label: Reporter.

She had always read her local newspaper growing up, but now she read the *New York Times*, the *Daily News*, the *Post*, *Newsday*, the *Norwalk Hour*, and the *Stamford Gazette*. She read the news and features, but she also surreptitiously did the crossword puzzles, read her horoscope, and followed Doonesbury, Brenda Starr, and Bloom County. She copied recipes, even if she never cooked anything. She read about crime and mayoral races; she devoured movie reviews and interviews with Hollywood royalty. She read about White House intrigue, Reagan's Star Wars defense systems and terror in Beirut. Newspapers were a buffet – you didn't know what you wanted until you turned the page and picked something. After several months, she thought I could write this stuff. And after another week, she thought, I want to write this stuff.

Tina soon realized she faced a conundrum. To apply for a job as a reporter, even on a small paper, she needed stories, clips, as they were called. But without working on a paper, she had no clips. She was politely told by the *Norwalk Hour,* which advertised for an opening, no journals and college English papers were not acceptable clips. What? No writing for the school paper? Sorry. No clips no job, no job no clips.

On her days off from the restaurant, Tina took the train into New York, walking through the neighborhoods, feeling like a bit of smoke, her still-new slenderness aiding the sensation she was transparent and windborne. She never had a plan, she simply wandered Manhattan, its bustle filling the blank slate of her thoughts. The passing aftershave of bankers, the aroma of sizzling meat from the street vendors, the reek of garbage carelessly piled at the curb, all this served to enforce the reality she was actually still alive.

She would have never noticed the print shop, a small storefront among other small storefronts, except for the sign, "Writer Wanted. Inquire Inside." Even then she might have just walked on, but she lingered too long trying to see what was inside, and what it could possibly have to do with writing.

"If you're going to come in, come in," someone barked as he opened the store door. "I don't bite."

Startled, Tina looked up and saw mostly hair. A beard resembling a nest of twigs, a lank ponytail, bushy eyebrows. Watery eyes behind smudged wire-rim glasses. Randy Cohen. The store owner.

For the next half hour, Tina listened politely as Randy launched into an explanation of what the writing job entailed. First, he had to tell her he was an old Commie, something he liked to declare loudly, even to the Suits, his term for the yuppies coming in for print work. He grew up in New York, left for the Coast to be a screenwriter, wed and shed three wives and returned decades later to take care of aging parents. Randy took over their print shop business, renaming it Red Ink, both to reflect his ideology and his financial condition. He expounded on all this to a puzzled Tina, as she perched on an ink-spotted chair.

Red Ink could have been just another print shop, but Randy explained he had a specialty that brought him calls from TV directors, Broadway producers, and Hollywood filmmakers, often at midnight. His last assistant helped him with this work, but he had made the mistake of sleeping with her (so he candidly told Tina, reassuring her that she would not have this problem, which made her nervously rearrange her bangs over a couple of Niblets). The assistant had quit in a huff because he refused to get cable TV, another plot by fascists to make workers pay for things that should be free.

"Look here," he said to Tina as he handed her the front page of a newspaper. It was the front page of the *New York Post* and Tina's first thought was how did I miss this?

FRIEND OR FOE?

ALIEN SPACECRAFT LANDS IN CENTRAL PARK

was splashed across the top, above a photo of a saucer-shaped spaceship. She realized the front page was a fake but it was perfect, with lottery numbers, weather and index. The paper even smelled of the dingy tang of a tabloid.

Tina read the lead story:

In what could be an invasion or a friendly visit from the beyond, an alien spacecraft landed in Central Park today about 5 a.m.

The craft was immediately surrounded by police and National Guardsmen, and thus far has remained closed and quiet. "We are waiting to see what happens," a source said. "I mean, do you walk up to a flying saucer and knock?"

The President called for the public to remain calm, saying the aliens have shown no overt signs of hostility.

Continued on Page 6.

She looked up at Randy who was grinning like a proud parent. "That is hot off the press," he said. "Special order from the director Spielsport or Spielsburger, something like that."

"It looks so real," said Tina hesitantly. It was the right thing to say.

"Exactly," Randy roared. "You can read the story. It's all there. Look at these." And he started pulling out other newspapers, some yellowed with age. There were front pages from newspapers from all over the world, *New York Times*, *Paris Tribune*, *London Times* and those with odd titles: *The McCaw Express*, the *Ossining Free Press*. Most had huge headlines: House of Horrors Defendant on Trial; Congress Bans Mutant Marriages; Victory for Allied Forces.

Randy continued. "No one touches our work on newspaper props. You look closely at some of the crap passing for props on TV today. It's mimeographed junk. Sure, they got the headlines but look closely and you see the text is just garbled, nonsense in three columns. We don't just do a prop. We do a newspaper."

Tina thought of the movie "Citizen Kane" and its "FRAUD AT POLLS!" headline. Had there been text under that iconic splash?

"Some say you can't read the print when it flashes on the movie screen. They're wrong. A real newspaper makes the movie real. When I worked in Hollywood, we knew a thing or two about getting the attention of the audience. Those capitalist pigs don't understand, all they can see are the dollar signs. We are proud of what we do here. I need someone to help write these stories. How's your grammar and spelling?"

"Good," said Tina.

"That's what we need here. And, of course, help out in the shop. Can you start tomorrow?"

That is how in 1984, Tina became the World's Best Writer of Fake News.

For the next year, Tina reported on plagues of killer snakes, the abduction of the President's daughter, the alleged suicide of a corrupt mayor, the giant tidal wave that engulfed London, and the earthquake that destroyed California. She still worked some nights at Mahoney's, but during the day she filled the copy machines with toner and worked on the terminals at the back of the shop, while Randy wrangled with a Suit about Reaganomics as the Suit placed an order for brochures. She got very good at "covering" trials, filling her stories with quotes from self-righteous prosecutors and angry defense attorneys, based on the real news stories she read. Sometimes she had to concoct an entire day of news for a full newspaper. The big stories carried her byline.

Randy would look through her work and print the final product, saving one for his records and one for Tina, before he sent the rest to California or Broadway. "This is a great clip," he would say, looking over "Wall Street Tumbles" and Tina would dutifully fold it and bring it home, wondering what kind of editor would consider hiring someone who wrote a story about "Mega Sharks Menace Cape Cod" or "Superman Convicted of Air Traffic Violations."

That editor turned out to be Maureen O'Malley, features editor of the *Stamford Gazette*.

CHAPTER THREE

Meeting Ms. O'Malley

THE STAMFORD GAZETTE occupied a squat red brick building near the train station. A billboard on top proclaimed: The *Gazette* Tells You Like It Is. Tina walked warily into the front door as if at any moment a security guard would haul her away for fraud. The sleepy man at the front desk just waved her toward the escalator when she said she was there to see the features editor. Tina had sent in a job application as a bit of a lark to the *Gazette* after seeing an ad for "Very, very creative and hard-working feature writer wanted" in *Editor & Publisher*. She had included samples of her Red Ink articles with her cover letter, figuring at least the editor would get a laugh. She described herself as enterprising and indefatigable, a word she checked for spelling twice in her dictionary to ensure absolute accuracy. She thought she would come up with words other than "creative" and "hard working." To her surprise, she received a call from the features editor asking her to come in for an interview.

Perhaps due to a sleepless night, Tina's face had it all: Niblets, two Nubbies, one Thunder Dome and what could be the start of a Sweat Bomb. She was tense, imagining any second the editor would stop mid-sentence and say, "I just can't deal with a face like yours."

Tina stepped onto a rumbling escalator, which deposited her at a long hallway with large photos, methodically lining the wall. Ahead of her was a sign for "Newsroom" over a double door. Someone had written on a Post-it note above it, "Abandon Hope All Ye That Enter Here." Someone else had crossed out "That" and written "Who." She pushed her way through the double doors into an open space, filled with desks arranged in crooked rows. Most were piled high with newspapers and folders that leaned like fortresses about to fall in battle. When Tina politely asked a man at the nearest desk where she could find Maureen O'Malley, he sighed with exasperation. "I'm not the receptionist, you know. I wish they would explain that. She's over there," and he jerked his thumb over his shoulder.

"Are you Tina?" came a voice from a slender woman in a miniskirt with short red hair, who was walking toward her.

"Yes, how do you do, Ms. O'Malley," Tina said quickly.

"Oh, I'm not her. My name is Sarah Gold, and I'm a features copy editor. I'll take you to her desk. We're supposed to escort people up, but the guards sometimes forget," said the woman. "Follow me."

Tina followed the woman as she weaved through the maze of desks, each with computer terminals with sickly lizard-green letters on a murky background. People were hunched over plank-thick keyboards or talking into phones or headphones. One man was leaning back in his chair with an unlit cigarette in his hand. "So let me get this straight," she heard him say into the phone cradled on his shoulder as she passed by. Tina thought they were headed to one of the small, glassed-in offices around the room's perimeter, but they stopped at one of the larger desks, where a woman was talking loudly into the phone cradled on her shoulder. She motioned for Tina to sit, and nodded at the other woman, who said softly, "Good luck," and disappeared. Tina slid into the dingy chair and waited.

Everything about Maureen O'Malley was emphatic, her height, her solid figure, her mass of chestnut hair framing a square face with porcelain skin. Her blazer had shoulder pads with the heft of submarine sandwiches, her nails were gleaming ovals of scarlet, and a green and coral scarf was wrapped precisely around her neck. "Okay, okay, Elektra. Yeah, that's fine. Let's say you get this in by Tuesday morning. All right? Good." She hung up the phone with a thud, and muttered, "Actually the deadline is Wednesday but she doesn't need to know that," and turned to Tina.

"Hi, I'm Maureen O'Malley," said Maureen, thrusting out manicured fingers to engulf Tina's small hand. "Thanks for coming in. I have your clips here… somewhere," and piles of paper seemed to shift maniacally on the desk. "Ah yes, here we are. Let's see. Loved your story on 'Martians Found on Moon.' "

"Ah well," said Tina. "For the movie, 'Shell-shocked'. As I tried to explain…"

"Yes," said Maureen, with a flip of her red-tipped fingers. "You did explain about the print shop. You really have a way with words, you know. And, by God, if Martians were discovered on the moon, these are exactly the questions you'd ask NASA. And of course, you'd get a quote from Ray Bradbury. Exactly."

"Thank you," said Tina.

"Of course, not everyone would recognize the creativity and excellent writing here," Maureen said, as her hands reined in her scarf which had attempted to drift out of position. "But not everyone wants – demands – creativity from reporters. Some editors would just bypass this. They would see non-conventional clips, yada yada. But I always look deeper."

"You need clips to get clips," Tina said.

"Who, what, where, when, why. Anyone can learn that. But to describe Armageddon. That takes imagination." Maureen held up a copy of Tina's *New York Daily News* front page: "This Is The End."

"I love this! The pathos. The dark humor. What would it be like to put out a daily paper when a comet is on a collision course with Earth? I knew right away you were an excellent writer. So why do you want to work for the Gazette? We're just mere earthlings here." Maureen laughed uproariously.

"I really hope to break into the newspaper business," Tina said.

"Perfect! What I want in this position is a fresh approach, new ideas, new ways of writing. We are going to make the feature pages pop out. None of this 'women's pages' junk anymore. We want the water cooler talk stories, even though we don't actually have a water cooler. Like defining a Miami Vice dress code for Connecticut Yankees. Or an expose about taking away Vanessa Williams' Miss America crown because of a few nude photos. That's just fucking unfair, excuse my French. Subway shooter Bernie Goetz: hero or a thug? You know what I mean."

"Sounds great," said Tina, who wondered how she would ever come up with an idea that wasn't a movie prop.

"You're indefatigable. I love that word. True?"

"Hard working," said Tina. "And creative."

"Love it! So," said Maureen. "Are you up for a tryout here?"

"Sure," said Tina, who wasn't at all sure. But they talked more and agreed Tina would come in the next week. Even as Maureen shook her hand goodbye, her other hand was reaching for the phone.

A few days later, Tina found herself staring at an implacable enemy: a blank computer screen. Words that had come so easily when she wrote for Randy Cohen were gone, gone, poof. She felt like she was digging into a handbag, probing to find the hard edge of keys she knew were in there but could not reach. She tapped her fingers on the thick squares of the keyboard. The screen was a chasm, dark with a greenish tinge and a relentlessly blinking cursor. Greg's face came back, more fearful than Brugger and Bagger. He was the writer. He had been the master of words. The only cliché she had ever heard from him was, "We'll always be friends." For the tenth time, Tina picked up her notebook, filled with observations and quotes from "Paranoia: The Last Look Back to 1984," an art exhibit, which she had been sent to cover.

The show had been staged in a Stamford warehouse, accessible only by a freight elevator. Tina had to wait until someone came down to go up. On the third floor, she stepped into a large room, illuminated by throbbing red lights. Paintings had been hung on bare-board walls or pushed under ragged couches where they had to be pulled out to view. Chairs and tables were painted as well; the tables were black and white on top and you were supposed to crawl underneath, sliding like a sardine into the circle of other viewers to see the bright globs of paint underneath. Other pieces were made of irregular wooden boards spray painted with neon colors and decorated with bits of steel wool and plastic dolls heads. They had titles like "Emotional Weapon," "Big Brother's Panties," and "Newspeak Spoken Here."

Both the crowd and the artist wore black and sipped glasses of pale wine. The artist, who called herself G. Gotham, stood out with her eyes circled in black like a raccoon, and a fake razor blade, colored red and studded with rhinestones, on a chain around her neck nestling precariously between her breasts. She projected aloofness, greeting well-wishers with a cool half smile. When Tina introduced herself as a writer from the *Gazette*, those raccoon eyes fixed on her and Ms. Gotham poured out a stream of thoughts on art, censorship, and media mind control. Tina struggled to jot down the exact words.

So she had it. She had it all. Quotes. Descriptions. Comments from the art dealer who called Gotham's work "A seething indictment of alienated culture" and the guy (he was cute) who said it was a load of dribble but the booze was free. She paged through her notebook again. The cursor blinked, relentless, impatient. And then she wrote one sentence. And then another: the who, the what, the where, the when, the why. Then another sentence. She was typing, backspacing, erasing, typing.

Sarah Gold wandered by and leaned over her shoulder to ask, "How are you doing?" Tina pointed at the screen and Sarah bent forward to examine the screen.

"Hmm," she said, one eyebrow rising above the other. The energy drained from Tina, a balloon deflating. Then Sarah said, pointing to the fourth paragraph, "I think your lead is here. That's your first paragraph. That's the most interesting. Come back to the details later." Sarah turned and walked away, and Tina stared at the screen, the words blurring.

She thought of the articles she wrote for the movie newspapers, the stories that had to sizzle on the screen and reveal in a flash of type what the hype was about. With the copy and paste function – how much easier than a typewriter! – she moved the paragraph Sarah had liked to the beginning. And began again. Fingers moving hesitantly on the keyboard. Then faster. When she finally pressed save, she messaged Maureen (Sarah had shown her how to do this): "Slug: 1984ArtShow in features Q."

Maureen hated it. That's what Tina thought at first when the editor called her over and showed her the edits she had made. Crosshatches now marked the copy like the ragged stitches on the Frankenstein monster's face. But Maureen said, and Tina would never forget this, storing it like a miniature photo in a locket, "Not bad for a first story. So tomorrow I have something else for you to cover."

At six the next morning, Tina scampered to the corner drugstore and leafed through the *Gazette*. She found her name on page 31, the front of the feature section, under the headline: "George Orwell Meets G. Gotham and It's Paranoia at First Sight." She looked through another paper as if she couldn't believe her name would appear more than once. She bought five copies.

Three weeks later, Randy was actually gracious when Tina said she had found a job as a feature writer in Stamford. He ranted for only ten minutes about fascist newspaper publishers and how they exploited reporters. As a parting gift, he gave her a certificate declaring Tina the "Best Fake News Writer Ever." Maureen later insisted Tina get it framed.

A few months later, when Tina was shopping in New York, she decided to drop in at the print shop with some real clips to show Randy. A sleek fern bar was in its place. No one there seemed to know anything about Red Ink and Randy Cohen.

CHAPTER FOUR

Elektra Shock Therapy

THAT ELEKTRA PAPADOPOULOS talked too much was apparent to Tina immediately after they started hanging out together. She knew because Elektra said it herself. "I talk too much, yeah, yeah, but there's so much to say. I'm making up for my childhood when I wasn't allowed to talk at all and I think I have enough time deposited in my conversation account. Hey, that's an idea. Conversation accounts, you get so much time to talk. That could be an article!" She was a mutt from a mutt house in New Jersey, she told Tina. Her Greek father had died when she was six, the youngest of three daughters, and her mother had remarried a divorced Italian with two boys. Everyone always spoke at once at the dinner table.

"I started calling it the Mutt House 'cause everyone was always woofing and howling about something." Growing up in Asbury Park, she was Ellen Bellucci but when she decided to leave New Jersey and move to New York, she had a fight with her stepfather and decided to change her first name to Elektra and use Papadopoulos again.

Elektra spoke in torrents of words that left Tina feeling as if she was sitting by a roaring stream. Tina was happy to just listen. She was exhausted from daily feature assignments and reeling from trying to grasp the often illogical but necessary rules of Associated Press style.

Tina first met Elektra at a meeting called by Maureen who wanted her freelance writers to meet Tina and plan for the coming year. Everyone would come to the office at 5 o'clock,

Maureen would have pizza and soda for all. The freelance critics filtered in, marble-hard eyes on Tina, who was wondering if writing about invading extraterrestrials really qualified her as a reporter more than writing about theater, opera, art, and film. All the freelancers had hoped to be hired full time, but Maureen made it clear that writing about opera was not a full-time job. Nor was writing about theater. Theater critic Leticia A. Frank was particularly miffed, but she seemed to brush off the slight as another example of how so many dolts were insufficiently educated in and knowledgeable about the tradition, power, and grandeur of the theater. Leticia plopped her generously appointed body, smothered by what looked like a leopard print tent, into a chair and glared at the shaggy haired rock critic, smelling of cigarettes and wearing a fraying leather coat, seated next to her. He reminded Tina of Greg, with his quick movements and eyes that flitted from person to person. Tina could sense him evaluating her and determining she was not worth fucking and therefore not worth speaking to.

William, a features copy editor, walked into the meeting with a folded *Wall Street Journal* under his arm, and a bowtie perched below his chin. Tina would later learn he had been a philosophy major at Harvard who thought he could dabble in journalism until he finished his novel. Sarah appeared and smiled at Tina in a friendly, but distracted way. Tina could see the rock critic looking shrewdly at Sarah's legs and tight jean skirt as if they were a band he was supposed to review.

When Elektra rushed in last, the atmosphere lightened. "You would not believe the traffic. Oh my gawd," she announced, heaving a huge bag on the table.

"This is Elektra, who does features and celebrity interviews," Maureen said, her gaze softening. Tina was fixated by Elektra's smooth olive skin and frothy hair; a cascade of raven curls brushed her shoulders and flowed over her forehead. Her lips were slathered with cherry red and her azure-lidded eyes danced around the table, joyously acknowledging the other writers.

Maureen began the meeting by declaring that the features section was going to rival the *Times* in depth and quality. The movie critic interrupted to say she hadn't had a raise in a year, and then the rock critic asked if he could smoke, and Leticia said she would leave if she had to breathe second-hand smoke, and the art critic said he saw at least two typos in his last column. Tina admired how Maureen adroitly complimented and herded the writers at the same time, until finally everyone was discussing what they would do for the next six months.

At one point, William cleared his throat and Maureen turned to look at him, which silenced the other writers. "I think we really need to do some kind of feature story on AIDS," he said. When Maureen frowned, he quickly added, "I know that news has been covering this and the medical reporter has done some stories, but I think features should take a look at its impact on the arts."

"You know the joke: what's the worst thing about getting AIDS? Convincing your parents you're Haitian," said the rock critic, triggering general laughter. Tina noticed neither William nor Sarah smiled.

"Well, it's a good idea," said Maureen. "Anyone interested?"

The room was quiet. And then Tina spoke up. "I could work on this; I've been reading a lot about the issue."

Maureen frowned again. "That's a pretty big topic when you're just getting started."

"I can help out," Sarah said. "William and I can pull out a lot of contacts for her."

"All right, go ahead," said Maureen, as Tina wondered what she had gotten herself into. "And now, what are we going to do about Madonna and her 'Like a Virgin' hit? Is this sacrilegious or just silly?"

When the meeting ended and the writers filed out, Elektra bounced up to Tina. "Welcome, welcome. You'll like Maureen, she's a great editor. She really, really helped me when I first started. Sarah can be spacey but she has great ideas and she knows AP style backwards and forward. William is okay, even if he looks goofy with that stupid tie but he saved my butt when I misspelled Chappaquiddick. I spelled it Chappyquickdick. Can you believe it?"

"How do you like interviewing celebrities?" Tina asked when Elektra paused to pull out her lipstick. Turns out "celebrity" was a loose term. Even small newspapers were besieged by public relations representatives pushing for features on up-and-coming musicians, book authors on tour, and actors and actresses who appeared at the Stamford Center for the Arts. Elektra specialized in these interviews. She had interviewed Paul Newman and Joanne Woodward. "They were dolls." Christopher Walken was spooky. When she interviewed David McCallum, "I totally embarrassed him because I was such a *Man from U.N.C.L.E.* fan and he wants to live that down." By this time, they were outside the newspaper office and Elektra suggested they go for a drink.

If Maureen was emphatic, Elektra was vivid with her bright dresses, eyeshadow and skyscraper heels. "Oh my gawd, you wouldn't believe it. It was hysterical," was the equivalent of the connector "So then," in Elektra's rapid parlance.

Over drinks that night and subsequent nights, Elektra told stories of growing up in New Jersey, and working as a secretary in Manhattan. At one office she was given a new typewriter even though the old one was perfectly fine. Then she could not get the new IBM to work and she picked it up and threw it across the room. "And oh my gawd, you wouldn't believe how heavy those things are and then it turns out it wasn't plugged in, and needless to say, I was not going to that office anymore, but the girls gave me a farewell party and I kicked back three rum and cokes and got up on the bar to do a go-go dance. It was hysterical." At the next job, she remembered to plug in the IBM machine but forgot Mr. Andersonville drank his coffee black, Mr. Bernstein drank his coffee with one pack of sugar, and Mr. Beauregard required two packs of sugar in his tea. "I mean, how the hell could anyone keep that straight?"

Neither of Elektra's sisters had gone to college. They were expected to party and then settle down with a husband and start a family. Her brothers would enter the family's restaurant business – the hard choice was Greek or Italian. Something never felt quite right to Elektra about those options. "I liked hanging out with my girlfriends but they all started getting married and I just never stayed with anyone long enough to get a ring. Guys were all wham, bam, thank you ma'am. They all wanted blow jobs but go down on a woman for more than thirty seconds? Forget it."

She decided to move to Bridgeport and attend Connecticut Community College, working as a waitress to get through school and sharing an apartment with roommates. "I didn't know what I wanted but they asked for a major and I just put down writing because I didn't think you could major in reading. And then this English professor, such a nice lady, told me my essay on fake Greek food was hilarious. It *was* funny, I have to say. She said it should go into the campus newspaper. And then I wrote another piece on trying to acid-wash jeans myself and how to use a Sony Walkman."

She moved to a cheap studio apartment in Stamford, started working for Maureen, and continued to pitch stories to local newspapers and magazines. "Once I stood on a street corner with a sign, 'Will Write For Food.' I didn't get an assignment but some guy asked me to dinner and another guy gave me $5."

There was nothing Elektra wouldn't write about. When a bus driver saw her running for a stop and ignored her, she wrote about how simple courtesy was dead. She turned her pining over a lost love into an erotic story she sent to *Hustler*. "But there was too much plot and not enough fucking," she admitted. Both she and her girlfriend Kathy ended up spending the night with a guy on his boat and then they ran into him in a bar and he wouldn't speak to them and she drank her wine down to minimum impact and maximum effect and threw it in his face. This became another erotic story for *Hustler*, and apparently the plot-to-fucking ratio was right because they bought it. She was always pitching magazine stories about the life of a carefree single woman.

Lately, though, she was writing lots of freelance articles for Maureen. "Maureen scared the bejesus out of me at first," Elektra said. "But she is the best editor." Maureen, she said, realized Elektra's fearlessness was an asset when she was assigned to do celebrity interviews. Even if Elektra talked a lot, she would listen with even more intensity, fixing her large dark eyes, with their sapphire lids, on her subject's face, encouraging celebrities to spill their stories. Her speech patterns screamed New Jersey, but her writing style was pure Manhattan.

Tina let herself drift in Elektra's bends and loops of conversation. Bruised by Greg's rejection, Tina was warmed by Elektra's tales of date and toss: This one snored too much. This one was too cheap. This one had a mole on his penis, which was too distracting during blow jobs. Elektra picked and chose and never looked back. "And then I fell in love! It changed my life. I never knew how much love could do for me."

"Who was the guy?"

Not a guy. A little brown and white cat that a co-worker was giving away.

"She was white with a large brown patch. So I called her Sundae. You know, vanilla ice cream and chocolate. Oh my gawd, it was like she knew we were meant to be together. You wouldn't believe it, but she saved my life."

One night, she was out in the city with friends. "These guys started buying us drinks and when it was closing time, they said, come to our place and party and do some coke. We said no, it's getting late, but then we were going to go. This guy was rubbing my back and we got in a cab and then I thought of my Sundae, all alone and crying for her dinner. I screamed to stop the cab and I jumped out and they said what are you doing and I said I have to get home to my cat. The men all laughed. But I left and then my friends jumped out after me."

"How did that save your life?"

"Because those guys were bad news. I found out later. One of my friends met a girl in a bar who got raped by them. She had gone to their apartment and they all jumped her when she passed out. She woke up stark naked and bruised. And she couldn't go to the police because, you know, they would just say she went to their apartment and what did she expect. If it weren't for Sundae, that could have been me."

"She sounds like a lovely cat."

Elektra's face twisted; a change as sudden as a clap of thunder. "She was my sweet darling and one day she stopped eating. The vet said her heart was failing and I spent hundreds but they couldn't save her." Elektra began sobbing as Tina, flustered, didn't know what to say. Elektra grabbed a napkin and dabbed at her eyes, leaving swaths of blue and black on the paper.

"I know, I know," said Tina. "When our dog was hit by a car, I was heartbroken."

"Sundae was my angel."

"Did you ever think about getting another cat?"

Elektra took a deep breath. "So there was this guy I met

and he was gorgeous but he turned out to be such a loser. He worked at a garage and I met him there one night and we were going out to some concert and I heard a sound. 'What is that?' I say. 'Oh, we found some kittens here.' 'Oh, where are they,' I say. 'We put them in the dumpster.' 'You put them in the dumpster!' And he goes, 'Yeah, who wants cats around?' And I shriek at him, 'You son of a bitch, where are they?' And he pointed and I leapt into the dumpster, you should have seen what I did to my nylons and I was yelling get a box, get a box. I found the little kittens and got them in a box. I started to go and he says, where are you going? I'm going home to feed these kittens, and he says, what about the concert? And I say fuck the concert, you son of bitch kitten killer and I took off.

"I got the kittens home and got them to start eating. I mean it was karma, wasn't it? Sundae saved my life and now I saved their lives."

"So you have one of them?"

"Three cats," said Elektra cheerfully. "My three babies."

CHAPTER FIVE

Maureen's Deadline

THE DAY AFTER the features meeting, Maureen was navigating the morning traffic to the *Gazette* office; the commute gave her twenty minutes with Howard Stern on the radio, which was enough. She recalled with satisfaction Tina's work, the girl had a gift; she just didn't even realize it. But Maureen would step in and nurture Tina as she had all her other writers. She thought about Tina's blonde hair and slight frame. "I bet she eats so slowly. That's why she is so nice and thin. God, I'm such a horse. Hey, I'm driving here!" She leaned on the horn, gunning the battered Toyota through the yellow light, muttering, "I'm gonna be late."

She wasn't actually late. Indeed, she was never late because she hated to be late. Lateness was laziness. Time on the road, when not at her desk, not on the phone, was wasted time. Her father had been keenly aware of time. He taught Maureen the importance of getting things done when they needed to get done. He liked to say he never missed a deadline. Which was odd, because he was almost always late coming home from the newsroom to the harsh glare of his wife's disapproval. Maureen and her brother, James, didn't care that he was late. Dad would tell them the details about the latest mob murder or anti-war protest which he covered that day as a reporter and columnist at the *Boston Herald-American*. Even at home, he had a radio turned on day and night to pick up police broadcasts.

Throughout her life, whenever Maureen heard the wail of a siren, she thought of her father. She could see him, cigarette dangling from his mouth, steering the station wagon with one hand, coffee cup in the other, chasing the sound. When she scratched behind Hercules's ear at night, the cat's bulk sprawled across her lap, she thought of how her father was the one responsible for convincing her mother decades ago to let her and her brother keep the kitten that they found in the alley behind their Somerville triple decker. Since then, except for her college years, she had always had a cat in her life. She always knew she wanted to work for a newspaper like he did, and studiously ignored her mother's frequent, and often fierce, suggestions that she should think about another line of work.

Even though her father had died when she was a junior in high school, his presence remained a visceral sensation well into her thirties. When she walked into the *Gazette* newsroom, she could see him at one of the desks, battering loudly on the steel blue Smith Corona he loved.

He had experienced chest pains at dinner and her mother rushed him to the hospital. Maureen believed him when he said after his discharge that not even a heart attack could stop him from being a reporter. He did request an extended leave from the paper to recover. A couple months later, the day after Maureen proudly told him she had been made editor of the high school newspaper, he fell asleep in an easy chair watching TV, the police radio on in the background, and never woke up. Maureen was certain it wasn't the long nights and pressure that eventually stopped his heart. No, she insisted, he died from having to stay home, having to stay away from the newsroom when so much was happening. A blaze that killed nine firemen. Battles over busing. The stabbing of a Harvard student in a red light district. That's what broke his heart, Maureen knew.

Maureen intended to major in journalism but she planned to get out of staid old Boston, with its regional prejudices and decaying downtown. She loved her mother but she wanted to escape the mental cold-water showers that her mother believed it was her duty to pour on Maureen's ambition to be a reporter like her father. When she was accepted into Northwestern University's Medill School of Journalism just outside Chicago, she visited her father's grave to tell him.

In a sophomore English class on "Childhood Classics Revisited," Maureen wrote a paper on "Class Prejudice and Social Warfare in *The Secret Garden*." Another student, Sarah Gold, examined "J.R.R. Tolkien's Visions of Utopia." Students were asked to present their papers in front of the class. Maureen had never read any Tolkien and doodled on her notebook when Sarah talked about the Undying Lands and the Valar, but Sarah had adored both *The Secret Garden* and *A Little Princess* and resented any rebuke of her favorites. She accused Maureen of inappropriately projecting radical feminism. Maureen insisted Sarah was applying a false narrative of social realism. They argued. The class woke up, and the professor was pleased.

The next semester, in another English class they battled over *Pride and Prejudice*. Maureen defended Jane Austen as a proto-feminist, a savagely critical and astute observer of human nature. Sarah dismissed Austen as a defender of conventional patriarchal conformity because nothing ever really happened in an Austen novel except girl meets boy and girl gets boy and everyone marries.

"Marriage should not be the sole object of a woman's life," she declared.

"Of course not," Maureen retorted. "You just don't get the context of the era." This time the professor cut them off, but they continued arguing after class, waving their papers. "If you want a heroine, read *The House of Mirth*," Sarah said. "Lily Bart preferred death to a stupid marriage."

"I think Lily was the ultimate silly woman," Maureen replied.

Noticing all the red marks on Maureen's paper, Sarah flaunted her own clear copy, saying, with a smirk, "At least I know how to spell."

Although embarrassed, Maureen shot back. "If you're so damn good, then come to work for the *Daily Northwestern*," she said. "The campus paper needs good copy editors. Come on, put yourself to the test." Sarah looked startled. She said she would drop by. To Maureen's surprise, she did.

By the time Maureen became the editor of the *Daily*, Sarah was her second in command. Maureen trusted Sarah with her deepest, darkest secret. Maureen was not a great speller. She could spot errors in other people's copy from across the room, but when going over her own writing, she missed so many misspellings and typos that another editor said Maureen could not even see i before e. Sarah's superb editing skills were often put to the test by Maureen's copy. Maureen watched with a touch of envy as the lean, lithe Sarah turned heads. Sarah seemed to always attract a heartsick lover, guys whose puppy eyes would follow her as she moved around the newsroom. But Maureen noticed Sarah had stopped speaking up in class. She was still a killer on the copy desk, but as their senior year progressed, Sarah became quieter. She seemed increasingly stunned by campus life.

In a long night of talk over cheap wine and saltines, Sarah confessed how she longed for the tone of authority Maureen interjected in her every sentence, even when ordering pizza toppings.

"You know what you want and when you want it. I'm getting more and more flustered," Sarah said. "This summer I went to California to visit my high school friend, you know, Jasmine Woo."

"Yeah, her mom was black and her father Asian, right?"

"Well, they separated. Jasmine told me. She didn't seem

too upset. And anyway, Jasmine was living in this group home and it seemed really cool at first, but it was kind of creepy the way the guys seemed to pick a different girl to sleep with every night. Jaz told me not to be so uptight, but…" and Sarah stuffed another cracker in her mouth. "Anyway, I wasn't into it and Jaz got upset with me for being, oh bourgeois or something like that. I mean, everyone was so, so smelly. It just kind of got on my nerves. This guy was pressuring me and I lied and said I had my period. He told me I was frigid and to get over myself. I kind of just left the next day and I haven't talked to Jaz since. I get it, marriage is a trap and all that, I mean I would die before ending up like my parents. They really should divorce. But there has to be another way. And I'm bummed about Jaz. We were really close."

"I really didn't have any close girlfriends in high school," Maureen said. "Just boyfriends."

"Jasmine and I got really stoned before our prom," said Sarah. "Speaking of which," and she pulled out a joint.

They continued to talk until they both fell asleep on Maureen's bed.

After graduation, they wrote to each other weekly for the first year. "Dear Space Jock," Maureen would write. "Dear Bossy Bitch," Sarah would respond. Then the letters trickled away.

Without her back-up editor, Maureen gave up reporting to be a newsroom editor. She toiled at several regional papers in the Midwest and then jumped on an opening for a features editor at a small but prestigious Connecticut daily, the *Stamford Gazette*. Now she would build her empire.

She hired, honed, and polished a cadre of part-time freelance critics who shuddered with fear and pleasure at the sound of her voice on the phone when she called to make an assignment. She recruited Terry, the restaurant critic, Jeff, the rock critic, Frances, the art critic, and Leticia A. Frank, the theater critic, who once complained her byline was misspelled when the "A." was accidentally left out of her name. She brought in a talkative creative spirit from New Jersey, Elektra Papadopoulos, who made up in enthusiasm what she lacked in polish. She fought for a full-time assistant editor and lured Sarah, who was then working for the Dallas office of the Associated Press, to Stamford.

Maureen found directing freelancers was a lot like dealing with cats. They were temperamental, territorial, ferocious but loyal and endlessly creative with their tales of why a deadline was so hard to meet. Yet she, Maureen, could get them in line. And now, she had Tina. Her empire was complete. The newspaper's top editors would finally recognize her ability. Twice before she had been passed up for promotion in favor of Bob from the copy desk, and Taylor, brought in from *Newsday*. Taylor was considered a wunderkind by the editor and, coincidentally, the nephew of the publisher. She shrugged it off, and pressed on, knowing she would succeed eventually. She would do it for her dad.

Even as she waited for recognition, her gaze went south, to New York City, toward the Holy Grail, *The New York Times*. Someday, she promised herself she would move from the minors to the majors. Someday, Maureen told Sarah she would get a job at the *Times* and they could share a big apartment in the city. This had to happen soon, she insisted. She encouraged Sarah to apply to the AP headquarters in New York. Sarah said she would think about it. "You're the one with the deadline," she told Maureen.

CHAPTER SIX

The Lost Kingdom of Arianna

IF SARAH PROTECTED Maureen from embarrassment from a misspelled word, Maureen defended Sarah's dreamy, sometimes decidedly unworldly, demeanor that didn't blend easily into a newsroom even if she was a sharp wordsmith. Maureen attributed Sarah's quixotic aura to those ridiculous fantasy and science fiction books she was always reading. Such a waste of time.

Sarah flicked off Maureen's disdain with placid composure, saying Maureen should really give Ursula K. Le Guin a chance. Only decades later, when they were living in Stamford, did she explain to Maureen about how as a child she created her own world that seemed more real than anything in her actual life. The far, fair land of Arianna had been her refuge as a child and then became something more over the years.

Sarah could still picture herself in her childhood bedroom, the closed door muffling her parents' arguments, with Arianna spread before her in a landscape of exploration, danger, and acceptance.

The crystal towers of Arianna were nestled along the Roaring River, the Thick Forest on one side, the Clever Cliffs on the other. Snap-a-Birds hung from their beaks on the cliffs, taking off in undulating flights into the valley. There, among the Bombillo trees, lived trolls with bulging brown eyes and purple hair, Sir Dragonette, a three-foot high dragon, tiny but fierce, and the magical Star Horse, who streaked like a meteor across the sky. The people of Arianna lived in square houses, cut out from milk cartons, nestled in the trees. All the citizens gathered at the white towers for celebrations or to hear the goddess Athena who ruled the kingdom from atop her bed with wisdom and benevolence. Until mom poked her head into the bedroom to yell, "Sarah! Didn't you hear me? Time for dinner." And a tidal wave would consume Arianna, sweeping the kingdom into a box pushed under the bed.

Sarah Gold remembered her childhood as one filled with dread and ferocious joy. Her father gave her books that lined her bookshelves; her mother quizzed her every day about her homework and complained about her messy room, tangled hair, and muddy shoes. Her sister, who was five years older, mostly ignored her.

When Sarah's parents fought, they flung words like grenades; it didn't matter if shrapnel hit Sarah or her sister. On the rare days when they were not fighting, the house seemed tilted, as if on a precipice waiting for a landslide. The family lived in a suburb, a false little place with a cheerful, welcoming face on the outside and a hard nut of resentment inside. Still, their neighborhood was beautifully landscaped. Large elm trees shaded orderly streets and tulips were planted with precision on traffic islands. Sarah's home was on a cul-de-sac with large stucco houses, each with emerald swaths of grass in the front and backyards hidden by tall fences. None of the kids in the neighborhood played on the front lawns. Everyone hung out in the alley behind the houses, preferring to hit baseballs and play tag on the rough concrete and gravel rather than risk the ire of grownups who fertilized and clipped the lawns. The alley was better anyway. The Roths had put up a basketball rim on their back driveway and didn't mind the chalk marks for hopscotch and the occasional baseball sailing into their yard. Sarah always found someone to play with since the boys let her on their teams once she showed them how fast she could run.

If no one was around, she would just hang out by herself bouncing one of her mother's tennis balls against the Roth's garage door, thump, catch, thump, catch. Anything to stay out of the house where the tension floated like dust motes. Sarah was allowed to walk to the library by herself. She read books about the Greek myths and the Oz series and one day the librarian put *The Lion, the Witch and the Wardrobe* in her hands. That led to the rest of the Narnia books, *The Last Unicorn, The Hobbit, The Lord of the Rings* and then science fiction and other books her sister ridiculed. At night when the parents fought, Sarah would close the door to her room and go to Arianna. Her charm bracelets became Snap-a-Birds, which hung by their beaks, their clasps, from cliffs or slightly open drawers. She put out a glass unicorn missing a leg, a rubber dragon, a plastic wolf with a chewed-off tail, and her collection of trolls with their glass eyes and fluffy hair. A tarnished pony pin became the Star Horse, guardian of the kingdom.

Her mother did not want any pets in the house, not even a parakeet. Sarah collected miniature china cats and they roamed through the kingdom. Tales were spun and spun again with different endings. Eventually, the Five Sisters of the Stars, separated at birth, found each other in the evil Kingdom of Katunna where lived the Warrior and her horse, the Martyr and her dove, the Seductress and her snake, the Gardener and her wolf, and the Thief and her cat. Banding together they escaped and traveled to Arianna where they became the Queens of the Realm, great and good and elusive as God himself. Together they had a child, who would become the Princess of Arianna.

Walking to school each day, Sarah was watchful. Someday she would find a way into the secret garden, a tunnel to Narnia, a bridge to Oz, or a ship to Middle Earth. She kept her eyes on the ground, eyes primed for the half-buried key, the gold ring, the stone marked with runes. She passed through childhood, waiting to be spirited away. What did this world matter? There were worlds within worlds, a closet with a portal, a phantom tollbooth, a mysterious road, a mirror that flowed into liquid when you pressed on it. Sarah knew one day she would speak the spell, find the door, match the key, and find herself in the elsewhere, and her real life would begin.

She grew out of that expectation in high school when she started hanging out with Jasmine Woo. Jasmine wore tie-dye dresses she made herself and went to peace marches with her parents. She confidently flirted with boys mesmerized by her long, ebony hair and dark eyes. She showed Sarah how to roll a joint and how to ask older guys outside liquor stores to buy them Boone's Farm.

In history class, the students, led by Jasmine, argued with the teacher about Vietnam and Cambodia. In English class, Sarah read Virginia Woolf, Fitzgerald, Faulkner, and Hemingway but, encouraged by Jasmine, she plunged into *Stranger in a Strange Land, In Watermelon Sugar, Cat's Cradle*, and *Slaughterhouse-Five*.

Sarah was recruited to both the track team and volleyball team where she got the nickname Space Cadet for her tendency to daydream during the coach's pep talks. The name morphed into Spike Cadet after Sarah developed a ferocious focus when playing close to the net.

Sarah also hung out with the school's basketball team since she could outshoot them in pick-up games. She cut her hair short one day to annoy her mother. With Jasmine, she skipped classes and joined the other kids who snuck out to smoke in the gully behind the school. Being high loosened her tongue, she found herself explaining to stoned dudes about the clues to Paul's death in Beatles lyrics, how UFOs might be visitors from the future, and the meaning of "grok." Girls giggled, but the guys would say, "Oh wow," as she sat crossed legged, tugging on her short skirt over her tights. Being high helped to dissolve the veil between the worlds. Arianna faded and was replaced by something resembling the landscape of the Yellow Submarine, where women wore flowers in their hair and longhaired musicians sang of peace and love.

Then the coach caught her and Jasmine toking before a game, and she got kicked off the volleyball team. She left with a shrug. She told her parents she now hated volleyball and had quit the team.

Sarah decided she would major in literature in college; to her surprise, her mother approved of English majors. She said she had been one and it was a good safe choice before getting married. Sarah told her she was never getting married; what good was it? Couples just fought all the time. Her mother retorted, "This is your father's fault" before storming away. Armed with high SAT scores, Sarah was accepted at Northwestern University, said goodbye to Jasmine, who was taking time off to work for George McGovern for president and who declared if Nixon were re-elected, she was moving to a commune in California.

Sarah left home without cleaning her room. When she visited during the Christmas break, she found her mother had pulled the box out from under her bed and thrown out Arianna.

CHAPTER SEVEN

Introducing the Cats

ELEKTRA'S CATS WERE named Sugar Pie, Sammy, and Eddie. Maureen had a cat named Hercules. Sarah had a cat named Carrington. Tina learned all this on the first night the four of them went out together, some months after she was hired. Maureen wanted to have dinner at this new Italian place and needed Elektra's help. Maureen had her doubts it was real Italian food; there were white sauces on the menu. Was that Italian? She wanted to taste more than one dish. So she rounded up Elektra, Sarah, and Tina, and they met at the place after work on Thursday. After Maureen and Elektra drilled the waiter with questions, the place was deemed to be Italian, but not red-sauce American Italian. They ordered four dishes, plus appetizers, and circled the plates around the table.

Tina was still rather intimated by Maureen, but the women split a bottle of Chianti, and Tina found herself chiming in on current events particularly after Elektra ran out of breath. This was not like being out with sorority sisters. Elektra, Sarah, and even Maureen paused and listened to her. They let her finish her sentences. They laughed or gasped when Tina found a choice word about a current event or new movie. They all nodded when she said her mother couldn't believe her favorite actor, Rock Hudson was gay, but that just underscored the points in her AIDS story. "Good story," Maureen interjected. Now Rock was dying of AIDs. Sarah said the truth about Rock Hudson really buried the 1950s when everyone was supposed to live in the suburbs with two kids and a dog. Which led to a discussion on cats. All the women had one or two, Tina lost track and so she jumped in with what for her was logical observation.

"I didn't know you were allowed to have cats in apartments," Tina said

"Studio 54? No one seems to care," said Sarah. "We all live in Studio 54."

"Studio 54?"

"That's not the real name," said Maureen. "Elektra started calling it that because it's all studio apartments, except for a couple of one-bedrooms."

"Maureen has a one-bedroom," said Elektra.

"I was lucky," said Maureen.

"She got me my studio and I really, really love it," said Sarah. "It's like a bit of New York in Connecticut. Complete with weirdos. Do you guys remember the time I was drying my clothes in the dryer in the basement and I went upstairs, and when I got back all my underwear was gone."

"Happened to me, too," said Elektra. "Bastard got some Victoria's Secret specials."

Tina thought Studio 54 seemed a rather dubious place for a single woman to live.

"I think I figured it out," said Maureen. "I think it's an old guy who has been there forever. I went over to talk to him and dropped a few hints about calling the police and it stopped."

Once again, Tina was impressed by Maureen's command and pleased that somehow this imposing figure liked her writing.

After finishing off the dinner, Sarah said they should try this new nearby fern bar to see if it was really as trendy as those in Manhattan. They all agreed it indeed had ferns in the window, but that was about it. Maureen ordered a glass of burgundy, Sarah wanted a glass of chardonnay, and Elektra ordered a Sea Breeze.

"What's a Sea Breeze?" Tina asked. "Vodka, grapefruit juice and cranberry juice," said Elektra. "Grapefruit juice kills the calories in the vodka." Maureen shook her head, but Tina said she would have one too. The bar started to glow with a warm light, making Tina forget she was a fat girl with a bad complexion and a boyfriend who had dumped her. Elektra started talking about Sundae, her angel cat, and her current trio of darlings. Sarah agreed she much preferred snuggling with her cat Carrington than a snoring man. Maureen said Hercules snored. They finished their drinks, Tina thinking Sea Breezes were much better than her mother's martinis, the only other cocktail she had ever tried.

Maureen suggested Tina come over to visit Studio 54 and meet the cats; it was walking distance. They could even watch "Saturday Night Live" even though everyone knew it wasn't good anymore.

Studio 54 was a plain brick building with white columns the color of dingy laundry flanking the entrance and a foyer smelling of fried meat and Pine-Sol. Dark wood doors lined the hallway and Elektra led the way to the third door on the right. Stepping inside the apartment, the women were greeted by loud meows. "Sit," said Elektra, pushing aside jackets, skirts, dishes and a bra from the couch and the two chairs. Books, newspapers, and magazines were stacked in a precarious tower on the small table near the tall windows. A cat scratching post stretched like a carpeted staircase from floor to ceiling. The walls were splashed with posters from the Metropolitan Museum of Art, sunflowers, water lilies, and a cornfield rendered in blunt strokes. "Sorry, I haven't had time to clean this year," Elektra said, bundling the clothes and the bra and tossing them toward the bathroom.

Sugar Pie and Sammy talked as much as Elektra but in

cat speak and in stereo. Tina could not tell them apart. "Are you hungry?" Elektra asked them. "Do you want a treat?" "We dooooo," the cats said. Elektra shook out a treat from a large selection on the counter and threw one toward the cats and Sugar Pie (or Sammy) caught it. She tossed another and Sammy (or Sugar Pie) caught it. "More, more," said the cats. Maureen, Sarah, and Tina took turns tossing the treats, many of which skittered under the couch. "Oh leave it," said Elektra when Tina attempted to retrieve one. "It has friends down there."

"But where's Eddie," Maureen asked slyly. "Yes," said Sarah with a huge grin. "We still haven't met Eddie."

"Eddie. He's very shy," said Elektra who was attempting to open a bottle of wine. "Eddie. EDDIE. Come out. Come talk to our friends. Eddie!"

Elektra poured the wine into plastic cups. "Sammy, where's Eddie? Sugar Pie? Where's Eddie?" The cats stared at her. "More treats," they said.

Eddie didn't show up. Turns out he never showed up. Maureen and Sarah had already started to call Eddie Mr. Ed, like the famous horse who talked only when Wilbur was around. "Mr. Ed does not appear until he has something to scratch," Sarah would sing. Elektra swore Eddie would appear the minute everyone left.

They each had a glass of wine while they waited for Eddie to appear and then they walked up a flight of stairs to Sarah's studio on the second floor with Elektra carrying the now half empty bottle of wine.

Tina stepped into Sarah's studio, and immediately thought it had to be bigger than Elektra's. She quickly realized it wasn't, the place was just more sparsely furnished. There was a futon that doubled as a bed and couch, and a leather easy chair. The wood floors gleamed. Tall oak bookshelves lined two walls, filled with hardback books, pottery and curious, colorful figurines. Wine glasses were neatly arranged on one shelf over a filled wine rack. A cat sat on the easy chair, a smudge of darkness against the sandy brown. "This is Carrington," Sarah said, pulling out wine glasses. Carrington had a coal-black coat with golden patches, like embers in a dying fire. Carrington, Sarah told Tina, as the other two clicked glasses, had traveled with her from Texas, where Sarah found her hanging around her home. With languid grace, Carrington stretched, rose, and jumped off the chair and came to Sarah, rubbing her neck against her leg. She allowed herself to be petted, then retired to a corner where she watched the women with disdainful eyes. Tina kept glancing at Carrington, unsure if the cat was amused or about to attack.

Over the futon hung a poster of a man with smoky eyes and a fierce mustache. A sombrero and sash of bullets was slung over a shoulder. "That's Emiliano Zapata, the Mexican revolutionary," said Sarah when she saw Tina staring at it. "I spent some time in Mexico, studying Spanish."

The women finished the bottle while discussing if Madonna was an example of female empowerment or a cheap boy toy. "I like her moxie," said Tina, delighted when the other women nodded.

Elektra said she was hungry again and Sarah, as usual, didn't have food, so Maureen invited everyone to her place for Nacho Dorito chips and a chance to meet Hercules.

Maureen's living room was precisely arranged with a couch, loveseat and coffee table, all shades of black and tan. The counter next to the sink in the small kitchen was taken up by a drainer, neatly stacked with creamy ivory plates. Unlike the other two apartments, there was a separate bedroom, where Tina noticed piles of clothes and towels on and around the bed. It seemed Maureen had a yin and yang approach to home décor. The bedroom was chaotic while the living room was orderly. Hercules met them at the door. He had long black and white fur and a clouded eye which gave him the rakish air of a pirate with an eyepatch. He weighed, Maureen said, about 20 pounds and had a ridiculously high-pitched meow. She picked him up, staggering a bit, and hugged him. When she let him drop to the floor, the room shook. Maureen had, she explained, adopted him after her cat Matilda died. She fully intended to get another small female cat, but there was something about the Buddha-like calm and quiet dignity of Hercules sitting in the cage at the shelter that caught her attention. When she lifted him for the first time, she was surprised how calm he remained. She sat him down on her lap and he looked deep into her eyes. When she brought him home, he sniffed around a bit, and padded majestically into the bedroom where he jumped on the bed and curled up by the pillows as if he had always lived there.

Now Hercules solemnly went to each woman requesting they each scratch behind the ears, while Maureen brought out chips and another bottle of wine. Tina gently patted the cat's head, hoping she was touching him correctly. Maureen pulled out the cork with a thwack and poured the wine into one wine glass, two mugs and a paper cup, and settled herself on a chair with the paper cup; Hercules jumped into her lap and sprawled across her skirt.

This was the routine, she explained. Herc would wait until she stirred in the morning and pat her cheek until she rose to feed him. When she watched TV, he would curl up on her lap, which made things difficult when she left the remote out of reach. At night she would crawl into bed and Herc would jump on her stomach and stare into her eyes, while she scratched his neck and stroked his magnificent chest.

When she came home exhausted, Hercules was there. Pet

me, you will feel better, he would say. When she sat at the kitchen table to eat and read, Herc would curl at her feet. Herc did not fear people, not even children, she said. When a neighbor introduced her troublesome five-year-old boy in the hallway, Hercules padded up to the boy and rubbed against him and sat still while the boy dropped cracker crumbs on his head. Herc never panicked. When Maureen accidentally locked him out of the apartment, he waited outside the door until she returned, and comforted her with purrs when she sobbed, "Will you ever forgive me?"

"You didn't really cry, did you?" Sarah asked.

"Oh, she did," said Elektra. "I would have."

Tina couldn't imagine Maureen tearing up, but she watched as her hard-edged editor smothered Herc's head with kisses, which he bore patiently.

With tongues fully lubricated, the contest began anew: men versus cats. Elektra kicked it off.

"So I was dating this guy Brad and I really liked him, but all we did was have sex, and one day I noticed Sammy and Sugar Pie were more loving than he was and made me realize he was just using me and I told him to get lost."

Maureen nodded, hugging Hercules. Sarah said Carrington was always there to listen but was not too demanding. She could leave out plenty of food and water if she had to go away overnight. Carrington was perfectly fine with that.

"Hercules is far more reliable than John," Maureen said, sipping from her paper cup, as Hercules shed white hair on her charcoal Armani skirt. "He never loses his cool."

Maureen explained how she was now dating this guy, John, a business consultant. When they finally spent the night together, John complained the next day he woke up with that cat on top of him, staring at him. He insisted Hercules hogged the bed and groused he never got enough sleep because the

CEO was always on his case and he could never relax.

"Hey," Maureen declared, waving her cup and spilling wine on Hercules. "It's time for *Saturday Night Live*. Herc, buddy, do you want to watch SNL?"

"I think he would prefer *Wild Kingdom*," said Elektra, tossing back a chip.

"Carrington loves *Moonlighting*," said Sarah, attempting to connect her mouth with her mug.

Tina didn't have any cat tales to add but she found herself laughing uproariously at her friends' stories and running commentaries on SNL, which turned out to be more amusing than the actual skits. When Maureen got up to go to the bathroom, Hercules padded over to Tina and jumped in her lap, a huge furry weight. She found herself putting her arms around him and hearing a rusty purr. Maureen returned and smiled her approval.

"Oh, he likes you," said Elektra. "He knows a cat person."

"Oh no," Tina said. "I don't have any plans to get a cat."

"You forget that, like nature, cats abhor a vacuum," Sarah said, waving her glass. "When one cat goes, another appears. I learned this back when I was living in Dallas."

CHAPTER EIGHT

Cats Abhor a Vacuum

IN COLLEGE SARAH would never have dreamed she would end up in the Lone Star State hanging out in cowboy bars. But after graduating Northwestern, her life became a twisting river and she was content to float in the current. She thought about looking for Jasmine and joining her commune, but had lost track of where her friend was. She found that, while jobs for English majors were sparse, there was a demand for newspaper copy editors, especially ones willing to work later shifts. She was offered a job as night copy editor at a newspaper in Idaho, and took it, figuring it was halfway to California.

Her hometown had been green and gray, the spinach green of manicured lawns and shade trees, the sheet metal tone of overcast skies and high-rise apartment buildings. Idaho was brown, tan and dusty. The unrelenting turquoise sky and scrub desert around Twin Falls were both utterly monotonous and strangely soothing. The managing editor told her not to wear short skirts to the office but otherwise, she enjoyed the work. Since she usually worked afternoons to midnight, she would hike during the day in nearby canyons, following icy streams snaking through the baked ground. At night, she dreamed she was hiking through the imaginary world of her childhood, the land of Arianna, now turned into an arid landscape where streams, alive with dancing flames, wound through rust-colored canyons.

Sarah became intrigued with a camp of migrant farm-workers, just outside the city's limit, and pressed the reporters to do a story on it. None were interested, so Sarah did it herself, finding a ten-year-old child who did the translating from Spanish to English. After she wrote the story, Sarah applied for and received a National Press fellowship to study Spanish in Cuernavaca, Mexico. The editor reluctantly let her go on a leave of absence.

She returned to Idaho, fluent in Spanish but something profound had happened in Cuernavaca, something she folded up and stored away. She quickly found a job in Dallas at the Associated Press. Dallas was huge, raw, and raucous. Sarah bought a pair of cowboy boots and polishing the black stitched leather became a soothing weekly ritual. She rented an apartment carved from a ranch house owned by an older couple. Every night she would smell cigar smoke from the room where the owner watched TV with his cat, a huge black beast with matted fur who hung out on the porch when not in the house. Sarah tried to pet him once. He smelled of smoke and his fur was as rough as steel wool.

Dallas had gangly men who would buy her drinks, tell her she was a cool drink of water, and plead to take her home. Every now and then, she consented, and spent the night with tequila shots and bouts of frantic pounding followed by snoring. She always left before dawn, whispering, "Goodbye cowboy" in a sleeping ear and walking to her car in the sullen air. When alone at night, she dreamed about the Star Horse of Arianna, who would descend from the sky, and tell her how he loved her sad, beautiful eyes and fierce spirit.

The landlord met her at the door one day. "Have you seen Oliver?" She shook her head, surprised at his concern for a cat he didn't seem to take care of. "He hasn't come home," said the man. She later heard him calling for Oliver in the neighborhood. When she saw the landlord a week later, he told her he found Oliver in bad shape hiding in the bushes and had taken him to the vet. "He's not coming home," said the landlord, his eyes damp. "My wife will be happy; she never liked him. Now, I have to smoke alone."

A few days later, she took home a cowboy, a sweet young thing who said he had some cocaine. "Is this your cat?" he asked as they staggered up her front stairs. A cat with dark fur spotted with gold was sitting on the porch. For a second Sarah thought Oliver had come back to life, but this cat was smaller with shorter fur. It wove around the cowboy's feet, making soft mewing sounds.

"No, it must just live around here," Sarah said, frowning.

"Nice kitty," he said, scratching behind its ears as it arched its back. "Are you feeding it? They won't leave you if you feed them."

"How do you know?"

He winked. "I know pussies, darlin'." He actually didn't, and he disappeared the next day in a pickup truck festooned with a Confederate flag. The cat, however, was back the next night. When Sarah climbed the stairs to her front porch, it was sitting on the top step. She reached down to stroke its head. "Go home," she said, and went into her apartment. It was there the next night. And the next. Just when Sarah expected to see it again, it disappeared.

Sarah often worked the three to midnight shift, keeping an eye on the stories and messages being spit out by the telex machine. It could get hectic; she had to track the national and international wire and prepare to deploy the reporters working in the office or to contact the stringers spread through Texas. Bit of news floated by on the wire, legislation from Congress, announcements from President Carter, plane crashes, unusual murders, and dispatches from Israel, Europe, the Soviet Union, and Guyana.

The Guyana story caught Sarah's eyes and in a few minutes

the staff was gathered around the TV in the room. The reports were confusing and horrific. A congressman and a group of reporters were shot while investigating a cult led by a religious man from California. Following that, cult members in Guyana committed mass suicide, apparently by drinking cyanide-laced juice. Even the jaded reporters were shocked, although jokes about Kool-Aid began circulating. Sarah read as much as she could of the dispatches. The news videos of the scene were ghastly, the bodies piled like a jumble of rags, brightly colored shirts, red pants, dark jeans, nestled into a lush green jungle. One shirt caught her eye, a tie-dye pattern that seemed familiar. She couldn't place it until the next day when she realized it was one of Jasmine's designs. She tried to put the image out of her head. It was not possible. Or could it be? She no longer had a number for Jasmine. She called information for the number of the Woo residence and dialed it. The phone rang and rang and Sarah was about to hang up when it was picked up.

"Hello," said a man's voice. Sarah recognized it.

"Mr. Woo, this is Sarah Gold."

"Oh, Sarah," said Jasmine's father. "Oh, Sarah."

And Sarah knew Jasmine was gone. "I'm so sorry," was all Sarah could say, over and over again. Sarah called her mother and they talked for an hour, the first time in many months they had exchanged more than a few words. Her mom told her Jasmine's mother joined this crazy Jim Jones guy and got her daughter to come along. Jasmine later moved to Guyana.

"I always thought she was troubled," her mom added after a pause.

"Why do you say that?" Sarah said. "She was so cool, so free. Everyone liked her."

Her mother sighed. "There was something in her eyes. Even your dad saw it. But we didn't say anything; we knew she was your friend."

Sarah didn't get off her shift until long after the bars had closed. It was past 3 o'clock on Monday morning and the streets were quiet, as if bracing for the work week. After she parked and got out of her car, she paused to lean against the door and try to make out stars popping in and out of the clouds. She had a strange uneasy feeling, as if her parents' harsh voices were rippling on the slight breeze or that someone was calling her name. She thought of Jasmine with her lovely, long hair sleeping in the muck of the jungle. Why had she stayed with the cult? Had she drunk the poison willingly? Why would she do that? She turned to her porch, and there was the cat.

"Meow. Meow?" it said. It looked thinner. "Okay," Sarah said. "You can come in for the night." She opened her door and the cat ran in. Sarah watched as the cat walked around the house and then leapt into a drawer of her socks she had left open. "Remember, no pooping," she said, and went to bed to dream of Arianna, now deep in the jungle with crooked trees with bulging eyes.

In the morning, the cat was sitting by her front door. She opened it. "Go home," she said. "Go home." The cat looked at her and scampered off. She went back to bed. When she woke at noon, she decided to go out for groceries before starting her shift.

She ran into the landlord. "Joe, there's this cat hanging around. Do you mind if I take it in?

"Oh sure," said Joe. "Honey, you can have two cats. I miss ol' Oliver."

Sarah kept thinking about the cat. She had not fed it. It must belong to someone. All the cats in her childhood had belonged to someone even if they roamed the streets and alleyways, many of them dirty, furtive creatures. But someone must have deserted it. Someone must have left it outside or moved and never returned. There was something in the cat's eyes. She was lost. She needed help. At the grocery store, she bought a can of cat food.

The cat was on the porch when she came home. "Meow," it said. "Meow." Sarah sighed and opened the door. The cat just sat there.

"Come in, if you want to stay," Sarah said. "It's up to you."

The cat remained where it was. Then with a burst of energy, it ran up the stairs and Sarah walked inside and closed the door. The choice was made. The cat was home.

The next day she bought more cat food, a bag of litter and a box. She came up with a name a week later as she was sorting through her college texts to finally dispose of them and came across a biography of Virginia Woolf. She looked up an old number, and dialed. "Hey Mo! Just fine. I need to ask you about cats. You had a cat growing up, didn't you? Oh, you have one now? Yes, I adopted one or she adopted me. Carrington. Carrington, the cat. She seems to sleep a lot. Is that normal?"

What was normal for Carrington soon became normal for Sarah. At first, she would just watch the way Carrington slept, curled up like a fuzzy caterpillar, occasionally stretching out her paws, and resettling on her back, never opening her eyes. As she slept, Carrie seemed to smile, a curve of her mouth that intensified when Sarah stroked her belly. Sometimes her paws would twitch or her tail would lash, once, twice, and then settle in a half circle. Sarah started coming home after her shifts instead of going out for drinks with colleagues or teasing cowboys at the bar. She would pick up a bottle of wine and open her door to a purring cat who would rub her ankles with the side of her neck, as if marking Sarah as her territory. When Sarah headed to bed, glass in hand, Carrington followed and hopped up beside her. Finishing her wine, Sarah put down the book she was reading and watched Carrington, her eyes closed, her back pressed against Sarah's side.

Carrie wasn't asleep, Sarah decided. Nothing had to sleep so much. She was dreaming, cat dreaming. Once, Sarah woke with the feeling she had been running on a path through tall grass that twitched as she passed. Carrie was ahead of her or behind her. The more she tried to recall the dream, the more it faded, leaving only the sensations she had been where everything was as it should be.

When Maureen called about becoming her second-in-command at a paper in Stamford, Connecticut, Sarah thought about it. Dallas was bigger than Stamford, but Stamford was outside of New York City. There would be no cowboys there. She turned to look at Carrington, who was regally washing her face atop the couch. "Would you like to move to Connecticut?" Carrington paused, regarded her with curiosity, and returned to her beauty routine. "Sure," said Sarah into the phone. "I can be there in a month."

CHAPTER NINE

The Two-Cat Solution

WHEN TINA WAS ten years old her dog was hit and killed by a car. Everyone in the Montgomery family loved Dougie, all the boys, her mother, father, and Tina. But Tina was usually the one who walked and fed Dougie and slipped him bits of meat under the dinner table. One day she stayed late at school, and when she came home, her mother said there was bad news. Her younger brother had been walking Dougie when the dog pulled away and ran into the street. They buried Dougie in the backyard. She cried for two weeks. This is what she told Elektra when asked why she didn't get a cat. After all, Maureen had Hercules, Sarah had Carrington, and Elektra had Sammy, Sugar Pie and Eddie. Tina said she couldn't go through that kind of pain again. What if something happened?

Elektra was unconvinced. "Get two cats then. You'll always have one in case something happens to the other. Also they'll keep each other company and there's more to love."

Maureen agreed Tina should get a cat. "I don't know what I would do without Hercules." But not two. "They might be jealous of each other. They might fight all the time."

Tina just said she was more of a dog person. Also she was busy writing features for the paper now, honing skills she did not realize she had. Besides, pets were not allowed in her apartment complex.

Someone new moved into Tina's building. For several weeks, before and after work, a dark-haired man in the lobby had rushed by her, a blur of a shiny suit, red tie, briefcase and pungent aftershave. Tina usually ducked her head when she saw him, her hand on her chin, cheek or temple, saying a quick "Hello," answered by "Hi there."

One evening, Tina opened her mailbox to find a letter from her mother. She tore open the envelope and read it standing in the lobby. Her mother had lots of stories from home and had dotted her i's with little hearts. She was still smiling, when she caught a scent of something spicy, and the dark-haired man was standing beside her opening his mailbox. "You look happy about something," he said. "All I get are bills."

"Oh, just a letter from my mom," Tina said, wondering if she sounded like a teenager.

"I wish my mom would just write me and quit calling," said the man. "Hey what's your name?"

They started chatting. His name was Ricardo, but everyone called him Rick. He was a lawyer, the youngest in his firm, he added. Tina was able to say she was a newspaper feature writer, feeling she now had an impressive nametag. The man asked her what she was writing and Tina found herself talking quickly, reaching to pull at her bangs to make sure they covered a line of Pimplets that had begun clamoring for attention on her forehead. He cocked his head to listen, frowning in concentration, as Tina described her feature on the rise and fall of New Coke, all the while studying his dark eyes and the one lock that escaped his neatly combed hair and drifted over his forehead.

"Hey, since we're neighbors, why don't we have dinner sometime?" he asked.

"Oh sure, that would be nice," Tina said, hoping it sounded like every week some strange man asked her out to dinner.

"How about Thursday if you're not doing anything?" the man asked. He said he would drop by at 7 o'clock. Which apartment?

Tina had two days in which to panic and call Elektra, who helped her go through her closet twice before they both scampered off to the mall to see what was on sale. On Thursday, Rick knocked at 7:15. Tina, who had been ready by six, jumped to her feet, then slowly walked to the door. "You look nice," he said. Tina tingled.

They had dinner at a seafood place nearby; Tina hardly tasted her swordfish as they chatted about movies and theater. Rick loved jazz; he had played the saxophone all through college and been in a couple bands, but he was too busy now. Tina could see how Rick would be great as a performer; he had an aura like Kenny G with short hair. He would be describing a case, then turn to her and fix her with a gaze that made her forget what he was saying.

"What?" she said.

"Just like that," he repeated and put a forkful of salmon in his mouth.

In turn, she described the mad personalities of the newsroom and Rick laughed uproariously when she did a fair impression of the rock critic's pontification about the musicality of Peter Gabriel's "Sledgehammer" and how Maureen broke in to say, "Oh, come on, it's just about sex." Her college boyfriend Greg had never laughed at her jokes.

Rick walked her back to her apartment door and leaned over to kiss her. Tina worried her lips tasted fishy when he pulled back and said, "Goodnight, I'll call you soon."

It was too late to call Elektra so she curled up in bed, hugging her knees.

The weekend came and went with no call from Rick. No sign of him in the lobby. Then on the following Tuesday, they ran into each other at the elevator. "Sorry, I've been busy," he said. "Big case. Dinner tonight? Seven o'clock?"

Tina was ready at 6:30, with extra layers of foundation. He

knocked at 7:30 p.m. "How about going to that same place? I really liked it," he said. "Sure," said Tina, who quickly decided she would order pasta, not fish. Rick seemed to be looking around the restaurant a lot, not at Tina. But when he did look at her, he smiled with easy warmth and Tina would smile back. "I have an idea," he said. "Let's go to the Shady Lane Club; a buddy of mine is playing in a band there."

The Shady Lane proved to live up to its name. Guided by Rick's hand on her back, Tina stepped into a smoke-filled cavernous room, rippling with music and conversation.

"My man," said the bouncer to Rick. "My man," he said back as they grasped hands. "This is my friend Tina," Rick said. "Hmm, hmm, hmm," said the bouncer. "Miss Tina, you are most welcome." They found a table near the stage and Rick ordered two beers. Tina found the music a trifle discordant but nodded her head with other patrons and joined in the clapping. Rick waved to his friend on stage, who said something about his good friend being there with a lovely lady at his side. When another of Rick's friends came by to chat, Rick introduced Tina and put his arm around her shoulders as if, maybe, to show she was taken. Between songs, he would whisper in her ear about the music, the touch as intimate as holding hands.

Later, he walked her to her apartment, and they lingered by her door and kissed again. Tina was trying to decide if she should invite him in when Rick pulled away. "Another big day tomorrow; I'll call you." And he was gone. Tina could smell his aftershave on her blouse and she crawled into bed with it pressed to her cheek.

She ran into Rick the next morning as they were both rushing out the door. "Hey babe," he said. "Wish me luck today. Have a good one. Maybe I'll drop by tonight."

Tina spent a long time trying on different dresses – this was too prim; this was too revealing. "This would be a third date, right?" she asked Elektra. "Right," said Elektra. "Third date and you're not a slut." Tina decided not to stint on the concealer, but she had to do her face at least twice when the blush didn't look right. She was ready by 6:45. By 8 o'clock. Rick had not shown up. By 9 o'clock, Tina was too anxious to call it a night.

She knew what floor he was on and crept up the back stairs and peered into the hallway. I'll just walk through casually; I was visiting a friend on the third floor, she thought. She walked slowly down the hall, listening to the faint sounds of TVs and murmuring conversations. She paused by what she thought was his door. All seemed quiet. She was working up her courage to knock when she thought she heard a woman's laugh. Was that inside? Or next door? She heard a scraping sound, as if furniture was being moved. She pivoted and ran down the stairs, back to her apartment.

"But he didn't say for sure he was coming," Elektra said the next day. "Right? Something could have come up. Right?" Tina had to agree there was no commitment, hence no problem. She clung to the thought.

In the morning she ran into Rick as they were leaving. "Hey Tina, Tina, we won. Score one for the good guys," he said, grabbing her hand and pulling her in for a big hug. "A bit more paperwork today and then champagne's on me. See you soon," and he was gone, shiny shoes clicking on the granite of the front stairs.

"And that was it," Tina said to Elektra. Nothing for a week. No sign of him. Elektra alternated between cursing out men in general to saying really, nothing was wrong. He might be busy.

Friday evening, as she was coming home from the *Gazette*, there was Rick, standing outside the building on the front steps, smoking a cigarette. Tina halted, her heart beating. "Oh, hey," she said as casually as she could.

"Hi there. How ya doing?" he said, smiling broadly, and Tina could not help but smile back.

"So, what's your latest assignment?" Rick asked, fixing her with a stare that held her in place. Tina began to tell him about her latest assignment and then suddenly there was a tall woman, in a long burgundy coat, walking up to them. "Tina," said Rick, "I'd like you to meet my colleague, Angela." The woman seemed to regard Tina from three stories up, topaz eyes set with precision in an elegant face with perfect skin. "Angela, this is Tina who lives in the building."

"Hello Tina," said Angela, her voice cool and creamy as her complexion, a faint smile hovering on lips just a bit brighter than her coat.

"Tina, I'll see you soon," said Rick, flicking away his cigarette, and he and Angela walked off, with Rick eagerly talking as Angela moved effortlessly on high heels, adjusting the gold-link strap of her purse over her shoulder, the YSL logo catching a glint of the evening sun.

"Well, he did say 'colleague,'" Elektra said the next morning. "But I don't know. Could be an office romance. I dunno."

Tina wanted to hold out hope. She threw the blouse, now bereft of any scent, into a basket with the rest of her clothes and headed downstairs to the laundry room, where she saw Rick walking hand in hand with Angela out the front door, Angela's hair, tousled into a cloud of inky perfection, Rick in jeans and a leather jacket.

All the machines were in use and Tina took her basket back upstairs, sat on the bed and cried. She started to think back to college and about Greg, the man she thought she would marry. She called what she thought was his number and a woman answered. She hung up quickly, mumbling, "Wrong number."

She ran into Rick and Angela several times over the next week, trying not to notice how Rick's arm would be around

Angela's waist. Rick always greeted her, but he didn't really see her. She was the little fat girl with the awful complexion. That's what she was. That's what she always would be.

She struggled to keep her mind on her work. Maureen was coming up with choice assignments, each one pushing Tina into new territory, culture, politics, even music. Then, she came home to find a message on the phone machine from the apartment's owners saying they were returning in two weeks and they wanted to find the apartment in good order. And empty.

Tina sat on the bed and cried again. She resisted the temptation to call her mother and wail. Instead she turned to the one person who seemed to have all the answers. Maureen made a few calls. There was good news. One of the studios on the second floor at Studio 54 was vacant and did she want to rent it? Of course, she did. After Tina signed the lease, Maureen, Elektra and Sarah all helped to move her possessions, clothes, and some chairs she rescued from the curb. They ordered Chinese and ate, sitting on the floor in Tina's apartment and drinking chardonnay out of paper cups. Tina ordered a futon from Macy's, her first piece of adult furniture; in the meantime, she would sleep on a camping mattress Sarah lent her. Elektra gave her extra plates; Maureen had extra blankets. Sarah offered her a vase from Mexico with cheerful patterns.

The next night, Tina sat on the floor in her studio, her studio, and felt really hungry for the first time in months. She looked in her refrigerator, where Maureen stashed the leftover Chinese food. Tina ate it with relish, even if the rice was a cold block and the sauce had congealed around the bits of chicken. The floor, newly redone by the apartment management company, gleamed warmly. She would get curtains and maybe another chair. She wouldn't have to worry about running into Rick and Angela. Wiping her mouth with the leftover napkins, Tina started thinking about how Hercules would leap into

Maureen's lap, nearly knocking the wine glass out of her hand when Maureen was trying to make a point. She thought of Elektra, picking up Sugar Pie, hugging her, and saying, "Mommy's home." She thought of Sarah talking about Carrington and cat dreaming. She thought about her friends saying cats were better than men. Maybe she was a cat person after all.

Elektra offered to take her to the Stamford Animal Shelter.

The shelter smelled of pee and poo overlaid with bleach. Tina was certain she would be overwhelmed with choices, but it only took a few minutes and another minute to choose a name and Mindy Marmalade was in her lap, trembling, with her orange fur and eyes like green sea-glass. Her double-toe front paws looked like furry dumplings. Tina brought her home in a carrier Elektra lent her. Mindy stayed under the futon until about midnight when Tina felt her curl up beside her and press against her side. She reached out a hand to pet her and heard a rusty purr.

For the next three weeks, Tina rushed home to feed Mindy. The cat ran into the closet when trucks roared by, but she crawled on the futon every night. While Tina read, Mindy would nestle beside her. She chased the catnip mouse Tina bought until it disappeared and Tina bought another. She liked to play with Tina's shoelaces, the strap of her purse and rolled up bits of aluminum foil which began to appear in odd spots around the apartment.

When Tina left in the morning, Mindy was in the window, washing her face. She was by the door when Tina came home. Until the day she wasn't and Tina, terrified, started calling, "Mindy, Mindy." How could she get out? Why did she leave? When Mindy didn't appear, she called Elektra who rushed over.

"I can't take another Dougie," Tina sobbed.

"Don't worry," Elektra said. "We'll find her."

They heard a faint mew and Tina opened the closet door

and Mindy ran out. "But I looked there," Tina cried, sobbing with relief.

"Cats!" cried Elektra. "They just like to vanish." That night Tina kept reaching for Mindy who purred every time Tina touched her.

The two-cat solution now had its appeal. One cat. One back up. Still, Tina didn't want Mindy to be jealous. She didn't want Mindy to feel like she wasn't enough.

"You have to introduce the cats slowly, gradually. It can be done," Elektra said. "Sugar Pie and Sammy always get along and we all love Eddie. Eddie, Eddie, come out and say hello. Eddie?"

As Tina sat with Mindy on her lap, she asked her, "Would you like a friend to play with when I go to work?" Mindy purred.

At the shelter, Tina fell in love again. Sheena, Queen of the Jungle, black ripples on her gray fur, was lean, lithe, and fearless. Tina brought her home and nervously let her out of the carrier. Mindy sat in a corner, her tail lashing. Sheena sashayed around the apartment with, Tina thought, the smooth cool of Angela's high-heeled stride. As Mindy stared, Sheena sauntered into the bathroom and sniffed the litter box. She turned and headed toward Mindy. "You two have to get along," Tina said. "Be nice to each other."

The two cats touched noses as Tina held her breath. Then Sheena went on another inspection of the house. Tina later found both cats on the bed, Mindy licking Sheena.

She called Elektra rapturously. "They are getting along beautifully." Tina and Elektra had dinner to celebrate and Maureen joined them for drinks. Sarah showed up for dessert. Elektra said she and Tina should go to this new singles dance "'cause girls just wanna have fun."

"I don't want to go out just now," Tina said. "I have to take care of my cats."

The next night, Mindy was not at the door when Tina came home from work. She found Mindy and Sheena lying side by side on a chair. After dinner, she settled on the futon and flipped open Time magazine. "Mindy," she called. "Mindy, come here." Mindy jumped down, came over to the futon, and stared at Tina. Then she turned around, jumped on the chair, and curled up against Sheena. Tina watched them for a while, and during the night her hand reached for the spot where Mindy usually slept next to her. She was not there. Tina closed her eyes, trying to shut off images of Tony holding hands with Angela and Greg embracing a voluptuous actress.

When she returned from work, Sheena, not Mindy, was near the door. She kept meowing while Tina was putting out cat food. Mindy touched Sheena's nose with her own and gave her a quick reassuring lick. Later Sheena chased Mindy around the apartment, and they tussled over a catnip mouse which had somehow reappeared.

Sarah called, she wanted to see if Tina wanted to take in a movie. "So how are the two girls getting along?"

"Great, lovely," said Tina. "Just like sisters."

Sarah snorted. "Obviously, you've never had a sister."

After the movie, she told Tina about her older sister and their epic battles. Later, when Tina got into bed, she had to push aside Sheena who had taken the center spot. Sheena meowed huffily and Mindy looked concerned. Tina lay awake for a while, wondering if Rick and Angela were in bed together right that moment. She reached out for Mindy or Sheena but her hands only met empty air. She sighed and drifted off to sleep, dreaming of looking into Mindy's eyes. In the morning when she got up, the cats were cuddled on the floor together and barely looked at her when she said goodbye.

The next three days were a blur; the entire staff of the *Gazette* was pulled in to help cover the Challenger space shuttle disaster. Reports and editors gathered by the television, which repeatedly showed the explosion and those weirdly curling bone-white clouds of smoke and debris. Tina slumped home exhausted, trying not to notice how the cats were curled around each other and would not look up until she opened a can of food.

Elektra's celebrity interview with Kathleen Turner about her new movie was canceled. To fill the feature page for the next week, Maureen frantically sent Tina to a bookstore in Greenwich to stalk Erica Jong who was doing a signing for her new book but had turned down an interview request.

"Just hang out in the bookstore and see what people say to her," Maureen said before dashing into another news meeting.

Tina dutifully showed up at the bookstore early to leaf through the pages of *Fear of Flying* which Maureen assumed Tina had read. Now she understood what Sarah meant when she spoke of a "zipless fuck." When Jong arrived in a plainly cut dark suit with a creamy white blouse, Tina thought she was demurely dressed for a sexual trailblazer. She greeted the bookstore visitors, mostly middle-aged women, with aplomb.

"You saved our marriage," a woman told Jong and bent to whisper in her ear as the author smiled stiffly and the woman's husband (at least Tina thought it was her husband) shook his head.

Arriving home late, Tina wondered about how she would write the story amid a world reeling with unanswered questions. She fumbled with the can opener, thinking she would eat a mouthful of tuna fish and give the rest to the cats as a treat. As she dumped the fish into a bowl, Mindy pressed her nose to a crying Sheena. "Meeeow," said Sheena, and batted Mindy's nose away.

"Stop," Tina said sharply. Mindy backed away, looking at Tina, with hurt eyes. "You have to get along with each other."

She put down the bowl. Sheena hissed when Mindy came close.

"No hissing," Tina said. She put more fish in another bowl as Mindy arched her back and rubbed against her legs. "We all have to get along," she said, setting down the second bowl.

Losing her appetite for tuna, she grabbed a handful of crackers, sat down on the futon and opened a brand-new magazine Sarah gave her called *Spy*. Mindy jumped beside her. Sheena jumped to the other side. Pay attention to me, Mindy said. No, pay attention to me, Sheena said. With a hand on each cat, crackers forgotten in her lap, Tina read *Spy*, bewitched by how cruel snark made for entertaining journalism.

When she finally crawled into bed, she navigated her body between the two cats on opposite sides of the futon. They hissed at each other once or twice as Tina called out sleepily, "We have to all get along." By the morning she found Mindy was pressed against her thigh. Sheena had crawled on top of her.

Maureen loved Tina's "Fear of Fans" article and the newsroom started to get back to its normal level of stress. On Sunday morning Elektra woke her up with a phone call because she had an idea for a humor article called "My Cat is Better than Your Boyfriend" and she wanted to know what Tina thought about it. They spent hours trading funny lines, as Tina sprawled on the futon with her cats.

"So how are the girls getting along?" Elektra asked.

"Great," said Tina. "Just like sisters."

She reached over to pet Mindy on one side and then Sheena on the other. They were each gazing up at her. Both were purring.

CHAPTER TEN

A Conversation with Jane

WHAT FRESH HELL is this? It's not even rush hour. "Move, move. Right turn on red, bozo. What are you waiting for? Go, go, go. We can do this." The light changed, Maureen roared past the slow car and made a hard right on the ramp to I-95, north toward New Haven.

She wanted to blame John for her bad mood. This morning, when she called for what she hoped was a brief call, he had to tell her again what the CEO said, why it was wrong, why it was stupid and why the guy was a jerk. John used profanity with an effortless energy that made it almost poetic. "So I'm busting my balls, and in this meeting, he rips me a new asshole like I don't fucking know what I'm talking about and the marketing director – he is always rubbing her back like they must be fucking – and she hates my guts so she is agreeing with him… "

"John," said Maureen.

"Like she fucking knows something. She knows nothing. The CEO knows nothing. I got two employees who are complete flipping morons…"

"John," said Maureen, a bit louder.

"This other VP who is forty and looks sixty doesn't fucking know how to string a fucking sentence together…"

"John!" Maureen barked.

"Right, right. So how are you? What's going on?"

"Okay. I have some issues at work but," and Maureen took a deep breath, which allowed time for John to say, "You know you are doing a great job. You always do a great job. But you don't work with friggin' morons like the CEO who calls me in the middle of the fucking night…"

"John, I was getting back to you about dinner tomorrow. Are we on?"

"Okay, so let me explain. You know I have a huge meeting in the morning. The CEO is gonna get his balls handed to him by the goddamn board tonight and we're going to meet in the morning and then I have to organize …"

"John. Dinner. Focus."

John, with an aggrieved tone, said, "I'm trying to explain. I'm trying to explain that I have to get that report done for the marketing department and this bitch who is probably going down on the CEO right now is out to get me. So tomorrow's off, kiddo. But I miss you. I want to see you."

"Okay, maybe the weekend."

"Great. I could really use your help on this report. I'll take you to dinner and we can talk about it."

Maureen resisted. She clenched her jaw. But it popped out. "What kind of report?

John, naturally, could not answer this directly. Not until he relayed the circumstances of how he was given the report to do and what was said when it was given to him and the unreasonable expectations about getting it done in two weeks by idiots who never wrote a decent sentence in their lives. Eventually he got to the description of the report and Maureen made a few acute observations.

John first told her why everything she said was wrong until he started thinking about it and came to the same conclusions. "I don't know what I would do without you. You are the best," he said. "I can't wait until this weekend. I'm getting hard just thinking about it."

"Bye, John."

Maureen had to admit she wasn't quite sure why she continued to date John. He burned with a dark energy, a ferocious perception of eternal rightness that took no prisoners. A disagreement between them could flare into an argument, like the flick of a burner on a gas stove. And then it would be gone. While he never backed down from a disagreement, neither did Maureen, and sometimes she felt like they wrangled like professional wrestlers, with crowd-pleasing strangleholds and backflips, as part of an elaborately choreographed battle. No matter what, John stuck around. They might go for weeks without speaking but eventually John would call with a question or Maureen would want a name from John's prodigious Rolodex and they would go out to dinner. She didn't see, as she told Sarah, a future with John, but he seemed vitally interested in her career; slights against her were slights against him, he with the great good sense to be her lover. She liked the energy they both brought to the bedroom; here they closed the door against disagreement. But sometimes Maureen wished for something other than a fellow warrior at her side, someone calmer perhaps, surer, less shiny.

Maureen jotted down John's name in her Filofax and turned back to her computer. She had to prepare copy for tomorrow and to speak briefly with the managing editor who was nervous about her freelance writing budget. Leticia A. Frank called and kept her on the phone complaining about a headline. Maureen managed to extract herself and run to the bathroom, but the tampon machine had run out. She stuffed her underwear with toilet paper and dashed to her car; she had to pick up her dry cleaning and deposit her check. Then it was on to I-95. She had a meeting at two o'clock with the director of the New Haven Theatre company about getting access to review shows there. Oh shit, she forgot she had to get cat litter today. Hercules was a patient cat, but he liked a clean litter box and made it obvious when it was not up to snuff. She hadn't balanced her checkbook and she was worried some of the mail piled on her kitchen table contained bills needed to be examined for errors and paid. As she braked when the traffic slowed, she realized there was a run in her just-purchased nylons, the expensive brand. She threw on her blinker to move into the left lane where traffic was moving just a bit faster, but the car behind her made a quick turn into the lane forcing her to slam on the brakes. "Asshole," she shrieked. She was going to be late. God, how she hated to be late.

Jane Austen spoke up then. Miss Austen often spoke up when Maureen was driving and stressed about arriving on time. Miss Austen could always calm her, her measured voice honed by Maureen's tendency to re-read *Pride and Prejudice* when she couldn't sleep.

"It never fails to astonish me how very emphatic you are with your solicitations to fellow travelers despite the undeniable futility of any possible effect upon your circumstances."

"I'm late," Maureen muttered.

"Your desire for promptness is commendable, and certainly were I the party to which you are so rapidly approaching, I would be most appreciative. Perhaps you should, however, direct your attention to the carriage bearing down on the right side."

Maureen yelped and turned the wheel to the left slightly.

"However efficient this mode of horseless transportation is, it is neither elegant nor tranquil. One travels at such a pace that one cannot enjoy the scenery passing by and one must be constantly on guard less calamity befalls."

"Jane – may I call you Jane?"

"Let us jettison formality, even if we have not been formally introduced."

"Yeah, people are just way too informal today. It really bugs me that the copy assistant Joey calls me Maureen and he calls Ken, Mr. Conroy. I'm a senior person and Joey is only 20 or 21. It shouldn't get to me. But it does bother me."

"You cannot gently but firmly correct him?"

"Oh God, no. I would be considered a class A bitch if I did that."

"And you would prefer not to be perceived as a female canine."

"No, but it would be better if the whole office were more formal. And if …you asshole!" She opened the window and screamed, "HEY, YOU CUT ME OFF."

"Your energy in defending your right of passage is delightful to behold, even with what can only be considered uncouth parlance. Why the haste, pray tell?"

"I don't like being late and I am tired. John kept me on the phone way too long. God, I wish he wasn't so needy. Two nights ago at the video store, I met this guy while we were both browsing in the documentary film section. We both reached for "The Front Line," the documentary about the war in El Salvador. He said he would call. So I stayed up late by the phone."

"If he calls while you are indisposed, will he not leave his card?"

"No, no, I mean on our phone message machines, those things. I just wanted to be home. I don't want him to leave a message because then I'll have to call him but I think he's the kind of guy who likes to call but not be called. Anyway I hate to call because then I might have to leave a message and wait for him to call back and I hate it when men don't call back so if I'm home I can pick up and not have to call him."

Maureen paused. "If you know what I mean," she added.

"I regret I don't. It does, however, occur to me if you sufficiently impressed him, he will call upon you. Or perhaps he has a betrothed already and yet seeks the pleasure of an imaginary conquest. You are, after all, currently allowing yourself to be courted by Mr. John."

"You know, you write so well about the battle of the sexes. Even though it was, like 200 years ago, it seems like things haven't changed much. There is still this tension, this dance between men and women that plays out again and again. I wish I had a Pump Room to go to instead of a bar, or I could go to a ball, not a singles dance. It seemed easier when I was younger. Guys sort of came to me and I could pick and choose. It's not the same now."

"Youth does have its exquisite appeal, particularly when matched with a sizable dowry. I confess I am rather surprised you did not find a suitable match when you were in the full bloom of young womanhood. Did you not have suitors when you first came out in society?"

"I did have a boyfriend in high school, but I guess you could say I outgrew him. And then there was Fred. I suppose I could have married him."

"And why did you not?"

"He was just too dull. And then there was Sebastian in college."

"What was amiss with his character?"

"He had no direction in life. He just wandered off."

"And were there no other suitable gentlemen in want of a wife?"

"Well, I really adored Paul. He dumped me for the instructor he met in an EST training seminar. He told me he was trying to get his head together. He obviously was working on another part of his anatomy. And now there's John. I guess I like him, but he takes up so much energy. I'm always having to be supportive. Still, he seems to really like me and that's better than nothing, right? Sometimes you have to settle, don't you?"

"Perhaps. However, 'better than nothing' is not necessarily the way to regard a gentleman to whom you will pledge your everlasting devotion. Then again … "

"But Jane, I don't know, I – hold on." Maureen made a hard right and screeched into the parking lot. She had arrived in New Haven on time.

CHAPTER ELEVEN

Origami

IN GIRL SCOUTS, Tina learned how to braid lariats, cajole neighbors into buying cookies, and fold little bits of paper into flowers and animals. Tina wasn't crazy about lariats or cookie sales, but she really liked origami. As she, Elektra, Sarah, and Maureen began to spend more time together, Tina began to think of them as four corners of a piece of paper folded differently at different times. Fold the paper in one pattern and you get a lotus flower or when she and Elektra popped over to Mahoney's Pub for Sea Breezes and French fries. Fold the paper into another configuration, and it was a butterfly as when she, Elektra and Sarah went to the movies. They would sink into the seats, inhale the hot breath of popcorn, and get lost in *Brazil, Jewel of the Nile*, or *Back to the Future*. Fold the paper into a jumping frog, and that's when Maureen would ask Tina to accompany her to an art opening or concert to scarf down handfuls of cubed cheese, pick at grapes, hover around the shrimp, and troll for feature ideas. Then there was the crane, the most elegant pattern, when four of them would meet for dinner and often ended up hanging out at Studio 54 in Maureen's apartment. Thursday became crane night.

On Friday and Saturday, maybe after an early movie, Elektra and Tina headed out to single bars or clubs. Elektra and Tina once spent an entire Saturday evening waiting to get into Limelight. Finally Elektra started complaining loudly, which turned out not to be something the doorman didn't appreciate. Maureen might join them depending on her status with John.

Sarah would come if she were between "cowboys." Maureen usually wore her blue silk peplum dress with its assertive ruffles at the waist. Tina favored black jeans tucked into cowboy boots and a sparkling bodice. Elektra called it the "Madonna home on the range" look. Elektra generally wore an oversize white shirt with black zigzags and spirals, a Keith Haring rip-off, she explained, matched with a black belt and shiny leather skirt. Sarah turned heads with a sleek mini-dress resembling a glittering snakeskin. "Would you believe I got this at Macy's on sale?" she said, every time.

They shouted over the pounding music in giddy tones and sipped watery drinks as they waited for a man to brave their formidable line up and ask one of them to dance. When a great dance song played like "You Spin Me Round" by Dead or Alive, Aretha's "Freeway of Love" and Prince's "1999," they would push their way through the sweaty, perfumed crowd to dance together.

After yet another Thursday night in which they talked about how men today were total losers, Maureen decided they needed to discuss something serious once in a while. Apparently, a lot of women were forming groups in which they all read the same book and gathered for potluck dinners to discuss. Maureen decided to form a book club and invited her friend Cheryl who invited her friend Diane. They set a date to talk about *The March of Folly* by Barbara W. Tuchman at Maureen's apartment. Cheryl, Maureen explained, was the real estate broker who dabbled in apartment rentals and helped her find Studio 54. Cheryl arrived teetering on stiletto heels and in jeans so tight, that Elektra later whispered to Tina that Cheryl must have a steel-plated crotch. She slipped off her heels the minute she sat down and rubbed her feet. Diane came a bit later, the others were halfway through their glasses of white wine, saying she had to stay late to discipline one of her employees for making long-distance calls surreptitiously from the office. "She should know this costs us money, both in phone bills and productivity," said Diane, unbuttoning her snug jacket with a huge sigh that fluttered the ruffles of her sallow yellow blouse.

The women made a stab at Tuchman but soon veered into topics like Imelda Marcos' 3,000 shoes. "I love pumps but there are limits," said Cheryl. They analyzed Tammy Faye Bakker's eyelashes. "Why doesn't she hire an image consultant; everyone is doing that," Diane said, who had dripped chardonnay on her blouse which seemed to just blend into the fabric. Everyone agreed the next book should be a novel and *The Prince of Tides* was chosen.

At the next meeting, after a quick pit stop on the characters in *The Prince of Tides*, the talk veered into less literary topics. Diane, her ring finger sparkling, said she was absolutely fixated on finding the best honeymoon spot. Cancun was overrun, Jamaica was getting dangerous, but there was a Club Med in Haiti, right? She had just nine months before the wedding. "I just hired a personal trainer to get me in shape and he is fabulous," Diane said.

"That's what I did before my wedding," Cheryl said. "Do you know what Roger got me for my birthday? A pager! So we can always be in touch."

"Oh, I am so obsessed about what I should get Teddy for his birthday," Diane said. "Maybe a Calvin Klein pullover? What do you gals think? What do you think a man would like?"

Tina shrugged and Elektra rolled her eyes.

"Can we get back to the book?" Maureen asked.

The next month, during what was supposed to be a discussion of *The Name of the Rose*, everyone confessed they hadn't finished reading it. Diane said she was way too busy trying to narrow down the wedding decoration colors. Cheryl said she was trying to close a deal on a house in Westport; she also had to host a dinner for the executive team of Roger's company and figure out what to do with the wives after the meal.

Maureen also had an excuse. She had the flu and Hercules hadn't left her side even when she was puking. Then Elektra jumped in to say Sammy and Sugar Pie played patty cake together and omigawd, how she wished she had a way of filming that because it was so cute. Tina chimed in with how Sheena had discovered gravity and was teaching Mindy how to push objects off the table. Sarah said Carrington had a gravity phase too and she lost one of her best Mexican figurines. Cheryl fiddled with the strap of her Coach bag and Diane became fixated on the bottom of her glass of wine.

When Elektra started to explain how she thought Eddie was coming out of his shell, Cheryl said, "Oh, let's not talk about cats anymore." "Yes, let's not," said Diane.

"You know," said Cheryl, her voice deepening as if she were summing up the fine points of a property to a neophyte buyer, "I don't think men really like cats much. You might keep that in mind."

"In mind for what?" said Sarah, who was deep into her third glass of chardonnay.

Cheryl blushed suddenly. "I thought you guys were all big into the dating scene. I mean, single women and their cats, it's a bit, you know, kind of a turn-off. Not that you don't have cute cats," she added, glancing nervously at Hercules who was lounging at Maureen's feet. "But, you know, it's like you know, old maids and their cats."

"How about we read this new book called *The Handmaid's Tale*?" Maureen jumped in, as Elektra was opening her mouth.

"I heard that was really depressing," said Diane. "Can't we do a light, fun read?"

Maureen managed to convince the group Margaret Atwood was an important writer about women. So a date was set to meet at Tina's place the next time.

However, both Cheryl and Diane called Tina to say they would not make it for the next meeting. Or ever again. They were each too busy. Diane had a crisis as the band she had booked seemed to have broken up. Cheryl said the day after the last meeting, she discovered Hercules had peed in her shoes judging by their smell.

Tina commiserated, saying, "Those really are pretty shoes; can't you get them cleaned?" and they chatted about the benefits of shopping in New York versus the Stamford Mall.

"You know, Tina, sooner or later you are going to have to focus on finding the right man," Cheryl said. "It's not easy, you know, to get a commitment, especially these days. Didn't you see that study that said a woman over 40 was more likely to be killed by a terrorist than to get married? Diane didn't get her fiance to propose until I got her to lose ten pounds and to add highlights to her hair. I'm not saying get rid of the kitties. Still you have to have priorities. Talking about cats with your friends is fine, but it's like a starter home. Eventually you have to really invest in a real house. Diane and I used to do everything together but sooner or later things change."

Tina thought of her sorority sisters, how they swore to stick together after college but how her letters to them did not seem to be returned. She only received engagement or wedding announcements. She thought origami would be different.

Maureen just shrugged when Tina said Cheryl and Diane were dropping out. Elektra was delighted, and Sarah said she didn't think they really knew how to read anything but romance novels.

The Cat Talk Book Club met once more. But rather than read *Old Possum's Book of Practical Cats*, they just went to see the musical *Cats* because after four years, it was likely to close soon.

CHAPTER TWELVE

The Ghost Kite

WHEN MAUREEN WAS twelve and her brother, James, was ten they found a kitten mewing in the alley behind their house. It had long black fur and white paws the color of dirty snow. They named it Fluffy. When they brought it home, their mother said to get that animal out of here. They pleaded and promised to feed and take care of it. Mother said absolutely not, she already had enough trouble keeping the house in order. Maureen's father was reading the paper or hiding behind it as he had a tendency to do when Mother was lecturing the kids. James started sobbing, clutching the crying cat, and Maureen ran out of arguments on the benefits of having a mouse hunter in the house. Her father put down the paper and said in a soft tone she would remember all her life. "Molly. Let them keep the cat."

So it was settled. There were conditions. Maureen and James would have to pay for a litter box and cat food out of their allowance. They had to clean the cat box daily. "Otherwise, it goes back to the street where you found it," Mother said.

With four people crammed into the top floor of a triple-decker in Somerville, even her father had to agree that cat box odor could not be permitted. After a couple of smelly weeks, Mother finally laid down the law. Maureen and James must clean the box every single day or Fluffy would go back to the alley.

So they squatted near Fluffy's box, trying not to gag, and

eyeing the lumpy hills and twisted ridges barely hiding what lay beneath. Maureen handed her brother the scoop purchased with the box. "Scoop it," she said.

"Why me?" he said.

"You're younger." In those days this was impeccable logic. "Just do one scoop and then I'll do one. One scoop."

Jimmy gingerly ran the scoop through the gravel, capturing one brown nugget. "Now shake it out and put it here," Maureen said, holding out a bag. "Now, I'll do it," and she took the scoop and made an emphatic sweep. "See, I got two." She handed the scoop back to Jimmy who scooped with more energy.

"I got three!" he said, squeaking with delight.

And they traded off. "I got one. That makes three." "I got two, that makes five" until the box was clean.

This launched the game of poop patrol. Taking turns, Maureen and Jimmy would each try to get the most poops in one scoop. Strict rules for the game evolved. You could only do one straight scoop, no zig zags. Poops smaller than a dime were worth only half point. No touching the poops for the tally. The most poops at the end of the game won. They began to check the box in the morning, after school and before bedtime, each seeking to be declared the day's champion. Soon Mother complained they were cleaning the box too much. She forced them to individually clean it on alternative days. Even so, they would hiss at each other. "I got three!" "So, I got four." Fluffy didn't seem to care one way or another.

Fluffy died after Maureen went off to college. But even now, decades later, when she cleans the box for Hercules, she mutters, "That was two. That was three." And sometimes she ended phone conversations with her brother with "I got three." He would usually spit out, "So, I got four" and hang up before she could counter.

Thus, Maureen learned early on that shit happens, but sometimes the more you get, the more you come out ahead.

MAUREEN DIDN'T WANT to fly to California during winter. She didn't like the way taking a break in a warm climate disrupted her Zen-like acceptance of New England's cold winters and cool, elusive springs. When Sarah once talked her into a sojourn to Cancun in February, it threw off Maureen's placid acclimation to bone-numbing chill and she didn't warm up until May. The heat was temporarily welcome, however it instilled in her body the false hope spring would arrive soon.

But now she had to disrupt her winter stoicism to fly to San Francisco to attend the fifth birthday party of her brother's son. Her mother had gone every year but this year she was too tired to go and besides, Maureen should get to know her nephew. That might not seem burdensome, but Maureen now had to get her nephew a present.

"What should I get my nephew for his birthday? What do you get a five-year-old boy? I mean, I haven't seen him since he was born," she groused to Tina. Everyone in the newsroom had to hear her lament. She asked Sarah who said she should get a book. Maureen asked William, who said, "How about a book?"

"I always send him a book," said Maureen.

"Then, how about a toy?"

"Last year I sent him a Rubik's Cube for Christmas and he already had two. How do I pick out something he doesn't have?"

"Why don't you call his parents and ask?"

"Well, I called my sister-in-law and she said, please don't spend a lot, and another book would be fine, but remember he's already reading at the second-grade level. I asked my brother and he said to get something without a ton of assembly." She did not add how she said, "I got four" by way of goodbye. Her brother just said, "You win" before hanging up.

"You'll think of something," William said.

Maureen walked to the Stamford Mall, wishing she could ask John, but he was immersed in a new initiative and put her off every time she called. What was she doing with him anyway? Why wasn't she hunting for real husband material?

She took the escalator to the second floor and paused outside a novelty store, remembering when she taught her younger brother to play checkers and then chess. She showed him how to put your face in the water when swimming, and how to grip a baseball bat. She told him it was okay to push a boy who called you "booger face." It was not okay to pinch your older sister for calling you "pest butt." She told James which were the good teachers at school and which were to be avoided. She showed him the proper way to inhale a joint.

As teenagers, they were comrades in battle against their ever-vigilant mother who patrolled the walls of the home against a world that could not be trusted. When their father was home, the wall would crack and a smile would seep out, bringing a strange light to the kitchen table. Their father often worked late, covering breaking stories. When he missed dinner, their mother retreated behind her fortress, brooding, waiting, silent, anticipating impending disaster.

At the dinner table, Maureen would talk about what she said in class and complain about the stupid jocks who teased her. Her brother agreed or argued or made fun of her, until she screamed at him to shut up, and he, delighted to get a rise of her, repeated his point, their voices rising to full volume until their mother said, finally, firmly, in a tone chilling the air like opening the freezer door, "That's enough."

Afterwards Maureen and her brother watched TV. They had made up a game called Guess The Product in the Commercial Before It Is Mentioned. Because commercials repeated and repeated, this simply meant who could say Charmin or Alka-Seltzer fast enough and then they would argue, until the voice, like that of doom or God, would come from the other room. "That's enough." When their father came home, they would pounce and demand stories until Mother gave the command. "That's enough."

Three days after their father died, Maureen and her brother held hands during the wake, numb, as his friends spoke to them quietly. It seemed like the entire city stopped by, the publisher, the mayor, even. Their mother, now justified in her premonitions, greeted everyone warmly. Later at home Maureen and her brother tried to watch TV. "Coke," said Maureen. "No, Pepsi," said her brother and they began to cry and wept, through the commercial break and through the next break and the next until their mother came in from the kitchen. "That's enough," she said, her voice cracking.

While Maureen went into the newspaper business, her brother went to the West Coast for college and stayed to work in the computer industry. He quickly married. Maureen bought an expensive present and a slinky, sequin dress for the wedding, thinking that as the older sister, she should have walked the aisle first. A year later, he had a son. She visited again, conscious she had relinquished forever her position as the trailblazing sibling, a feeling that grew more intense after she turned thirty without a fiancé in sight. And now her brother's son was five years old.

Maureen had no qualms about corralling a reluctant source, running a meeting, or editing a story while talking to a reporter on the phone, but she was forced to admit to herself that children put her on edge. When confronted with the offspring of acquaintances, she awkwardly shoved out a manicured hand for a shake, watching bewilderment and apprehension in the young eyes.

But this was her brother's son. She pictured Kenny saying, "I'll always remember when Aunt Maureen came to California and gave me this great present for my birthday." She thought about this all through the flight to California.

Jimmy was still at work, as Maureen drove up in the rented car and prepared herself for pleasantries with his wife, Penny. Penny, who was a few years older than her husband, switched to a part-time job when Kenny was born, and now devoted herself to his gym jamborees, piano lessons, and soccer games.

Maureen knocked on the front door and stepped inside, disoriented as always by the bright light that poured through the large windows. Penny rushed to hug her. "You can leave your shoes here," pointing to Maureen's heels. "Jackets go in the closet; plenty of room there. Come in, come in. Are you hungry? I have leftovers or I could make something."

Penny ushered Maureen into the living room. Kenny was curled in a chair, head bent over a picture book. He looked up when Maureen came in, carefully marked his spot with a strip of paper, and shut the book. He stood up. "Hi," he said, extending a hand. "How do you do?" His mother beamed. "This is Aunt Maureen. She came to visit when you were born," she said.

Maureen took the small hand in hers. "How do you do, Kenny?"

Penny said, "Why don't you call her Auntie Mo."

"I am fine, Auntie Mo."

"I'm fine too, Kenny."

They stared at each other. Kenny looked at his mother. "Can I go back and read now?"

The birthday party was as raucous as two dozen five- and six-year-old girls and boys could manage. Penny organized games and snacks; there were balloons, sparklers, and a clown with ragged clothes and holes in his two-foot-long shoes. When

Maureen finished helping Penny hand out plates of ice cream cake and her brother led the kids in a kazoo chorus in the yard, she sunk into a corner of the couch.

About a half hour later, Kenny, sniffling because he had been tripped by a bigger boy, came into the living room. The party carried on outside. He walked over and sat down beside Maureen on the couch and rubbed his eyes. They sat silently, listening to the happy screams coming from the backyard.

"You okay?" Maureen said.

"Yes," Kenny said, looking at his hands.

"Are you having a good time?"

"Yes," he said, looking up with a quivering lip.

"I am too," Maureen said.

They sat there together for another few minutes until other children started streaming in. It was time to unwrap presents, Penny announced. The first present was a Koosh ball. The second, third and fourth presents were books, which made Kenny's eyes light up, even though (as Penny whispered to Maureen) he had read most of them last year. Maureen, who had been tapping her red fingered nails on a table, tensed when Kenny grabbed the long, thin package wrapped in green paper. Kenny tore it open and pulled out the sticks and the triangular square of cloth, red and gold, with a dragon snaking across it. Kenny stared at the various pieces.

"It's a kite," Maureen said. "We can fly it in the air. You'll see. It will be fun."

"Thank you, Auntie Mo." Kenny went on to the next present, which turned out to be another Koosh ball.

By four o'clock, the kids, slack from the sugar rush letdown, were picked up by their parents, and Penny and Maureen tried to locate all the paper plates, running with melted ice cream, which had found their way into odd places throughout the house. Kenny, having sorted through his presents, setting them neatly side by side, returned to reading his book. He looked up.

"Mom, dad," said Kenny. "Can we go fly the kite now?"

James had just settled down with a beer. "Can we?" asked Maureen.

Her brother set down the beer. "Sure," he said.

The kite was assembled. Penny found a ball of string. A tail was attached. Eventually the four people, three big and one small, set out for the park a few blocks away. James carried the kite; Kenny jumped and skipped but at the end of the block, at the curb, he obediently stopped and reached for the nearest adult hand to cross the street, Maureen's.

The park stretched several blocks, with a baseball diamond at one end and tall trees flanking the other. The red dragon on the kite gleamed in the late afternoon sun.

"What do we do?" Kenny asked. "What do we do?"

Her brother pulled his son close. "See here. we tie the string on here. Here we put on the tail." "That's too much tail," Maureen said, frowning. "We can always take some off as needed," said her brother. "Now watch." He lifted the kite, quivering slightly in the breeze. "Kenny, hold the string. And stand still," Kenny picked up the ball of string and gripped it with both hands. "Let the string out but hold it tight," Maureen said. James lifted the kite, held it over his head and ran, tossing it into the air. "Go, go, go," Kenny yelled. The kite lifted upward, spun, and took a nosedive to the ground.

"All right. A bit less tail," said her brother. He knelt by the kite and shortened the tail.

"Now, hold on, Kenny," Maureen said. James lifted up the kite and ran backwards, tossing it into the air. For a second Maureen saw her brother as he was when they were kids back along the Charles River in a harsh Boston spring, trying to get a dime store contraption into the unforgiving air.

The kite's edges fluttered as it caught the wind and they

all started to yell. "Up, up, up," screamed Kenny. "Let out the string," Maureen cried. The kite rose higher and higher, zigzagging slightly as it ascended. "Keep it steady," said her brother. "Let out the string." Kenny let the string run through his fingers, dropping the ball. The kite rose and rose and rose, becoming a speck in the sky, a dot of red and gold. "It's flying," Kenny shrieked. "It's flying." Penny applauded. Maureen shaded her eyes to see the kite which had soared higher than she had ever seen a kite fly.

Then, the kite seemed to stop moving. It shuddered and began to fall.

As everyone yelled directions, the kite dived, heading like a bullet toward the row of trees at the edge of the park. It hit the tallest branch, stopped and sagged, the string piling like spaghetti around it. "Pull the string," her brother yelled. "Let it out and then pull," yelled Maureen. "Nooooo," Kenny cried.

They worked for an hour, pulling the string back and forth. The kite just lodged itself deeper into the branches, which embraced it in a leafy hug. There was no way to reach it by ladder. They finally gave up and Kenny stopped crying when Penny said they could go home and finish off the ice-cream cake. They all had big bowls, mounds of vanilla and chocolate ice cream topped with broken cookie crumbs. Only then did Maureen speak up. "I'm so sorry, Kenny. I am so sorry about the kite." Kenny looked up, ice cream and cake ringing his mouth. "That's okay, Auntie Mo. It wasn't your fault. It was the tree."

Maureen came back the following year for Kenny's sixth birthday, a quiet one at home this year. James, Penny, and Kenny all insisted on coming to pick her up at the airport. They drove back past the park, as Kenny turned to look out the window.

"Remember that kite?" her brother asked. "How it got stuck in the tree? It stayed there for a long time, all through the winter and spring. It kind of turned from red to white and it got pretty ragged there toward the end, but we could see it for a long time. In fact, it may still be up there."

"It looks like a ghost," said Kenny. "A kite ghost."

"Yeah, it really hung in there," James said.

"We look for it every time we go by," Kenny said "See," he pointed. "There it is. That's the kite tree." He waved as the car passed by.

For his birthday, Kenny said he wanted a pet. Maureen suggested they go to a local shelter to pick out a kitten. Penny was dubious, but Kenny promised to clean the litter box every day, particularly after his dad promised to show him a cool game he could play with it. Penny thought the game sounded weird, but she gave in, and they all piled into the car to head to a local animal shelter. Kenny chose a frisky little tabby who made him laugh by chasing its tail. He insisted on holding it in his lap on the way home.

As Kenny got out of the car, the cat leaped out of his arms and ran up the tree in the front yard, sending everyone into a panic. As Maureen, Penny, and Kenny shouted directions, James, teetering on a ladder, tried to reach for it. He managed to pluck it from a branch and hand it down to Maureen. Kite the Cat settled in after that. She was there to welcome Kenny home from Boston after he graduated from college.

CHAPTER THIRTEEN

The Day of the Dead

COLE CONCLUDED, "And that was a happy moment: when I learned he was fired and I got promoted." He looked at Sarah, his eyes sly and triumphant, as if daring her to challenge his knife-edge cunning.

Sarah was beginning to think this Cole had possibilities. She had met him when she went in for an interview at the Associated Press headquarters in Midtown. One of her AP Texas buddies was now working there and had recommended her for the general desk. She agreed to an interview but really, she didn't want to leave the *Gazette*. Maureen, however, encouraged her to give it a shot. "I'm not going to be here forever, you know, and you have to think about the future. That's what keeps me going."

"I don't really want to move into the city right now. What if I can't find a place that allows cats?" Sarah said.

"So commute by train with the rest of the herd." When Sarah delicately pointed out Maureen still needed back-up editing, Maureen said she could promote William as needed.

So Sarah went in for an interview and to retake the AP test, which was ridiculous because she even dreamed in AP style. The editors were impressed she spoke Spanish and told her the New York desk was often a stepping-stone to a foreign posting. While she was hobnobbing with her Texan friend, he introduced her to a former AP staffer, now in advertising – "he's a PR guru," her friend said – while the man, who had the build and heft of a linebacker, smiled broadly in complete agreement. They all went out for drinks and Cole, that was his name, later called her. Turned out he lived in Greenwich.

Cole intrigued her. Not so much on the first date; his bulk and coarse, sandy beard, as well as his arrogance put her off. They did have a lot in common. They talked about the line dividing news, advertising, and public relations. Cole had great personal gossip about the New York desk of the AP. He was adroit with words and persistent with his points, albeit with a charmingly teasing tone, spiced with just a hint of mockery, as if really, when you get down to it, everything was just a game to be won or lost. She agreed to a second date. She first disliked his formidable authority about everyone and everything, and yet this evening, she found his self-assurance compelling, even alluring. She guiltily warmed herself with the heat of his convictions. She found herself hoping he would apply that heat to seduce her.

"So that was a happy moment? When you managed to get someone fired," she asked Cole, trying to shake him just a little bit.

"Oh yeah," Cole said, without hesitation. "Yeah."

"Was it the happiest moment of your life?"

"Now, that's hard to say. Probably not. But," he took a sip of the wine, "Among the top ten."

"What was your happiest moment?" Sarah pressed.

"Dunno. What is yours?"

"Mine?"

"What's your happiest moment? I'd love to know."

Sarah looked at Cole's thick, strong fingers, curved around the stem of the wine glass. She pictured those hands cupping her breasts, the weight of his thighs against hers. Yes, possibilities. She fingered her own glass, now empty. "Mexico, I think. When I had a fellowship in Mexico."

"You had a fellowship in Mexico. What for?"

"To learn Spanish."

"To learn Spanish?"

"Si, to learn Spanish."

"And so, senorita, what was your happiest moment? Drinking tequila? Dancing at the cantina?"

Sarah was thinking of a Spanish word for hope. Esperando? No, that meant "waiting." Esperanza. Esperanza. She opened her mouth to respond, swept back by a memory escaping from the mental box marked "Mexico. Open with caution."

DURING HER STINT on the Idaho paper, she had applied for a fellowship from the National Press Foundation to study Spanish in Mexico. Someone at the foundation admired her migrant Mexican farm family article, and in a few months, she was headed to Cuernavaca, Mexico and one of the city's many language schools. She would live with a host Mexican family.

Two weeks of disorientation followed. Walking to the school. Doing Spanish drills. Trying to be polite to strangers. Trying to be polite to the family who pressed food upon her, which she ate because she had no way to say, thank you, it's delicious, but I'm now full. For the first time in her life, Sarah had no words, an odd state for someone who worked with words for a living. As an editor, she always had an expertly placed question, a single phrase of inquiry, a follow-up remark. Now, she had nothing. Just gestures, nods, an apologetic grimace. Nouns and verbs, ever her servants, eluded her.

After a while, she could utter bits of phrases that would make the family stare perplexed, then laugh. She tried to grasp the difference between por and para, between pero and perro, and, most of all, between soy (I am) and estoy (as in I am here). She messed up beso (kiss) and vaso (glass) and cansada (tired) and casada (married). All merriment for the teachers who saw such mishaps over and over again. Other students at the language school struggled too, except for those from Switzerland, languid young men and women, who came to Mexico simply to add another language to their repertoire of French, German, and English.

Sarah latched onto Margaret from New Jersey, who was quickly becoming fluent. With her dark hair and chocolate eyes, Margaret even looked a bit Mexican. Margaret was determined to experience the "real" Mexico before she went back to teaching junior high school in Hoboken.

Sarah found the Mexicans of Cuernavaca were largely tolerant of the students who came to the language schools. The teachers, most of them struggling to stay in the middle class of a country split into rich and poor, were amused by students like Margaret who begged to be taught the swear words and street slang. When, finally, Spanish started to lodge itself in Sarah's head, she found herself more relaxed, ready to flirt, and effusive with hands and facial expressions; she would say she didn't have the words to say she was unhappy. She smiled easily now, as this made her halting words more comprehensible. Mexico came into focus.

When she walked to school, the air sizzled with heat, she smelled tortillas, grilled chicken, the fumes of passing buses, and the occasional hint of human excrement wafting from an open drain. She would study on a bench in the zocalo, an odd Mexican word for the city square, which was filled with vendors tending roasted meats, wrinkled women in shawls and aprons hawking slices of mangos dusted with chili, and mariachi musicians, looking shabby and splendid in their studded pants and boots. They did not actually play in the square but hung out there waiting to be hired.

Students would gather in the zocalo around sunset for a cheap meal and beer. She usually ordered her favorite, tacos de pollo, chicken rolled in a sturdy corn tortilla topped with a pale sauce, nothing at all like the Mexican food served in the States.

As the sun went down, grackles with ebony eyes and shiny feathers would start singing – or screeching, depending on who was joking about it. The whistles, hoots and raspy chortles were matched by the students' babble of tongues as they slipped in and out of Spanish. On weekends, groups would band together to visit the small towns in the area, to climb the odd pyramid or visit a special market. Led by Margaret, they always sought the "authentic" Mexico, not the tourist spots where clueless gringos barked orders in English. The school's teachers would smile tolerantly when the students bragged of their adventures.

The teachers called Margaret, Margarita. Most of the students were tagged with Mexican nicknames. Sarah earned hers after she asked the teachers, "What does 'guera' mean?" Men and boys in the street would wolf whistle at her and sometimes hiss "guera" as she went by. "Blondie," she was told. It didn't make sense. "Rubio" meant blonde, and Sarah had red hair. But, she decided, guera simply meant someone not Mexican. So Sarah's nickname became Guerita.

Margarita loved to try odd food stands, stomach issues be damned, and to wander into shops and bargain with the merchants. She was always dragging Sarah to the marketplace where produce and crafts were sold. Sarah was aghast by the ceramic skulls and small, skeleton figures sold alongside ornately decorated plates and cups. The skulls glistened with rainbow patterns; floral designs circled empty sockets. Tiny brides and grooms were decked out in veils and tuxedos and tucked into spangled boxes, their dead faces fixed in wide grins. There were dead musicians playing trumpets and guitars and elegant skeletal women with feathered hats shading skinless faces. Margarita explained these represented the "Día de Los Muertos" or "Day of the Dead," a holiday in Mexico combining an Aztec ritual of remembering deceased family members with the Catholic

All Souls' Day. It was a time, she explained, when the dead came back to visit their families; it was a true Mexican tradition. The figurines, these calaveras, made Sarah uneasy. They seemed determined to carry on despite being dead; their faces were twisted into grins, joyful and defiant.

The teachers would sometimes talk about Mexican history (so sad! so beautiful!) as the students tried to make sense of the Colonial period, independence, the war with France, the war with the United States, and the Mexican Revolution. The teachers would talk, but only when pressed by the students, about the precarious economy, the falling peso, which could wipe out their salaries in an instant, and the government promises never delivered. Sarah would see the teachers talking among themselves in low voices, worry creasing their faces.

Sarah's Spanish improved. Her Mexican family told her, laughingly, she needed a Mexican boyfriend to really learn the language. Sara watched enviously as Margarita started dating a young instructor from the school, even though Margarita had told her about a boyfriend back in the States. Margarita also moved into a local, cheap hotel, a favorite among students, Hotel Peñalba or Hotel Sin Aqua as the teachers called it as the generator was not turned on until well into the morning and there would be no hot water without it. Margarita was often late to class, rushing in with wet hair, saying she had to wait for the generator. The hotel had a restaurant in its courtyard with a resident parrot and a depressed monkey on a chain. There was a poster-size photo of Emiliano Zapata. He used the hotel as a headquarters during the Mexican Revolution, and his stern visage looked over the tables where students and tourists drank Coronas. The sound of typing poured from a room occupied by an exiled activist from Uruguay. Sarah found the bearded, bespectacled man fascinating but could not follow his arguments about the pedagogy of the oppressed.

It was at the Hotel Peñalba where she met Alejandro.

Alejandro had hair as black and shiny as the grackles in the zocalo. His eyes seemed to be laughing, as if he could see beyond the present to jokes told in the future. He and his brother were friends with the instructor dating Margarita, and they came along with a group of students meeting at the hotel one evening. Sarah was transfixed by Alejandro's laughter. The group drank and chatted as the sun went down and the sound of the grackles from the streets eventually grew quiet. Sarah struggled to produce her best Spanish. "How long have you been studying?" Alejandro asked her. "You should know more by now." Sarah sighed and fell silent. The group broke up when the waiter insisted the restaurant was indeed closing and even American students could not get another round. As they were walking away, Sarah felt someone take her hand, and she looked into the dark eyes of Alejandro, lit by a streetlight. "Come have dinner with me tomorrow," he said.

He picked her up at the school in a car, he apologized it was only a Volkswagen. Soon they were speeding through Cuernavaca. They ate at Las Mañanitas or "Little Mornings," Cuernavaca's famous restaurant, ordering ceviche with the piercing note of fresh cilantro, fish with chili sauce, chicken with mole as dark as earth, matched with Superior, which Alejandro said was the best Mexican beer. Alejandro, an engineer, talked about how strong Mexico would be if the government weren't so corrupt. He talked about buildings, roads and infrastructure, he asked what did Sarah plan to do? Sarah said she was a journalist, a periodista, but she wasn't sure she wanted to return to Idaho. The potato-studded plains seemed infinitely remote. She wanted to improve her Spanish, that was the goal, she said.

Alejandro seemed to like her answer. "So what do you think of Mexico, then?" he asked.

"I love Mexico," Sarah burst out. "Me encanta." She tried to explain how she wanted to experience the real, authentic Mexico. She loved the food, the people, the city, everything. She was just a bit spooked by the Day of the Dead figurines in the marketplace.

"Día de Los Muertos," said Alejandro. "This is a very Mexican thing. When I was little, my parents would set up an altar in our house and put out photos of my grandfather and grandmother. They would put out food too and when I woke up the next day, I would run in to see if it were eaten, like Americans do with Santa Claus and cookies. It was a joyous thing; I felt like my grandparents were watching me."

"But there are these skeleton figurines of women with big hats and long dresses."

"Ah, La Catrina. That's what she is called. The wealthy woman. La Catrina appears in Mexican art. You have heard of the famous artist Diego Rivera, no?"

Sarah nodded. She and Margarita had made a trip to art museums in Mexico City, which featured the work of prominent Mexican muralists.

"Rivera put La Catrina into his artwork and so did Jose Clemente Orozco, another great Mexican artist. You should know his work, as well. La Catrina represents the rich society lady who dresses in finery and feathers, who thinks she is better than the poor, los campesinos. But death comes to her as well. Death comes to us all, yes, even to rich American mujeres."

"Pero, no soy rica," said Sarah, remembering to use the feminine form. "I'm just a poor periodista."

"Perhaps," said Alejandro. "Perhaps not in Mexico."

They talked until the restaurant closed and held hands as they walked to the car. Maybe it was the cerveza, maybe the jasmine-scented air, or the hot kisses in the front seat of the VW, but Sarah agreed when Alejandro said he would take her to a hotel. They made love on the narrow bed, Sarah shedding her clothes without effort. Sex required no language, no translation.

When he dropped her off afterwards, he explained he was going away, as many Mexicans did, for Semana Santa, the week leading up to Easter. But they would meet at the Hotel Peñalba the day after he returned. Would she please meet him there?

Sarah also went away for Semana Santa. She and Margarita, who was having second thoughts about her instructor, took off for Merida and the Yucatan. Sarah insisted on doing most of the talking; she pictured herself impressing Alejandro with her improved vocabulary and whispered into his ear. Returning to Cuernavaca felt like returning home. Sarah brought souvenirs for her Mexican family.

Sarah arrived at Hotel Peñalba early. She ordered a Superior in the courtyard restaurant and tried to read a Mexican newspaper. A couple needed a recommendation on a place to eat and she told them about Las Mañanitas. She puzzled over the paper; she sipped her drink, and the grackles started their sunset song. She could hear the clatter of the typewriter from the Uruguay exile. From his corner, Zapata watched over the room. She was now thinking in Spanish. Estoy. I am here. Soy, I am. I am here and my lover is on his way. Soy. Estoy.

Why did she think she could put that moment in words? Why now, years later, did she try to describe to Cole a moment of sublime happiness, an afternoon where everything was as it should be. Never again would she feel that overpowering, unreasoning surge of pure joy, that absolute certainty of bliss, not without fleeting anticipation of dread. Gripping an empty wine glass, she tried to explain what she immediately realized Cole would not, could not, understand.

"So your happiest moment was waiting in a hotel courtyard," said Cole. "That's odd."

"Waiting for someone who never showed up, whom I never saw again," Sarah said, acutely aware she had foolishly strayed into precarious territory. "The moment before I realized he was not coming."

"Why didn't he show up?"

"Just one of those things."

"Ah, one of those things."

"It was just Mexico."

"Ah, Mexico."

"It was a long time ago."

Sarah wouldn't tell Cole about the last month of the fellowship. She did not try to reach Alejandro after Margarita flippantly told her she found out he was not actually single, just sort of separated from his wife. She didn't tell Cole how when she returned to the States, she had an abortion, reasoning if she told no one, it didn't really happen. She didn't tell Cole that since then she never stayed with someone long enough to let him leave her. Instead, she honed the art of disappearing.

The waiter appeared. "Would you like another drink?" he asked.

Sarah looked at Cole. "I would," he said. "Same?"

"Same."

"So," Cole said. "You never went back to Mexico?"

"Well, yes, actually, " Sarah said, back on firmer ground. Soon, he might see the figurines on the shelves in her apartment. A skeleton bride and groom. A fleshless musician playing guitar, another playing drums. A wizened lady with purple feathers on her hat and tiny parrot on her shoulder. Every winter, she returned to Mexico and she always bought calaveras. She told her friends she wanted to keep up her Spanish, but she really wanted to become La Guerita again. Mexico had taught her Spanish and how things could be both beautiful and sad, how the skull was never far below the pretty, painted skin.

Nothing was forever or even until tomorrow. When she spoke Spanish to waiters and hotel clerks, she laughed and flirted, lacking the words to be sad. Esperando, esperanza. Waiting. Hoping. The words would dance on her tongue, joyful and defiant.

She now saw Cole was watching her intently. "We all have these sublime moments," he said suddenly, softly. "Fleeting. We just have to grab them when we can." And he reached across the table to take her hand.

Two weeks later they celebrated Sarah's new job at the AP by going to a Mexican restaurant. Later, in her studio, they made love as the figurines trembled on the shelves and her stack of wine glasses tinkled faintly. "Espero," she thought. "Espero."

CHAPTER FOURTEEN

Running on Full

TINA'S WEIGHT WAS creeping up. She could feel it when she zipped up the Calvin Klein jeans costing more than anything in her closet. She could sense it when she pulled a sweater over her head. When she was with Elektra, Maureen, and Sarah, she could forget she was a fat girl with pimples. Now she was on the verge of becoming that again.

She bought a paperback on the Beverly Hills Diet and one on the Scarsdale Diet and a Weight Watchers cookbook. She decided to eat only lettuce for a week. On the second day she polished off an entire bag of potato chips. She vowed to give up bread, butter, burgers, chocolate, and ice cream. She ordered a salad when the women went out to dinner on crane night, but she always accompanied them to a great ice cream place which had opened near Studio 54. Of course, they didn't have ice cream; they all ordered this new "healthy" frozen yogurt. They would take their cups of pink and white cream to a table to eat with relish and self-righteousness.

The more Tina tried to focus on dieting, the more she thought about food, and the more ravenous she became. Every vending machine called her name. She stopped keeping food in the house, but she would often stand in front of the open refrigerator and stare inside, as if a low-calorie chocolate cake would manifest itself.

She had lost her fear of the bathroom mirror. Elegant bottles of Clinique clarifying lotion and moisturizer lined her sink; every Niblet and Nubbie disappeared under carefully matched foundation and powder. But after reviewing and cataloging the state of her complexion every morning, she adopted another routine for an even-more heartless master. She had to step on the scale; an implacable machine offering either disgrace or dispensation. Her weight might be up, it might be down or the needle, the damn needle, might be the same. Once the needle was way down and Tina joyfully danced as she dressed for work until she realized she disrupted the base setting the previous day when she kicked the machine.

On Thursday, Maureen wanted to try a new Japanese restaurant. Sarah was able to make it. She said she was doing fine on the new job, just getting used to the new office and the long commute, and she was off on Thursday night. And she liked sushi. Elektra balked at the idea of raw fish and ordered chicken teriyaki. Tina ordered a seaweed salad and miso soup. The salad slipped down her throat like slimy worms and the miso tasted like salty dishwater. She tried to keep from looking at Elektra's plate of fragrant meat and the ovals of rice with ruby red flesh set before Maureen and Sarah.

"So what's a good way to lose weight?" Tina asked. They were splitting one order of ginger ice cream, and Tina was trying to take as little as possible with every dip of the spoon.

"Champagne and celery," said Elektra. "You lose calories eating celery and the champagne keeps you happy."

"That's not too healthy," Maureen said. "I'll tell you, I've been on every diet and I still have this stomach. I really hate my thighs, but I can never change them. I tried jogging with Sarah but I think I strained every muscle in my body."

"Because you went too far, too fast," Sarah said. "I warned you."

"How long have you been running?" Tina asked Sarah.

"Well, I ran track in high school and I'm not as fast as I was then anymore but it feels good. Usually I go over to Cove

Island. Why don't you come out with me? We'll go slow," Sarah said, looking at Maureen, "and see if you like it. You really clear your mind and the calories melt away."

Tina didn't exactly care about clearing her mind but the idea of melting calories, watching them slide off her body like spring snow, was irresistible.

On Saturday, Sarah met Tina at Cove Island beach, which had the loop Sarah favored. Persistent if weak waves nipped at the shore and the sand wet from the night's rain. Walkers passed by with determined faces. Runners had blank stares, their ears covered by headphones connected to Walkmans carried in sweaty hands. Tina wore a pair of her old stretchy pants and a sweatshirt. Sarah was in sleek blue tights with a matching blue jacket. Sarah examined Tina's sneakers and shrugged. They started out at a slow pace, but in a few minutes, Tina was gasping for breath. "Let's walk," Sarah said. And a few minutes later, she shouted, "Let's run." They ran and walked and ran and walked, with Sarah shouting encouragement. When Tina collapsed after two loops, Sarah showed her how to stretch her legs and then she took off effortlessly to run three more loops.

"Let's go shopping," she said to Tina, when she finished, shaking her head and sending beads of sweat flying. "Let's get you some good shoes."

Two days later, $50 poorer – how could sneakers cost so much? – and a very pricey T-shirt – what the hell was "wicking?" – the pain really set in, running from the tips of her toes through her stomach and back. "Did I break something," Tina asked Sarah. "No, it's always worse the second day. Take an Advil. It's much better than aspirin."

If not for her investment, and Sarah's frequent invitations, Tina might not have gone running again. But Sarah called and Tina felt she had to justify the money she spent. Sooner than she would have thought possible, Tina began to keep pace with

Sarah. Usually on the last loop, Sarah would say, "Meet you at the end," and take off with a burst of speed as Tina would slow down for a cool-down lap.

Early one evening, they found themselves pushing hard. They completed five loops and Sarah called out, "I'm taking one more, and she was off, while Tina slowed to a walk. When she finally stopped, she stretched and sat on a bench to watch Sarah let loose on the last lap.

"Whew," said Sarah, pulling up, her hair plastered to her forehead. "Let's sit for a moment."

The sun behind them was casting shafts of gold across the beach. Everything was bathed in light and possibility. Shadows from the park benches drew crosshatch designs on the sand. "What a beautiful evening," said Sarah. She stood up and twirled, stretching out her arms. "Feel the air. Feel the summer coming." Sarah whirled again. "Runner's high," she explained.

She bent down to touch her toes. "It's beautiful," said Tina, who was looking at Sarah, her lithe form and high cheekbones, her face alight.

"Great workout," said Sarah as she sat next to Tina.

"I wish I weren't so fat. I could maybe run faster."

Sarah looked sharply at Tina. "You're not fat. Why do you keep saying that?"

Tina looked down. She mumbled, "I was fat."

"Well, you're not now."

"What if I get fat again?

"You won't. You'll just run harder.

They sat in easy silence. Tina thought about the word "fat." Fat chance. Fat cat. Fat of the land. Fat, a word emerging from the tongue in a puff of air. "Fat," she said softly, sending the word into the twilight, letting it catch the breeze and drift away.

She turned to Sarah. "So how are things going with Cole?"

"Fine, fine, I think," said Sarah. "Fine. I had no idea a man so bulky and tall could be so adroit when horizontal. I just wish we could spend a little more time together."

"Why don't you?"

"Oh, well, timing. I'm still getting used to the AP. They change my schedule all the time. And he works late and he has his son on the weekends."

"So you don't see him on weekends, then?"

"No, but," and Sarah stood up and stretched. "You know, I often work on Saturday and Sunday, so it's okay. It's all right."

The flush was fading from Sarah's cheeks.

"I mean, I'm not really interested in marriage right now. I've decided that in a year or two I'm going to apply for a foreign post. I want to go to Mexico or Central America. So this is fine for now. I'm happy to take it slow, actually. He has talked about taking a trip to Cape Cod together. He has a friend with a house in Wellfleet. He's had a hard life, two marriages, a son. His last wife left him, from what he says. So I guess I understand why he keeps me at a distance. He says he's never marrying again. He said twice is enough. But I guess I really like him."

Tina had not heard Sarah talk about anyone this way. "Why so?"

"He is a mystery I'm trying to solve. He's always attentive, but he never reveals much. It's as if I'm always seeing him at a distance. But then in bed, the heat turns on. I have never been with someone who loves sex with me the way he does. He seems to know me, know my body. When we are making love, time falls away. There is nothing but him and me, all touch, no thought. We go on for hours – how many men do that? He knows where to touch me. I know where to touch him. When to move, when to stay. When we are together, there is nothing else. Before Cole, I never had sex that just took over every part of me. Oh, yeah, I've kinda been to bed with a lot of guys, you know, back in my wild youth, so to speak. And I learned not to expect much, but I've never been with anybody who gave me the feeling my entire body was breaking, dissolving, disappearing until nothing but the sensation exists. This has to mean something."

Sarah paused and sighed. "I think he thinks this way too. We can't keep our hands off each other when we are together. Every time we make love, I feel like we have melted into each other, that we are one person and our hearts beat together."

"And then?" said Tina.

"Then he rolls over and falls asleep," Sarah said softly. "I lie awake for a while. And in the morning, he says goodbye. It's like this sunset, all glory and gold and purple and then night falls. But someday, we will come together. Somehow. Or," she shrugged, "We'll just drift apart. And sail into our respective sunsets."

"But maybe he's the one," Tina said.

Sarah looked at the horizon, eyes both hopeful and resigned.

"Maybe. I don't know. And yet I want to stick with him. I just have this feeling about us."

"Oh, I bet he really likes you. He just doesn't want to talk about it. Guys are like that."

Sarah examined her shoes, but she seemed pleased.

Tina touched Sarah's arm. "Thanks for teaching me how to run."

"No, this is great. This is getting me out more. Time for frozen yogurt!"

"Time for yogurt."

Some weeks later, Tina decided to go running by herself. Her legs ached, and her chest hurt but she put the pain in a box as Sarah had suggested. Two men in very short shorts passed her, Tina sneaking glances at their lean frames. Energy surging, she passed two women in pink tights and a short, chubby man huffing determinedly along. When she finished six laps, the most she had ever done, she slowed down but kept walking, unable to go on, unable to stop. One of the lean men passed her and smiled. Her racing heart gradually slowed to match the languid beat of the waves at the shore.

CHAPTER FIFTEEN

Life is But A Dream

A FIERCE DEBATE broke out on Thursday night over Bobby Ewing's appearance in the shower in the season finale of *Dallas*.

"That can't be the real Bobby. No way," cried Elektra, pointing a french fry at Maureen as if it were a baton directed at a flutist who hit a wrong note.

"Patrick Duffy wanted to be back on *Dallas*, and they will make it work," said Maureen, her certainty fortified by secretive perusals of tabloids while waiting in line in grocery stores.

"But he was run over. I mean, Bobby's dead. He was buried!" said Tina. "How are they going to explain it in the next season?"

Maureen shrugged.

"I forget. Who really shot J.R.?" Sarah said languidly, her fingers stroking the glass of her empty wine glass as if she could pump it for a refill.

"Maybe Bobbie is an evil twin. Or a zombie," said Tina. "Or an alien being."

"Ridiculous," Elektra declared. Maureen was surprised at her writer's fury. Elektra had recently switched her blue eye shadow for green on the advice of a Bloomingdale's counter makeover and the emerald swaths under her eyebrows enhanced her wrath. "It doesn't make sense. It isn't logical."

"But it's a TV show, just a nighttime soap opera," Maureen said, as Tina and Elektra uttered overlapping indecipherable words of outrage.

"Maureen's more of a *Dynasty* fan," said Sarah, whether to

calm the debate or inflame it, Maureen could not tell.

"You lived in Dallas. What do you think happened?" Elektra asked Sarah.

"I lived in the real Dallas, alas. So no clue," Sarah said.

"I know this is fiction but the plot has to have, I don't know, some kind of logic. That's what makes it interesting," said Tina.

"*Star Trek* has the same issue," said Sarah, perking up. "The uniforms in the first motion picture were nothing like the show and then they changed them again in the next movie."

Elektra and Tina simultaneously rolled their eyes. "It's not the same thing. In science fiction, anything can happen," Elektra said.

"Just about anything can happen on TV," Sarah said.

Maureen's thoughts drifted; she was thinking there might be a good feature story in how fans might explain Bobby's reappearance; the paper could even run a contest for the person who came up with the best explanation. She was also vaguely aware *Dallas* was as real to Elektra and Tina as news from Washington while Sarah saw *Star Trek* as a blueprint for the future. TV created its own reality. Didn't Geraldo Rivera make a spectacle when he opened Al Capone's vault and found nothing? And yet everyone kept talking about it.

Maureen tuned back in when the conversation shifted to how villains, like J.R., were so much more interesting than the good guys, like Bobby, but you need the good to make the evil much worse. Elektra said Alexis was so much more interesting than Krystal on *Dynasty*. "And better dressed," added Tina. This could explain why women (and men) seemed to like bad boys or (bad girls) better. Which turned into a discussion of men in general. Maureen was definitely off with John, Sarah thought Cole might be becoming more committed, Tina had given her card to a guy on a recent assignment who looked a little like Rick but was not a lawyer, and Elektra declared the only man in her life now was Eddie.

Maureen arrived home a bit after eight o'clock and found Hercules patiently waiting for his wet dinner. She cleaned his box, and closed the door to her bedroom, which was strewn with clothes, before pouring herself a finger of rum and settling herself on the couch. She reached for the phone, dialed, and her mother, who didn't believe in phone machines, answered on the fifth ring.

"Hi mom," said Maureen, trying to keep her voice steady and cheerful.

"What's wrong?" said her mother.

"Nothing mom, why do you always ask me that?"

"It's late."

"Mom, it's 8:30. How are you?"

Maureen tried to call her mother every other week. She actually liked the calls, in the sense her mom gave her news of the neighborhood, the Red Sox and Mr. Connolly, her renter who, Maureen knew, was much more than a renter. Her brother didn't like the arrangement, but Maureen knew the retired bus driver did repairs around the apartment building that her mother bought after her father died. She needled her mother about living in sin. Her mother retorted that the real sin was the way Mr. Connolly's spendthrift daughters were always asking for a handout and she didn't need to join that family, thank you very much.

What Maureen didn't like was how her mother praised her brother for making a great living in this "computer stuff," and how he had a very nice wife, a wonderful son, and a big house in California. Mother never complained about Jimmy not calling because he was busy while Maureen didn't have an excuse for not picking up the phone.

Maureen managed to get her mother talking about Mrs. Donnelly and the McGrath kids. She told her mom about how she managed to get an interview with Tom Cruise for Elektra

STEPHANIE SCHOROW

and the publisher praised her in the newsroom for the series she conceived and directed on radiation poisoning; she was certain when the Sunday editor retired, she would get the position. She went on about what she would do and only noticed after ten minutes her mom had fallen silent.

"Are you there?" Maureen asked.

"Yes."

"What's wrong?"

"I was hoping you would get this newspaper stuff out of your system."

This was not a new conversation. Her mother had dropped hints for the past couple of years how Maureen should finally look for a career outside of journalism, something that paid more money or gave her more time for a social life, by which her mother meant dating and cleaning her house.

"Mom, I'm doing really well here."

She heard her mom exhale, a rush of air exuding coffee, Crest and cigarette smoke.

"Mom, I love this work. Just like dad did."

"Your father gave his whole heart to the paper. And what did he get? A heart attack."

"Mom, we have been over this. He smoked too much and never exercised and I really wish you would stop saying the job killed him. He just hated being at home. He missed it. Once the leave of absence was over, he would have been back and he would have been fine."

"You always say that."

"It's what I think."

"He couldn't go back."

"What do you mean?"

Silence. Then her mother said, "I think you should know now. He didn't want me to tell you. He didn't have a leave of absence. He was retired. Not his choice. He was made to retire.

It was the work of the new editor your dad thought was ruining the paper. You know your dad didn't hide his feelings. But your dad was so popular with the newsroom, the editor couldn't do anything. But then your dad had a heart attack, and they told him he could take sick leave but he could not come back. He was offered a package to go. He was told to take the package or he'd be let go with nothing. It wasn't a bad package. He took it. The money came in the week after he died."

"What are you saying? He was fired?"

"He was told to take the package."

"This can't be true. Everyone came to the wake. Everyone from the paper. The whole city came."

"Hypocrites. At least some of them."

Maureen tried to take a gulp out of her empty glass and shoved Hercules from her lap.

"You never told me. He never told me."

"He didn't want you to know. And then he passed away."

Maureen loosened her tight grip on her glass and then let it fall. It bounced on the floor, startling Hercules.

"You didn't tell me."

"What was there to tell? The package helped you and your brother go to college. I used some to buy the apartment building. "

"I thought the money came from your savings!" Maureen cried out. "And the scholarships."

"Yes, that too."

"Who was this editor? Who pushed him out?"

"Stop shouting. You know him. He got promoted a few years ago to a big New York paper. He lasted about a year there before the union got him fired. I don't know where he is now. You know him."

Maureen did know the guy. It was newsroom gossip how Joe Rossi declared he was going to shake up the staid New York news world only to be booted within a year. But she didn't realize how Rossi had treated her father. Her father was a news veteran. He was the best reporter on the paper. This should not have happened. And he didn't want her to know. "Nobody told me," she cried.

"Sweetheart, there's nothing to tell. You would have found out, but your dad passed away. Maybe his heart was really broken. When you wanted to major in journalism, I didn't want to say anything. I knew how much you loved your father. But I always worry about you. In the end the bosses didn't care about your dad's work, his years at the paper. He said they told him they were taking a new direction. I don't want this to happen to you."

"This is not going to happen to me."

"Your father was the best in the business. But that editor hated him for it. Sometimes talent doesn't make a difference."

Maureen silently wiped away tears.

"Hello," said her mother. "Are you there?"

"Yes."

"I didn't want to upset you. That's why I didn't tell you. But maybe you should know."

Maureen took a deep breath. Hercules took this as a sign he should jump back on her lap. "Mom, listen, don't worry about me. I can do this. I know it. "

"I hope so."

"Dad always said don't let the bastards get you down."

"I hated him swearing in front of you kids."

"Dad always said no matter what happened today, tomorrow there was another assignment."

"He did."

"Look," said Maureen. "I'm going to take the train to Boston next week for a visit. Okay?"

"If you can afford the time."

"Maybe I can take you and Mr. Connolly out to dinner."

"You don't have to take us out. You can't afford it."

"Mom, let me do this. We can go to Legal Seafoods."

Maureen knew this Boston landmark restaurant was her mother's soft spot.

"Oh, all right."

"I will be there next week."

It was late but Maureen compulsively called Sarah. Sarah made reassuring sounds while Maureen talked. Maureen finally realized Sarah was falling asleep and let her go. She sat on the couch with Hercules on her lap. "I'm here, I am always here for you," he purred. "Don't let the bastards get you down," she whispered, scratching behind his ears.

CHAPTER SIXTEEN

Building Castles

A MEDIEVAL CASTLE loomed above them, rough bricks cut with precision. Then, a Renaissance cathedral with ornately chiseled masonry built less for the glory of God than the egos of men. Next, the wings of a stone eagle rose skyward as it perched on a graceful archway. There was a cobblestone street, elevated, flipped sideways and turned into a wall. There were delicate, airy railings as if elves had immigrated from Middle Earth, discovered Art Deco, and wove steel like a spider web. There was concrete rickrack plucked from a giant's sewing kit and studded with medallions as if the structure awarded itself its own medal.

The bridges over the Merritt Parkway were each different, Cole explained, as he expertly navigated traffic on the narrow highway. It was a beautiful road and he liked driving it even if it took a bit more time to get to Cape Cod. Sarah started making up stories about each bridge; Cole added details such as the sexual peccadilloes of the king in the castle or how the elves probably worked without a union contract, which was why the structures still stood.

The trip to the Cape had finally come about and Sarah was reveling in the thought of spending several days with Cole. Their lovemaking had gone from very good to revelatory, but they had never spent three nights in a row with each other. This would bring them together.

Both Sarah and Cole told each other they were not into marriage. "Twice is enough," said Cole. "I don't believe in it," said Sarah, thinking of the many women she had known who put their careers, jobs, and dreams on hold for a man. She was focused on her new job at the Associated Press. Cole was in a demanding position which often pulled him into meetings on nights and weekends. It was a perfect relationship.

Two things bothered her. She and Cole were together on her bed, naked, sitting up face to face and drinking wine out of each other's glass, when Carrington, who usually watched from a nearby chair, jumped on the bed and rubbed her back against Cole. Sarah was delighted. "See, she likes you! You can pet her now." Cole touched the top of Carrington's head, not so much a pet as a kind of pinch. "I don't really like cats," he said. "They are sneaky."

"Sneaky?" Sarah asked and laughed. "Carrington isn't sneaky."

Carrington never again approached Cole.

Something else nagged at Sarah, even after she told herself it didn't matter. While they mostly met at Sarah's place, Sarah would sometimes drive over to Cole's apartment in Greenwich; his second wife got the big house. Cole had asked her why she wasn't spooked by the grinning dead Mexican figurines in her home, yet his place featured garish masks from Brazil and brooding bronze heads from southern Africa. His father had been a diplomat.

Sarah was intrigued by Cole's choice of furnishings; he had a four-poster bed, which came in handy for ties and scarves. The living room was furnished in variations of black and gray; the table, the chairs and side tables were slate, the rug was the shade of a storm cloud and soft on her knees. A side table was covered with photos, mostly of Cole's son, Henry.

"Why do you have a photo of your wife here?" she asked on her third visit, picking up a frame.

"It's for my son, to make sure he knows his parents still

care for each other," he said.

Later, while she was kept awake by his snores, she got up and went into the living room to examine the photo of Cole and his ex. Cole had his arm around a slim woman with short brown hair and a shy smile, pulling her hard against his side in a gesture of joyous possession. His face was glowing and he was laughing. Cole had told her his wife had left him and she was the one who broke up the marriage. Sarah didn't quite believe him. Almost every divorced man she had ever dated blamed his wife for the breakup. Seeing the exuberant look on Cole's face in the photo made her think he was perhaps telling the truth. She carefully put the photo back, fighting a sudden urge to lay it flat on the table.

When they were finally able to schedule the Cape Cod trip, Sarah thought this was it. This would be the weekend they finally connected; everything would come together. They would finally say "I love you." Sarah leaned her head against Cole during the long drive.

The cottage smelled of salt air and decaying fish. Cole attempted to make a fire, gave up, and said he knew of a great seafood place nearby. They had white wine, oysters, sea bass, and split a crème brûlée for dessert. The cottage was still cold when they returned, at least Sarah thought so, but Cole insisted on opening another bottle of wine, saying it would soon get hot. She drank slowly, grateful she would have two days with Cole, two days to not only make love but talk to each other and maybe get that damn fireplace going. They crawled still dressed into the bed, piled with quilts and made a game out of taking off one piece of clothing at a time. When she climaxed with a howl, she saw a glowing full moon behind her eyelids, ripe and bursting. When he came, she could feel him falling into her and she held him until he fell asleep. The snoring kept her awake for a little while but soothed with wine and the sensation she and Cole had finally connected in both mind and body, she fell asleep.

Sarah woke, stretched, and thought of Carrington. Maureen promised to feed her and Elektra said she would look in. Carrington is fine, she thought. She reached for Cole and found him with an erection. This time the lovemaking was relatively short. Sarah was anxious to take a walk on the beach. They managed to get themselves out of bed, and dressed and ready to go out for breakfast when the phone in the cabin rang.

Cole answered it and turned his back, speaking softly, as Sarah pretended to finish getting ready. He hung up. "I'm sorry, but I think we have to leave early," he said.

"How early?"

"Like now."

"What's wrong?"

"Some issues with my son. His mother wants me to deal with him."

"Doesn't she know you're out of town?"

Cole didn't answer. "I'm sorry. Could we leave in about half an hour?"

"I thought we were going to stay for another two nights."

"That was the plan. But things change. I'm sorry. We have to go."

"You know I asked for these two days off."

"I'm sorry but I have to get back. I have to be careful until the divorce is final."

"What are you talking about? You mean you're not divorced?"

"Not yet. Almost."

Sarah did not know whether to scream or cry. "You told me you had been married twice. You told me your last wife left you."

"She did. The separation was her idea."

"But you're still married."

"Why are you getting so upset about this?"

"You didn't tell me you were still married."

"I think you jumped to conclusions."

"So this is my fault?"

"No, I just think you made assumptions. I am sorry, but we have to go."

"Okay," said Sarah, her voice like sandpaper.

"I'm sorry."

"Okay, I said."

They drove back in silence. Sarah was trying to remember exactly what Cole said about his marriage. Didn't he use the term ex-wife? Or did he just say, "his son's mother?" When Cole pulled up to Studio 54, she was ready to jump out and not look back.

"Hey," he said, reaching out to touch her shoulder, causing her to halt. "I really am sorry. I should have told you about my wife, but I just didn't want to think about it. I just wanted to think about you. Look, I had a really great time, even if it was short. We'll go back to the Cape. We will have a longer trip next time."

"Really?" Sarah asked.

"Really. I promise."

He pulled her in for a long kiss.

Sarah walked slowly up to her apartment. This was about his son after all. He was a good father. She was not one of those whiny, needy girlfriends. He was definitely separated, after all. Why did it matter? She opened the door and Carrington greeted her by rubbing against her ankles. And so what? She had Carrington. Cole was just another cowboy. That's what she told Maureen, Tina, and Elektra when they asked how the trip went. That's what she told herself.

CHAPTER SEVENTEEN

Petite Blonde Seeks Man Who Won't Play Games

THURSDAY'S CRANE NIGHT focused on personal ads. This was how people meet nowadays. Everyone is doing it. Everyone. Really. There was even something called video dating. Where else are you going to meet people? In a bar? In church? Oh please. There was no shame, no stigma anymore. Maureen remained dubious but intrigued. "Why don't you guys take out some ads and write a feature story about it?" she said to Elektra and Tina.

"Sarah?" She shrugged. "Why not?" Cole called once after the Cape trip to say he had to go to Atlanta for business and she hadn't heard from him since.

"How about you?" Tina and Elektra said to Maureen more or less simultaneously. "Maybe," said Maureen. "I'm still not sure about John. He can be fun to be around, and he seems to really like me, but we had an argument about nuclear power." Maureen insisted the Chernobyl disaster proved it wasn't safe while John said the Soviet Union was screwed up and she was being a ridiculous liberal again.

Maureen said she would write an ad but Elektra, Tina, and Sarah had to do it too. They would do it right now, together.

Tina's ad read: Petite blonde, who loves going to movies, long walks on the beach, cats, and great conversation over a glass of red wine. Looking for a warm, generous man who won't play games.

Elektra's ad read: Boisterous, generous, exuberant, free spirit, who loves music, long walks in the city, eating at Italian restaurants and cats. Looking for a partner for cocktails in the summer and Irish coffee in the winter.

Maureen's ad read: Would you like to meet a strong but loving woman, who will challenge you intellectually and support you emotionally? Adores all pets, especially cats. Looking for a guy to talk politics, movies, music, and theater over sushi and sake.

Sarah's ad read: Tall redhead who loves cats. Wants a good fuck.

"Sarah," they all screamed when she read hers.

"Well, I think it's good," said Tina. "But I think you should take out the cat part."

In the end, they all took out the cat part. Sarah's final ad read: Tall, toned, redhead who loves movies, running on the beach, and science fiction. Looking for a sensual, sensitive man who treats women with care and respect.

The next night Cole showed up with a bottle of champagne and chocolates, bursting with stories about Atlanta and how his lawyer had worked rings around his wife's lawyer. Sarah never placed the ad.

Tina did and found herself over the next few months on a carousel of dates, as if set to the tune of "It's Raining Men." Here comes George; there goes Jimmy; here's Seymour and Angelo, round and round, up and down. George, the stockbroker with the polo shirt and jeans, hair as sandy brown as the Cove Beach shoreline, with a spray of freckles and cunning blue eyes. Jimmy, with a Yankees cap who punctuated every sentence with, "So whaddayya know." Seymour, the lawyer, all polite and deferential but who refused to lose an argument – any argument – political, musical or whether salad can really be a dessert as in France. Marty cut a striking figure in a black leather jacket but was incredulous she actually liked Madonna. "Rock music officially died with Sid Vicious," he said. "Bon Jovi?" Too popular. "Blondie?" Ripping off hip hop.

Tina adopted her own guidelines: Don't order anything with fish or pasta, don't have a second glass of wine and never, ever, speak of cats.

"When you're not writing, what do you like doing?" asked George, fixing her with those blue eyes and smiling.

"Well, I run."

"So you're a runner. No wonder you're in such great shape. How far?"

"Maybe five, six miles, three times a week."

"Cool," said George. "What else do you do?"

Tina was a bit flustered under his gaze. "Well, I am teaching my cats to fetch."

"You have a cat," George said.

"Actually two cats. Sheena and Mindy. Very smart. I am teaching them…"

"My ex-girlfriend had a cat. Nasty little bugger, he never liked me."

"My cats are very friendly."

"He once pooped in my shoe. Italian, too. Let's get the check. I'll call you later."

Then again, cats could come to the rescue. Jimmy insisted on walking her home, and insisted on bringing her to her door. Asked for, no, demanded a good night kiss and said, "No, really, come on," when Tina said she really had to get up in the morning. "Besides," she said, "I have to feed the cats." "How many cats?" "Ten." "Okay, I'll call you."

Maureen bugged her about writing a feature, but Tina demurred. All the dates only made her long for Rick, his cool manner, his easy smile, his scent. Sarah lied and said she hadn't received any responses she liked. "I should have gone with 'Let's fuck,'" she said. Elektra was curiously noncommittal. Maureen had no responses at all

Instead of yogurt after their run, Sarah suggested to Tina

they go for drinks. She said she needed it. The AP job was a bit rougher than she had expected. Also, when she called Cole to tell him she had a surprise Saturday night off, Cole said he had plans with his son and abruptly cut off the conversation when she suggested the three of them get together. She said she was so angry she was thinking about telling him to get lost for good. Tina didn't want to go anywhere without showering and applying makeup, but Sarah convinced her to forget the Clinique, and just go. "Come on, we have an exercise glow," Sarah said.

Wiping off their sweat with Kleenex plucked from a box found on the floor of Sarah's car, they drove over to Bobby Valentine's, a sports bar with nary a fern in sight. Tina was nervous about a Nubbie on her forehead, but Sarah said it was barely noticeable. They settled along the bar and ordered two white wines. Tina made Sarah laugh by recounting the latest battle between Maureen and Jeff, the rock critic. "He hates 'Til Tuesday and Maureen told him 'Voices Carry' was a great song."

"I agree," Sarah interrupted.

"And then Jeff starts going on about the taunt predator-prey dynamic in 'Hungry Like The Wolf,' and Maureen said Duran Duran could not stand up to the complexities of Talking Heads and they get louder and louder until someone on the copy desk stands up and screams, 'Hush! You do know voices carry.'"

Sarah ducked her head and said softly to Tina. "I think a guy behind you is looking at us." Tina turned around immediately. "Which guy?" she whispered. "The chubby one," said Sarah. "Dirty blond hair. Glasses." "Oh, forget it," said Tina.

The bartender approached, "A gentleman over there would like to buy you drinks." Tina groaned. Sarah said, "We'll have two Sea Breezes," whispering to Tina, "Come on. Free drinks." The drinks arrived and Sarah turned and raised her glass to the guy. "He is coming over," she trilled softly.

"Hello," said the man. "I hope I'm not bothering you."

"Oh no," said Sarah, who was drinking her Sea Breeze in gulps. "This is Tina and I'm Sarah."

"Hello Tina and Sarah," the man said, trying to shake hands while clutching his own drink. "I'm Thomas, call me Tommy." Tina thought his hand was like a moist marshmallow.

"Uh, what are you gals up to?"

Sarah tossed back her drink and said, with a slight slur, "I'm up to five-eight but working on five-nine."

The man laughed politely. With the jerky flow of someone trying to drive a standard car for the first time, the conversation lurched on. Sarah giddy, Tina silent. Tommy wiped his glasses with his tie.

"What do you do?" he asked Tina.

"I write features for the *Gazette*."

"Hey that's neat," he replied. "Did you see the really funny story about how in the future everyone will be fitted with a camera in their foreheads?"

"I wrote it."

"You did? It was so funny."

Tina asked Tommy what he did.

"I work over at IBM in the personal computer division."

"I love my Apple personal computer," said Sarah, who had ordered another drink.

"Uh, that's sort of the competition," said Tommy. "There are PCs and there are Apples."

"Oh, yeah, right," said Sarah. "But isn't the Apple Two E a form of personal computer? It's very personal for me."

"Hey, Sarah, I think we should be heading home," said Tina. She'd not seen Sarah this inebriated in public before."

"Excuse me, I'll be back," said Sarah and headed in a zig-zag toward the bathroom.

Tommy turned toward Tina. "Could I have your number?

I'd like to call you sometime." Tina sighed. "Sure," and she gave him her card. He gave her his.

Tommy looked at the small piece of cardboard. "So your full name is Christina," he said.

"I prefer Tina," said Tina.

Tommy didn't seem to hear her. "Christina. Christina," he said. "I'll call."

He returned to his buddies who slapped him on the back. Sarah appeared, smiling but unsteady. She and Tina walked to Sarah's car arm in arm. Tina drove.

"I really miss Cole, you know, I shouldn't, but I do," Sarah said.

"It's okay," Tina said.

"Hush, hush, voices carry," Sarah sang.

Slightly off tune, Tina continued the verse. "He wants me but only part of the time."

Tina stayed with Sarah until they were inside her apartment. Sarah lay down on the bed, singing softly, "He wants me if he can keep me in line" and passed out. Carrington jumped up beside her.

As Tina backed out of the apartment, a memory of Rick brushed by her, a shiver of desire and jealousy.

Tommy called Tina the next day.

For their first date, Tina suggested a movie and dinner. "At least," she told Elektra, "I'll get a movie out of it." Everything was going smoothly at dinner until Tommy, exuberantly making a point about his new Sony Walkman, threw out his arms and sent his wine glass flying into Tina's lap. Fortunately, it was white wine and Tommy apologized profusely. On their second date, they went to see the dance group Pilobolus and Tommy politely sat through it; they went for hamburgers afterwards. On their third date, Tommy suggested they try a hot new restaurant in New York and they took the train together. On the way home, Tommy slipped his hand in hers and walked her home from the station. Outside her apartment, he leaned in to kiss her. Tina lowered her head, dropped his hand, and said she had a very busy week coming up. A very busy week.

"Call me when you're free," Tommy said sadly.

Tina found herself waiting to hear from him. "You didn't tell him about cats, did you?" Elektra demanded. Tina shook her head.

"But he said call him right?" Elektra said. "So why don't you?"

Tina thought about it. She really did enjoy the dates.

Later, even after feeding the cats extra treats, they seemed to be watching her as if they expected her to do something. But what? She dialed Tommy's number. "Hi Tommy. It's Tina."

"Tina! I'm so GLAD to hear from you. How are you doing?"

"Fine." Tina waited. Then she took a deep breath.

"Uh, do you want to get together Saturday? You know, casual like?"

"Sure, let's go to Bobby V's and watch the game," said Tommy, his voice happy. "A bunch of my buddies are going there. Burgers and beer on me."

Tina hung up wondering which game Tommy was talking about. "The World Series begins on Saturday," said Maureen in an exasperated tone on Thursday night. "Don't you read the sports pages? Mets versus Red Sox. Come on. It's a big deal."

Elektra sniffed and said the only game she watched was the Stoopid Bowl because somebody would throw a party.

"The Red Sox have a great team," said Maureen. "I think it's their year."

"You're not going to root for the Sox over the Mets, are you?" asked Sarah with mock horror.

"The Sox haven't won a World Series in 68 years," said

Maureen. "This is it. They're going to do it."

"I thought you were happy to be out of Boston," Tina said.

"Yes, well, the Red Sox are a religion in Boston," Maureen said. "I don't go to confession but I'm still a Catholic. And God says I still have to root for the Sox."

At Bobby V's, Tommy and Tina joined the crowd at the bar near the TV and Tommy was more animated than she had ever seen him, enthusiastically whispering details to Tina about the players. The entire bar cheered and groaned and Tina found herself yelling along, even though the hits were few. When the Red Sox came out ahead, 1 to 0. Tommy swallowed the rest of his beer down and said abruptly, "Let's go."

They stepped out into the fall air, still scented with decaying leaves. The bar was emptying amid shouts of "Wait until tomorrow." Tommy reached for Tina's hand and they walked silently hand in hand to Tina's apartment. Tommy pulled her to him and kissed her, his lips plump and soft.

Just as Tina was about to work up the courage to ask him inside, Tommy pulled away.

"Do you want to watch the game together tomorrow? Unfortunately I have to go."

"Really?" Tina asked, attempting to be coyly seductive.

Tommy heaved a huge sigh and held on to Tina's hand. "I have to take care of the boys."

The boys. He must be a single father. Maybe he wasn't divorced. Maybe there was a wife.

"The boys? How old are they?"

"Leo and Bob are seven and Ratso is fifteen."

Ratso? Fifteen? Tina was miffed. "Why didn't you tell me about them?"

"I'm sorry, I should have said something, but so many people get freaked out about a single guy with three cats."

"Three cats?" asked Tina.

"I call them my boys."

"Three cats?" asked Tina.

"Yes, my boys," said Tommy. "You're not allergic to cats, are you?"

TINA DISCOVERED SHE liked baseball, especially when watched in a bar, with beer, burgers and fries. In Game Six, she cheered with an ecstatic Tommy when the Mets pulled it off in the bottom of the tenth. She had to console a traumatized Maureen the next day who was cursing this guy Bill Buckner. When Game Seven, the final game, concluded with Mets victorious, the customers in Bobby V's poured out into the street shouting to the heavens. Tommy picked up Tina, whirled her around and presented her very own Mets cap. He had been saving it as a surprise. They ended up kissing madly in the street and Tina invited Tommy over.

Mindy made a dive for the closet when Tina opened the door. Sheena mewed loudly until both Tommy and Tina petted her. Tina put some cat treats in their bowls, popped a cassette into the stereo, and turned off all the lights save one. Tommy said he loved her cozy studio. Tina struggled to open a bottle of champagne Elektra had left in the frig; Tommy took the bottle and popped the cork, sending champagne spilling over and on the floor; Tina rushed to get glasses.

"I'm so happy the Mets won. What a series," said Tina.

"Ah well. It's only a game," said Tommy, gallantly lying.

They clinked glasses. He was leaning in for a kiss when the sound of "Gack, gack, gack" followed by a gushing sound coming from the direction of the bathroom. Sheena had vomited.

"I'm so sorry," said Tina. "Let me clean that up."

Tina grabbed a dish towel but in the dark, she couldn't find anything. She gave up and joined Tommy back on the futon.

"So how long have you had Mindy and Sheena?" he asked,

refilling her glass.

Tina told him how she got Mindy Marmalade and because she wanted a backup cat she got Sheena, Queen of the Jungle. She asked, "So how did you get your three boys?"

Bob and Leo were kittens bestowed on Tommy by a sister whose boyfriend was allergic to cats. The four of them lived in relative harmony, as long as everyone knew it was Ratso's world. Ratso was the alpha male of the group.

"Why did you name him Ratso?"

Tommy paused but plunged in. His youngest brother was born when he was twelve years old and he asked his mom why she had given birth to a rat. "Ratso" became his nickname for his brother, Richard. Ratso preferred to tag along with his big brother, even though his older sisters doted on him. Ratso was his shadow at home. Then Richard fell ill with leukemia when he was seven and lived for only a year. Tommy took a semester off from college to be with his family. "Rough. It was rough."

Years later, he found a skinny, bedraggled cat limping around the grounds of IBM, too sick and exhausted to run away. He took the cat to a vet and then home, determined he would nurse him back to health. He did. He named the cat Ratso.

Tommy fell silent, and Tina reached for his hand and squeezed it. "I like the name," she said softly.

"Well, he's never quite lost the look of a street cat. And he rules the roost. He keeps Bob and Leo in line. I also think he still misses his balls."

A giggle burst from Tina, not so much a laugh as a release of giddiness.

"What? What's so funny?" Tommy said, now laughing too. He put his arms around her, making her laugh more. "Balls," she sputtered. "Baseballs." Clothes were shed, slowly. Hands reached to sweet spots and there were no more interruptions until they fell back on the futon, sending Mindy hissing to the floor.

Afterwards, they held each other, Tina's head pillowed on Tommy's bulky chest.

"You don't remember seeing me before the night we met in Bobby V's," he asked softly.

"No. When?"

"I've seen you running at Cove Island."

"Oh," said Tina, now recalling a chubby guy running there. "You run there?"

"I tried to run there. Then I sprained my ankle. I only kept going because I would sometimes see you there. Sometimes with your friend Sarah and sometimes alone. Once you took off your headband and the sun was lighting up your hair. You were flying, like some exotic bird, around and around. I didn't want to sit on a bench and watch. I mean I would look like a total creepy weirdo, so I just kept walking and watched as you passed me."

"Why didn't you talk to me?"

"Me, this schlubby guy who can barely run? I've always been this fat kid who got beat up in school and you were this, I don't know, this fair-haired nymph. I couldn't believe it when I saw you in Bobby V's. Of course, you wouldn't remember me, but then you agreed to go out. I still can't believe I'm here with you." He stroked her face.

Tina was about to say, "But really I'm so fat." She opened her mouth, but Tommy said, "Hold on, I gotta pee." He rose and Tina watched his bulk, gray in the dim light, padding away. There was a slight squishing sound. "I found the cat puke," he called.

CHAPTER EIGHTEEN

The Promotion

THERE ARE BAD days and there are gruesome days. Maureen was having a gruesome day. It started when theater critic Leticia A. Frank had balked at filing on an early deadline for her review of *Macbeth*. She screamed about drama and art and the muse and would not hear about how copy editors had to go home once in a while. The copy editors, who called her Morticia A. Frankenstein, were not in a mood to compromise. Maureen had to hold her temper and wheedle and cajole both sides until an arrangement was worked out. Leticia would call in some details and background at intermission, and add the opening paragraphs as soon as the play ended by using the lobby payphone.

She didn't want to tell Sarah this, but she really missed her former second in command. William was certainly a good editor, but Sarah had a way of massaging copy, just enough to make it shine, and let the voice of the writer through. The other day, William and Elektra had a loud battle over the phone about the proper use of the word "unique." They settled on "distinctive." Then the movie critic complained William had boasted about never seeing any of the Star Wars movies and he corrected Luke to "Mr. Skywalker" on second reference.

Maureen thought her day was turning around when Elektra triumphantly turned in her story, an interview with Glenda Jackson, who was, she said, the perfect Lady Macbeth. Then a shamefaced Tina had to confess she was still waiting for sources to get back to her. She would have to write her feature on the perils of surrogate parenting next week. Tina's mortification notwithstanding, Maureen cut her off abruptly as she had to figure out a replacement story and settled on an AP feature she had been hoarding; she sent it to the copy desk. She called Jeff, the rock critic, who picked up on the tenth ring, about his story due that afternoon on the subject of "Heavy Metal versus Glam Rock: Who will win the battle of the bands?"

"Why do I have to turn in something today that runs in two days?" he demanded.

"We have been over this. We need to do the feature pages early. It's not hard news. I've told you this. It was due two hours ago."

"Okay, okay. Just a few minutes," he said. Thirty minutes later, the fax machine whirred and Jeff's copy came through. Maureen rushed through the first read, which sparkled with insight but was filled with typos and insider jargon which she corrected with her red grease pencil. She called Jeff back to define the difference between "Thrash Metal" and "Death Metal." She slipped the edited copy through the slot leading to the typing pool. Someone there would get it into the Atex system and William would read it again in the morning before it went to the copy desk for layout and headline writing.

At 9 p.m., she went home to a hungry cat and a glass of wine. She saw her machine blinking. John had called twice. She would call him back tomorrow. After gobbling his dinner, Hercules hopped up beside her, licking his lips, washed his face and crawled onto her lap. Maureen clicked on the TV. The old movie, "All About Eve," was playing. Maureen scratched behind Herc's ears and glowed; once again she managed to get everything together. They fell asleep together on the couch.

Maureen was hoping to showcase her talents at juggling editing tasks before the announcement of the new Sunday editor. She was sure she would finally get a promotion, since the current editor had announced he was retiring. Like Sarah, she was ready to move on. This would be her final triumph before heading to the *New York Times*. The other applicants were the dweeby copy chief, who was talented but dull, and someone from outside the paper, an old friend of managing editor Ken Conroy, a woman who had written magazine articles but had no daily newspaper experience. Gabriel "Gabby" Juniper did the occasional Sunday feature, usually featuring escapades with her two young sons and devoted but clueless husband.

Gabby had talent and experience. This Maureen could not deny. She had been published in *Cosmopolitan, Esquire*, and *People*, and she had self-syndicated her own women's advice column. Gabby was invited to give a presentation during a brainstorming meeting called by the managing editor to en- vision ways to attract young professional women, these damn yuppies, who were not picking up the newspaper habit. Like Ken, Gabby smoked and the two of them sat next to each other to share the one ashtray. Gabby talked a lot about what young professional women wanted today. They wanted to succeed in their careers, but they also wanted husbands and families and to wear pretty clothes and keep up with the latest home design- er trends.

For the meeting Gabby wore a hot pink dress that hugged her hips and breasts with a smooth embrace. Around her neck hung a chunky necklace with beads like blue gumballs. Her shiny earrings dangled like fishing lures. Maureen found her- self distracted by the raven-black, luxuriant hair that curled and twisted over Gabby's head and onto her shoulders, each strand striving to free itself yet all tangling together to form an ebony halo. As she talked, Gabby would run a hand through her mane, pull it back, and release it, letting it fall forward in a dark waterfall.

"Women do want it all, and they are entitled to get it all," said Gabby, tapping her cigarette in the ashtray. "I'm not a feminist, but I want to get paid just the same as a man. I want to work, but I'm not going to argue if a man wants to open a door for me. There are some traditions worth keeping."

"Women want equality both in the workplace and at home," said Maureen who had worn a new Donna Karan power suit for the meeting.

"Of course," said Gabby, stubbing out her cigarette and running both hands through her hair. "Women want to read about how to dress for success, how to make quick, healthy dinners when they get home from work, and how to treat themselves to a lovely bubble bath on the weekends. My kids know to stay away for an hour when I shut the bathroom door."

The meeting went on so long Maureen had to excuse herself to get out the features for the next day's paper. Gabby certainly made an impression, but Maureen remained confident the managing editor liked her work and would realize Gabby and the Dweeb just didn't have her experience. Her Donna Karan suit smelled like nicotine for days.

Two days after her gruesome yet triumphant day, the managing editor called her into his office. "Sit down," he said. Maureen sat down with the certainty the job would be offered. Ken had been in the newspaper business for decades and had the ruddy cheeks and paunch to show it. He used to hang out with the staff at Mahoney's Pub, but he went on the wagon a couple years ago at the insistence of his wife, so he groused to the reporters, and now he just went home at night. He was never without a can of tomato juice he claimed was the secret to his successful detox. The copy desk said it was also the secret to his complexion.

"We've had a complaint about Jeff's story today," Ken said, gesturing for Maureen to sit down. "He used the phrase, 'Lick my love pump.'"

"That's a line from 'Spinal Tap,' " said Maureen. "The fake documentary about the fake heavy metal band. It's meant to be satire. Jeff used it in context about this beautiful song one of them had written and it had this awful name and…"

"Doesn't matter," said Ken. "It's not appropriate for the newspaper."

"But I thought we were trying to reach out to hip yuppies and such," said Maureen. She was truly puzzled.

"Lick my love pump?" Ken said. "You know better, Maureen. That was a huge mistake. Especially when dealing with Jeff."

"With all respect, Ken, I don't think…."

"Please don't argue with me."

"Who complained about this?" Maureen's answering machine often filled up with theater fans complaining about Leticia's harsh prose or the movie critic's infantile love of mainstream movies. She had heard nothing.

"That does not matter!" Ken leaned forward and slammed his fist on his desk. Maureen felt tears spring up; it was unusual for Ken to be this worked up. "This is not the kind of language we want in the paper. Do you understand?"

Maureen could not speak. Finally, she squeaked, "Yes, sir."

Ken smiled then, a benevolent, avuncular smile, as Maureen blinked hard. "Please just check with me any time you have a question about language. My office is always open."

"Okay," Maureen said and sniffed.

The managing editor stood up. "As I have often said, you are doing a good job, and we will put this behind us." He walked around the desk and put his hand on Maureen's shoulder, squeezing it gently. "Okay?"

"Yes," said Maureen. She stood up. "Thank you, sir."

She made a rush for the ladies room and ducked into one of the stalls. Tears stung her eyes, and she tried to wipe them without smearing her mascara. She took deep breaths, one after the other. She willed Miss Austen to appear, but Jane said something about the proper use of the King's English and vanished. Maureen washed her hands, letting the cool water run over her fingers for a minute, and returned to her desk.

Sarah laughed so hard when Maureen called to tell her about the complaint Maureen was forced to laugh as well. "Oh, that's ripe," said Sarah. "What! Did Emily Litella call?" Sarah put on a Gilda Radner voice. "What's all this about glove pumps?"

"I guess I should have known better."

"Don't worry about it. Did you misspell someone's name? Did you libel the mayor? Did Spinal Tap call to say they were misquoted?"

Maureen felt better, especially when Sarah said she had to leave because her love pump needed refueling. Hercules began pawing her as she hung up the phone and she was obliged to give him a treat and heave him into her lap. "Love you," she whispered, putting a finger on his nose. He licked her finger with his sandpaper tongue.

A week later, in the late afternoon, the managing editor called the senior editors into the conference room for an announcement. Maureen was confused. Shouldn't she have been taken aside first?

"I want to announce we have hired a new Sunday editor and I know all of you will be glad," he said, nodding at Maureen, "I have hired a woman. Gabriel Juniper will bring a new perspective to the paper."

Maureen froze her half smile into place as she dug her nails into her palm. Ken said a few other things about how well the paper was doing and despite a dip in circulation, he was sure the *Gazette* would come roaring back and newspapers had a bright future. After the meeting, Ken called her into his office.

"Mo, I know you wanted the job, but Gabby is really going to put us on the right path. She has maturity and good instincts about editing copy. But more importantly, Gabby represents a fresh new direction, and I know I can rely on you to help in whatever way you can."

Maureen tried to keep fury from making her voice tremble. "I understand but I have done an excellent job for years now, you've told me so. Gabby doesn't have any daily newspaper experience."

"But she brings a fresh perspective," Ken said. "A fresh approach. You're always speaking about that."

"What are you talking about?" Maureen shot back. "She's just pushing all the same old women's pages stuff. Clothes, food, kids. That's not all women are interested in."

"Maybe you're not interested," Ken said, leaning back in his chair, his hands gripping the arms. "Women care about that stuff. They're tired of strident militant attitudes, they want to be women again. Gabby gets it."

"That isn't the case at all!"

"We are not a platform for radical feminism. This is exactly the attitude that turns off readers."

"You mean it turns off men."

"Enough! She is a good editor with good instincts. You've done a fine job here but we are taking a new direction. You can accept it or you can get out."

Maureen began to speak. Instead, she closed her mouth and gritted her teeth. She stood up. "I understand. I will do what I can. Excuse me, sir, I have work to do," she said with a clenched jaw, turned and walked out. As she passed the dweeb editor, she could see him repressing a smile.

By concentrating on her work she got through the day. She wiped her eyes occasionally and snapped at William when he asked if he could leave early. Only when she returned home in the evening did she sit on the couch and let the tears flow. She had messed up. *The New York Times* would not come calling now. She had been passed over three times. Three strikes and you're out.

Hercules leaped up beside her and pawed her arm. "Okay, I'll feed you." She opened a can of food and a bottle of white wine. She spooned the food into his dish and poured the wine into a glass. She sipped the wine, her appetite gone. She finished the glass and poured another.

After the third glass of wine, Maureen felt the walls of the apartment closing in. She felt herself being pulled back to middle school in Somerville, when she didn't understand why the other girls and even the teachers didn't like her. Boys teased her unmercifully, this was expected. But the other seventh and eighth grade girls started to speak a language she couldn't understand. Her mother told her to try to fit in; her dad said to tough it out. So she tried. She had friends, but then her best friend, another "wicked smaht" girl, as both of them were sometimes taunted, moved away. Her remaining friends drifted into the orbit of those who knew how to apply eyeliner and who shrugged with triumphant disdain when teachers asked the class for a response. Maureen continued to raise her hand, producing knowing titters from the girls and groans from the boys. She knew she was doing something wrong; she just didn't know what. She seemed to always say the wrong thing. "You're not as smart as you think you are," a girl, who always seemed to have a black eye from her thick eyeliner, told her. "Yeah," said another girl. "You've really gotten pretty dumb about things." Maureen, who had known these girls since grade school, pretended not to care, but eventually when she went home, she locked herself in the bathroom and cried. A day after she had done something really stupid, telling the teacher, "No, really the test was not too tough" to jeers from the rest of the class, she could barely contain her hurt and embarrassment; no one would sit with her at lunch. After school she locked herself in the bathroom, and scratched at her arms, muttering, "Stupid, stupid, stupid, stupid." The pain seemed oddly comforting. She scratched harder, her nails leaving red marks on her forearms.

She opened the bathroom cabinet looking for something sharp and slipped out a single blade from the razor pack her father kept there. She stared at the red marks on her forearms and then quickly drew the razor against the inside of her wrist. At first there was only a white line, then blood began to bead up. The red scared her, but it was somehow thrilling. She quickly washed the cut with soap and water and put the razor in the bottom of the wastebasket.

When she tried to argue with Mr. Hanson about the school dress code the next day, he told her loudly to shut up and the class laughed as she sputtered with rage. Never mind everyone wanted the dress code to change; she was the one dumb enough to argue about it. She locked herself in the bathroom after school and cut herself again. It became a habit.

Pain wasn't the goal; it was the relief she felt when she cut. It gave her a sense of control over feelings she could not articulate. Cutting was making anxiety manifest and concentrated in drips of blood she could see and wipe away. She tried to explain this to her father who asked her why she wanted to hurt herself. He noticed the missing razors and then her arms and, bewildered, asked her to tell him what was going on. Flustered, she said she was all right and begged him not to tell her mother. When he hesitated, she promised to talk to the school counselor, Mrs. Stewart.

Mrs. Stewart's office was decorated with anti-smoking posters and a sign declaring "Good Girls Don't." She smiled distractedly as Maureen sat uneasily in the hard-back chair. Mrs. Steward shuffled papers and asked her questions. Trouble at home? No. Grades? No. Drugs? No. Suicidal thoughts? Well, what? What? Maureen stared at her hands. She wasn't trying to kill herself, she tried to explain. She wasn't even trying to hurt herself. She was trying to stop the hurt. She liked the feeling of relief that a slight trickle of blood brought her.

"Blood?" asked Mrs. Stewart. "That's awful. Why would you do that?"

"It gives me, I don't know, a sense of command. Like I'm in charge of the pain."

"But hurting yourself is a terrible thing to do. Why would a smart girl like you do such an awful thing? You need to stop."

Maureen said she would. Mrs. Stewart frowned, sighed, and told her to come back as needed.

Maureen did stop. Not at once, but the urge to cut gradually diminished. By the end of eighth grade, Maureen learned how to play the game of girls. She deciphered the code of groupthink and learned how to obey or disobey discreetly. In high school, she found her way to the debate team. A teacher chose her to head up the school newspaper. She had the first of a series of boyfriends drawn to her thick hair and expanding bustline. She occasionally would lock herself in the bathroom, get out a razor, and stare at her arms. She brought a packet of razors to college, just in case, but never used it. She kept it tucked into the box of pens, pencils and erasers in a desk drawer.

Now she had messed up. Failed. Fucked up. She was good, just like her father, but it didn't matter. You are not as smart as you think you are. She set down her wine glass and stood, letting Hercules jump to the floor. She opened a dresser drawer and dug for the box, now filled with pens that had run dry years ago. The packet of razors was under a stack of business cards collected from people she no longer remembered. She cradled the packet in her hand and a longing for her father swept over her. She threw a dish towel over her arm and sat on the couch, noting the floor needed vacuuming. She took a sip from her glass. She carefully extracted one razor, making sure the blade still looked shiny, with no rust. With a quick stroke, she drew the edge lightly across her forearm. A faint line appeared. She watched as the line began to turn red. She drew another line, now deeper, and then a third line. Drops of blood began to appear on the first line and soon, more drops were appearing along the second and then the third. Relief washed over her as the blood trickled out. She was in control of the pain now, not Gabby, not Ken, not anyone. Hercules suddenly jumped in her lap and a drop of blood fell on his white chest. Maureen put down the razor and quickly wiped the blood from Hercules with the dish towel. "Ma-oow," Hercules said, gently pawing at her.

She took another sip of wine. Hercules pawed at her again. The blood had picked up and was flowing smoothly now. Maureen laid the dish towel on her lap to keep the blood off the couch. She felt tension draining away, replaced by a wave of euphoria. She had been stupid, oh so stupid, but she was back in control, she could manage this flow, the hurt made manifest and directed. If her father were here, she would explain it to him again. She downed the rest of the wine in her glass. She picked up the razor and lifted her right hand for another cut when Hercules pawed her right arm with his claws out.

"Owww," Maureen yelped, dropping the razor. She shoved Hercules off the couch. "Are you trying to hurt me too?" "Ma-oow," Hercules said, in his ridiculously high-pitched voice. "Ma-oww."

Maureen examined the cat scratches, which were starting to bleed. She stood up unsteadily, both arms dripping blood, and walked into the bathroom. She washed her arms with soap and opened the cabinet to get rubbing alcohol. She methodically cleaned the scratches, leaning against the sink for balance. She squeezed antibiotic cream on Hercules's marks and then on the ones she made. The cuts had stopped bleeding, but they looked deep and raw. She sat back on the couch and Hercules jumped up beside her. "Okay," she said, her breath ragged. He crawled in her lap and she hugged him. "Okay." They sat there, until Maureen got up and climbed into bed, still in her work clothes. Hercules followed and curled up beside her.

As she drifted into sleep, Maureen began to think about how when she told her friends about Gabby, Sarah would be outraged, Elektra would be dramatically hysterical, and Tina would look at her with concerned, worried eyes. John would erupt in a poetry of profanity against corporate bitches. She would figure out something about the *Gazette*. She would deal with Gabby like she finally dealt with the girls in junior high who eventually all clamored to be her friend. Don't let the bastards get you down. She pulled Hercules closer, his rusty purring as loud as static on a TV with a bent antenna. Never again. She kissed Hercules' ear which he flicked rapidly. Never again. In the morning, she wrapped the razors in the dish towel and threw the bundle down the garbage shaft in the hallway.

Despite a pounding headache, Maureen was at her desk by eight o'clock. By nine o'clock, she had forgotten about the cuts and rolled up her sleeves.

"Hey, what happened to your arm?" the dweeb editor asked, as he walked by.

"Oh, my cat scratched me," Maureen said, rolling the sleeves back down.

"That's why I hate cats," he said.

Maureen walked into the morning meeting at ten calmly, and even smiled at Gabby, who sat next to Ken. They used the same ashtray as they talked about Sunday coverage. Maureen noticed how their hands brushed together when they tapped their cigarettes.

With sudden clarity she realized Gabby was indeed a tradi-
tionalist. She had gotten the job the old-fashioned way.

CHAPTER NINETEEN

Elektra Comes Clean

ELEKTRA DREW A deep breath. "So I have something to tell you guys."

Maureen, Sarah and Tina nodded. Tina was halfway through a Sea Breeze, Maureen was drinking a white wine spritzer, and Sarah was on her second chardonnay. Elektra always had something to say or confess. It was crane night, and they were tucked into a booth at the Italian place waiting for dinner.

"No, really," said Elektra. "I really have something to say."

Tina set down her glass. Maureen closed her Filofax and tucked it into her purse.

"You guys know about those personal ads we put in and I didn't tell you but I finally got a response and it was something really different. The message said, 'Hi, I'm Sam and I just love your personal ad. Do you want to meet for drinks?' And I'm thinking, this is a great coincidence 'cause I have a cat named Sammy. So I write back, sure, and I give my phone number.

"And you know I get a call and I say 'Hello,' and I hear, 'Is this Elektra?' and I say, 'Who is this?' and they go, 'It's Sam.' I'm thinking Sam really has a high voice and I say 'How are you doing?'' and they go 'Really well' and I say, 'You know I have a cat named Sammy' and they go, 'I have a cat named Ella,' and I go, 'Oh wow, my real name is Ellen, isn't this a hoot and a half.' And we're talking about cats, but there's something different about Sam and I say, 'So Sam, what do you do?' 'Well, I'm an actress.'"

And I say, 'Sam, are you a girl?' And she pauses and goes, 'Well, yeah. You didn't get that?' And I say, 'What are you doing answering my ad?' I could tell she was embarrassed and she says, 'Oh, I thought you said you were looking for a partner.' And I said, 'Yes, but, uh, a male partner.' And she goes, 'Well you should have said so.' And I say, 'Well, I thought I had.' And she says, 'Well, I'm sorry to have bothered you.' And I said, 'No, no bother. Hey, what plays have you been in?' And she said, 'I've done some off Broadway and off off Broadway. What do you do?' And I say, 'I'm a writer and I specialize in celebrities.' 'Oh, who have you interviewed?' And I'm telling her this and telling her that and we're talking and laughing. She seemed pretty cool. She finally says, 'Well I should probably go now' and I say, 'Why don't we have a drink? You may be famous one day and I can get the interview done early.' So we decided to meet at the Carnegie Deli because it seems kind of like the thing to do."

"You went out on a date with her?" Maureen broke in.

Elektra sipped her drink. "No, no, I mean I thought it could be a story. You know, you wanted a story about personal ads and I thought this could be funny. And so we met. She didn't look anything like a lesbian; she had really stylish hair and she wore a dress, although she did have these really clunky boots, but she had on makeup and I thought, oh, she's just kidding about being a lesbian. And we're talking and a couple of guys try to talk to us and we just laughed."

"Then she tells me about how she came out some years ago and her parents were furious. At first, they didn't want to speak to her, but her mother was starting to come around but her dad was still mad. And I'm going uh huh and then I told her how in junior high, Jennifer Ponzini and I were best friends, we did everything together. We were walking to school one day and holding hands. Patrick – he was the biggest douchebag in school and I always told him to get lost when he teased me – and he sees us and says, 'Hey look, Ellen and Jennifer are a couple of lezzies.' 'No we're not, you moron,' I say. 'Lezzies lezzies,' he yells. And I say, 'Go away, you moron,' but now there were other girls around and they were yelling at him and some were chanting, 'Ellen and Jenny sitting in a tree…' Jenny was crying and I jumped on Patrick and screamed, 'Stop it you asshole,' then another guy tried to get me off and I slapped him and everyone was screaming.

"Of course, I was the one taken to the principal's office 'cause he always hated me since I wrote 'I am a jerk' in the dust on his stupid car, and I got sent home and my mom grounded me for a month and yelled at me, 'You better not be a lezzie because your cousin Peter is a goddamn faggot, and he's breaking his mother's heart and he's not allowed to see Nonna.' I loved my Nonna.

"So at school, Patrick is always whispering, 'Lezzie, lezzie' to me and I was always beating on him and getting into trouble. And then one day, Jennifer wanted to speak to me and I told her to get lost and she was a fucking lezzie and she tried to infect me and she ran off, sobbing. I can't forget her face. Years later Patrick had the nerve to ask me to the prom in the lunchroom and I dumped my tray on his head and told him I was going to the prom with Michael Fitzgerald who was gonna kick his ass, but I can't forget Jenny's face when I told her to go away. And I start to cry.

"Sam is sitting there listening, really listening, and nodding as if she knew what I was talking about but then I get angry. Because I'm not a lesbian, I say. I've done the dirty with plenty of men and I like men and you can't like men if you're a lesbian. Right? Right? And she explains people can be bisexual and she dated men until she realized she was more attracted to women.

"And I'm saying, but I like makeup. 'No matter,' she said. 'I like wearing dresses and I would never cut my hair short and wear army boots,' and she just laughed and said you don't have to do anything. So that was lunch and then we had dinner another time. I didn't want to tell you guys because I didn't think this was anything but tonight we are going to go to a movie and have dinner and I don't know if I should go. What if something happens? What if I really am a lesbian? Can I get AIDS from just kissing her?"

Tina fought a sense of fury. How could Elektra really be gay after all the men she had dated? Why hadn't Elektra confided in her? She told Elektra all her dating woes. Why hadn't Elektra told her what was going on?

Maureen was bewildered. What would this do to their friendship? What if Elektra started dating women? What if Elektra came on to her?

Sarah was the one to speak. "Elektra, sweetie, I don't think you have to worry about AIDS from Sam; I mean, you always have to take precautions. But that's not the real issue. What do you want? Do you like this Sam?"

"I don't know. Maybe… but what does this mean? I kept thinking, what are you going to think about me? I kept thinking about Jenny and how the girls teased us."

Sarah put her hand over Elektra's. "Elektra, we are your friends. We all know lots of gay guys. Vincent, David, William."

"William is gay?" Maureen asked, shocked. "I did not know that."

"How could you not know that!" retorted Sarah, gleeful she bested Maureen in matters of fact. "Elly, you have to figure out what you want. You. That's all that matters."

"Sure, that's right," said Maureen, who wasn't at all sure. If Maureen were gay, she could never admit it to anyone in the newsroom. It would be a career killer.

Tina said, "I wish you'd told us. I wish we'd known about this." She crossed her arms over her chest.

Elektra sighed. "I didn't know what to do. I've been so

stressed out about this, like really stressed. But Tina, you're with Tommy now, and Maureen has John, and Sarah has Cole."

"How many cats does she have?" Sarah asked.

"Just Ella."

"Have you met Ella?"

"No, I mean, I want to visit her apartment. She lives in Greenwich Village, and I wanted her to come to my place, but I didn't know what to say if I ran into you guys. So we're trying to figure it out."

"Look," said Sarah. "Just take it slowly. Try to figure out how you feel."

"I guess I could ask to meet her at her place before the movie. We could eat in Greenwich Village just as long as it isn't Indian food. The last time I had Indian food I had heartburn for a week. What if she really wants to have Indian food?"

"Not all Indian food is spicy," said Maureen, who felt the conversation was slipping out of control. Tina remained sullenly silent.

"I'm sure there is something both of you can enjoy," said Sarah.

As Elektra reported the next Thursday, she and Sam were able to compromise on Italian, and Ella turned out to be a larger version of Sundae and just as loving. A week later, Elektra announced that Sam came to Studio 54, and "Sugar Pie and Sammy just adored Sam, absolutely loved her. You wouldn't believe how adorable it was to see her with two cats on either arm. And Eddie just loved her too, he curled up on her feet."

"Eddie?" asked Tina, Sarah, and Maureen in unison. "Eddie came out?"

"Yes," said Elektra, sounding puzzled. "Of course. We all had a great time together. I think this is going to work out."

CHAPTER TWENTY

One Sundae, Eight Spoons

THIS WAS, SARAH thought, the disaster Tina predicted and Maureen tried to avoid. The original idea was they would all get together to meet Sam. Then Tina insisted Tommy should come along as part of the crowd and Elektra said it was girls night out, but Tina said Tommy was her partner and should be there. Elektra said he was a man and would be totally out of place. Maureen said, "Why don't I bring John and maybe Sarah could bring Cole and we would all go to Bobby V's." Elektra said she would ask Sam and Sam was fine with it as long as Elektra agreed to meet all her friends in the city the next week.

John was surprisingly excited to meet Sam. "Do you think they will make out in front of us?" he asked. Maureen told him he better damn well behave himself. Cole, somewhat to Sarah's surprise, also agreed to come to dinner. It took a month to meld everyone's schedule, forcing Maureen to make so many changes she had to use a pencil with a good eraser in her Filofax. She managed to find a night when everyone was free.

Bobby V's was crowded; it was a game night and the waitresses were snippy about pulling two tables together for eight people. Her ill temper was infectious. Elektra was unusually silent, whereas John described in excruciating detail the project he had just finished and how the CEO was trying to take credit for it. Tina cuddled against Tommy, narrowing her eyes into slits of resentment. Maureen kept trying to break into John's monologue to steer the conversation elsewhere. Cole was his usual taciturn self; Sarah suspected he was enjoying the tension. The only person at ease was Tommy, who was happily digging into the nachos appetizer and trying to catch a glimpse of the TV above the bar. Sarah drained her chardonnay.

Sarah liked Sam; she had dark, shrewd eyes, and short, streaked blonde hair. Two tiny diamonds sparkled in each ear. She laughed easily at John's obscenity-laced tirade with a casual, "I know how you feel." She noticed Elektra was wearing less blush than usual and seemed to spend an inordinate amount of time trying to decide which nacho chip she would pull from the gooey pile. Maureen finally jumped in when John took a breath to say in a formal tone, "Sam, tell us about your acting. How did you get started?"

"Well," said Sam. "It all began in high school when I played Maria in *West Side Story.*"

This ignited Elektra, who started singing, "I like to be in America. Okay by me in America!"

Sam turned and smiled at her, saying, "That's it."

The Elektra switch flipped on. "You wouldn't believe how well Sam sings. Her voice is incredible. Oh my god, we were singing along to Blondie and she hits these high notes – I thought the glasses in the place would break. You should have heard how great she sounded." She would have gone on, but Sam turned and quietly smiled at her. Elektra ended with "She can really act, too."

"I was an economics major in college but my real love was theater. So after I got my master's, I thought, what the hell, I would head to New York and try my luck for a summer. And I kept getting parts," Sam said.

"What shows are you in now?" asked Sarah, trying to keep her tone casual and hoping to prevent Maureen from conducting what would sound like an interview.

Both Elektra and Sam looked at each other and laughed, causing Tina to press her chin into Tommy's shoulder. "A little something," said Sam. "Off Broadway."

"Way off Broadway," said Elektra. "It is totally hysterical!"

As Elektra launched into a description of the plot of the show, which turned out to be a kind of campy send-off of 1960s surfer movies, Sarah studied Sam's face. She seemed utterly comfortable in her skin, focusing on Elektra as any new partner should. Sarah could also see that Maureen, a self-proclaimed liberal, was rather flummoxed, and Tina was wallowing in self-pity.

"So the show is great, but I think it will be a short-term gig and then it's back to the cattle calls," Sam finished. There was another silence.

The food arrived. A salad for Tina, burrito for Sarah, fish and chips for Elektra, chicken for Maureen and burgers for the three men and Sam.

"Is it okay if I finish off these nachos?" Tommy asked.

"Can I get another chardonnay?" Sarah asked the waiter, ignoring Maureen's frown, Cole's hand heavy on her thigh.

"So Sam," said Cole. "The cliché is, of course, actors and actresses have to wait tables between shows to make a living. Would you say that's true?"

"Actually," said Sam. "I was able to take an inheritance from my grandfather and put it to work in the market. So I watch the Dow closely and buy and sell as needed. I don't always do well because I'm trying to keep as much in the market as possible, but it's a helluva lot better than waiting tables. Of course, the market is always a gamble, but I make money more often than not."

"Really," said Cole. Sarah noticed an edge of disbelief. "Where are you investing?"

"Well, mostly in the Fortune 500, energy companies like Exxon and Shell, but I also like technical stocks like IBM, of course," she nodded at Tommy, "but also Hewlett Packard and

Texas Instruments. And I'm sticking with Apple, even though that seems risky. And I'm in the Magellan Fund with Fidelity; I like what Peter Lynch is doing."

"What you should do is get into real estate," said John. "The market is booming."

Sam made a face. "That's a bit too much for me. Long-term, of course, real estate is a good investment, but I sense a bit of a bubble coming."

"You can't be timid in the market today," said John. Sam shrugged.

"Caution is commendable, but Reaganomics has done the trick," said Cole. "The Dow is rocketing. I would agree that it's time to be aggressive."

Sarah took a long sip from her glass to avoid the piercing look from Maureen, who was not a fan of the president.

"Actually," said Sam. "Reagan has run up the national debt and that doesn't bode well for the future. My broker is also a bit concerned about the reliance on computers that execute rapid trades for the bigger companies."

"So your broker tells you what to do," John said.

Sam turned to look at him and her smile twisted ever so slightly into a sneer. "We work together on investment strategy."

"But is that better than a computer?" Tommy asked. "No offense to your broker, but he can't crunch thousands of numbers in a second."

"That may be," said Sam. "But you are forgetting the volatile nature of Wall Street. My broker has taught me a lot. You have to take into account the psychology of investors."

"So investors need shrinks?" Elektra broke in.

Sam smiled at her. "Something like that, sweetie. I'm concerned things are just too hot now."

Cole shook his head slightly and said nothing. "So what do you recommend?" Tommy asked, leaning in. John also leaned forward.

Sarah could not follow what Sam said next but she noticed Cole was trying hard not to show he was interested. Tommy was, however, animatedly asking questions. "I can't believe you're still with Apple," he said. "I mean, I think they did the right thing firing Steve Jobs, but I would bet on Microsoft and Bill Gates to win the operating system battle."

"Here's my thought." Sam launched into another discussion.

"Hey, I gotta pee," said Elektra suddenly. "Back in a sec."

"Me too," said Maureen.

"Me too," said Tina.

Sarah followed them into the ladies room after setting her empty wine glass on the table.

"Isn't it great how everyone is getting along with Sam?" asked Maureen, leaning into the mirror to reapply lipstick. "It's going well."

Elektra was brushing blush onto her cheeks in defiant hard flicks of her wrist.

"It's great Sam knows all about finances, isn't it, Elly?" asked Sarah, looking in the mirror at her reflection and thinking she needed a haircut.

Elektra shrugged. "Yeah, yeah, I guess. She really likes to talk about the stock market and it just goes over my head."

"I just hate it when Tommy goes on and on about computers," Tina blurted out. "I just don't understand all that stuff and it makes me feel stupid."

"Well, you're not stupid," said Sarah, "And I don't really know anything about computer stocks but I think my Apple is much better than any other computer. So I'd bet on Apple."

"John never stops talking," said Maureen. "Not even during sex."

"Really? What does he talk about?" Tina interjected.

Maureen blushed. "Oh the usual. He kind of narrates things."

"A blow-by-blow account," remarked Sarah, putting on mascara.

"Sam loves to talk about finances. And feelings," said Elektra. 'You should invest in General Motors Electricity,' she says. And she's always asking me about my feelings. How do I fucking know how I feel?"

"I wish Cole would ask me about my feelings," said Sarah.

"I wish John would shut up about his feelings," said Maureen, who was attempting to tie her scarf in a casual off the shoulder bow. She gave up and stuffed it in her pocket.

Tina started to say "Oh, men," but stopped at "Oh."

"I'll say this," Elektra said. "No matter if partners are male or female, cats really are the best."

Thus fortified, the women returned to the table. All the men and Sam looked up eagerly. Apparently, talk on the stock market had petered out.

"How about dessert?" Maureen asked cheerily. Usually they ordered one with four forks. The men and Sam declined and the other women looked guiltily at each other. "If you want something, order it, sweetie," said Sam. "What the hell," said Elektra. "Let's all split a hot fudge sundae. Hey waiter," she called. "One sundae and eight spoons."

CHAPTER
TWENTY-ONE

The Surprise Brunch

TINA CALLED SARAH to see if she wanted to go running and complained again Elektra should have said something earlier. Sarah called Elektra to make sure everything was going well. Elektra explained in detail the party Sam took her to where she met strange but interesting people. Then Elektra called Maureen to ask about borrowing a vacuum cleaner and Maureen said sure and she would leave out a mop and pail as well. Maureen called Tina to talk about maybe she should do a feature on how to come out to your girlfriends. Tina called Sarah back to say she hated the idea but didn't want to say anything to Maureen and if they could change their running date because Elektra finally called her about going shopping but only, of course, because Sam hated shopping. Sarah tried to call Cole, who did not pick up, and then she called Maureen to say her shift at the AP had changed again. Maureen called John to make plans and he wanted to know if she had ever been with a girl and she demanded to know if he'd ever been with a guy to which John huffily said never. Maureen said, "Well, don't be sexist," and they made a date for Friday. Sarah called Maureen to say she realized she had Sunday morning off and now they could go to that all-you-can-eat brunch place at the new hotel Maureen wanted to try out. Maureen said the food was likely just average, but the brunch featured endless mimosas.

The lobby of the new hotel was decorated in beige, brown and chrome; if it were a person, it would be a wallflower, Sarah thought. As soon as the pale orange glasses were brought to their table, they joined the line snaking around the food stations. They each scooped up scrambled eggs, one piece of bacon, and heaps of watermelon, strawberries and blueberries. Sarah snagged a bagel, Maureen a croissant, and they returned to their table. In ten minutes, they each ordered another mimosa. Maureen decided to go back for a coffee cake. Sarah picked at her eggs.

"So," asked Maureen, carefully cutting the piece of coffee cake in two as if to deceive the world she would only eat half of it, "How are things with Cole?"

"Everything is all right," said Sarah, forking a blueberry. "We each do our own thing and get together every week or so."

She didn't tell Maureen the getting together was mostly spent in bed, drinking wine or doing blow and having sex. She didn't tell her how the sex was getting increasingly intense, with ropes and toys and play acting. Cole had even shaved her crotch. She didn't tell Maureen Cole had talked about having a threesome and when she jokingly asked, "Male or female," he smiled and said, "Either."

She kept asking about the Cape, about meeting his son, or even just going to the movies together. He always had an excuse and his refusals made Sarah feel as if she was turning into one of those needy, whiny girlfriends she so disdained.

"How's John?"

"Oh the same. We did have a good time at the Wynton Marsalis gig, that's the kind of jazz I like. But he can be so damn needy. He calls me over every little thing."

They sipped their drinks. Sarah thought how nice it would be if Cole were more needy. She could prove to him he could rely on her. She thought John was amusing but abysmally self-centered. She knew he often exasperated Maureen, but for some reason she stuck with him. Maureen told her that for all his talkativeness, he was supportive of her and willingly listened when she complained about Gabby. Still, Sarah would be relieved when John and Maureen finally went their separate ways.

Maureen thought about the first time Cole, Sarah, and she had dinner together. Primed by Sarah's stories of the fierce erotic attraction and their smoking bedroom antics, she'd been surprised when they finally met to see a round-faced man with sandy, thinning hair. He was tall, yes, and built like a football player, but a football player after retirement. His hands were pudgy, with sausage fingers constantly in motion. Sarah glowed during dinner, but Maureen had disliked the tone of her voice, overly forced and high pitched, her head cocked like a puppy watching its master. Cole ordered the wine and explained why he liked the vintage. He had talked about his new account with Volkswagen and how the stock market was roaring under Reagan. It was time to let go of the misguided liberalism of the 1960s. Everyone could get ahead if they were smart enough. His voice was mellifluous, sincere, engaging, and without a hint of doubt. The future gleamed and you only had to grab for what you wanted, no false modesty, no self-defeating altruism.

Maureen could see why Sarah said dating Cole was somewhat like dating Reagan. By the end of the evening, Maureen began thinking about investing in a mutual fund, thoughts that had only lasted until the next morning when she woke with a hangover. Sarah spent way too much time obsessing about Cole. How to finally meet his son. How to spend more time with him, all punctuated with the confusing coda, "Anyway, I really don't want to get tied down with anyone right now."

Maureen asked John why Sarah was so infatuated with Cole. John speculated Cole, being a big guy, had a big penis and that was why Sarah was so obsessed with him. John, a relatively short man, was very proud of his large penis. Big penis or not, Cole did not speak much, but when he did, it was with quiet authority. Yet Maureen sensed him hiding behind his bulk and bravado was a wall of flesh that guarded a scared little boy fearful of a changing world where he wasn't the center of attention. She didn't like the way he spoke to Sarah in an arch tease. He was clever, yes, but his remarks were often quick and biting. Sarah often seemed flustered by his comments. Yes, she would be relieved when he and Sarah finally broke up. Maybe they should talk about something else.

"And things are okay at the AP?" Maureen asked.

Sarah ate a mouthful of egg. She had talked rapturously to Maureen when she first started the job. Taking the train to Grand Central was a bit rough, but she could walk to Rockefeller Center. Just entering 50 Rock and taking the elevator to the fourth floor had been a thrill. Here was the international desk, receiving the dispatches from around the globe. Over there, the New York bureau and then the General Desk, which determined what would go on the national wire from bureaus around the country. In the middle of the room was the so-called "Glass House," where floor to ceiling computers connected the office to the world.

What Sarah didn't want to tell Maureen was how as she started to catch on to the procedures, culture and various personalities, she began to feel more uneasy, not less. The ground under her should have been becoming firmer, but it seemed to ripple with small tremors. She didn't want to tell Maureen that a tiny part of her mind was furious about leaving the security of the *Gazette*.

"Well, everything is going okay but what is really getting to me is how my shifts keep changing," she said. "Peter, you know, my crazy boss, keeps saying that it's all part of the job of being an AP newsperson and we have it easy compared to when he would work an overnight shift and get up and do a day shift. But for me shifting from day to night and back is pretty rough."

"Can't you say something about it? Don't you have a union?"

Sarah gave a little snort and shook her head. She found it hard to explain to Maureen, such an excellent manager of people and personalities, how an office always on the verge of a nervous breakdown operated. At the Idaho newspaper and the Dallas AP, the reporters all groused about the conditions, the editors and about each other but it was all considered part of the job. That was journalism. At the New York office, there was an edge to the daily grind. Many of the staff, particularly those who had been there less than five years, moved with jittery energy, always leery of making an error, skittish colts on the beat. The staff might joke, "You can't spell cheap without AP" and most people signed off messages with a happy "Cheers," but it was a false front. Sarah had always been relaxed under deadline pressure but she was now making unaccustomed mistakes in datelines or in the spelling of a name, huge gaffes for an organization that set the standards for the media world.

Maureen didn't quite know what to make of Sarah's reaction. "Is there anyone there you could talk to?" she asked.

"There's this gal Alexandria, Alex, for short. I thought we could be buddies," Sarah said. Sarah soon found no matter how tired, or exhausted or worried you were, Alex was more tired, more exhausted, more worried. No matter how hard you worked, Alex worked harder. Sarah and Alex sometimes would take quick lunch breaks together. Alex would confide in her about how desperate she was to have a boyfriend. No matter how many sad stories Sarah had about her love life, Alex had one sadder. Alex was an excellent newswoman but fidgety. She was a canary in a coal mine, anxious about the next possible misstep.

Just a couple weeks ago, it was a slow night. Peter had time to round up the desk editors and reporters and give a lecture about the high calling of the Associated Press and how they were not stenographers but reporters, damn it, and none of them had the moxie, the balls, the cojones, he had when he was on the beat. Sarah tried to sneak glances at her colleagues. To her it seemed so over the top, but everyone else was just quietly listening. Alex was nodding, quick flicks of her chin.

"And then Peter singles me out for letting the word 'gay sex' appear in a story on AIDS. 'It should be "homosexual sex,"' he says. 'You should have known that. That is the AP standard.' 'That's what the press release from the health department called it,' I try to say, but Peter cuts me off with, 'So you're taking orders from a PR flak? Huh? That's not being a newswoman. When I was reporting, I knew never to trust a flak' and off he went again. I wanted to say, 'Well, the New York Times uses gay for homosexual' but I just sat there. I should have said the actual release used the words 'anal sex' but I didn't want his head to explode."

Maureen shook her head sympathetically. She didn't quite get it; she knew Sarah was an excellent editor. Still, you had to be delicate about this AIDS stuff. She'd never known a group of reporters to act like sheep, more like stampeding buffalo.

"Are you making any progress about getting a foreign posting?"

Sarah shook her head. "No, and I'm not sure anymore. I'm not sure I'm cut out for the AP, after all. It was fun in Dallas but in New York, I feel like I'm always making mistakes. Peter rides my ass all the time, I mean he rides everyone's ass. Alex says not to take it so personally; it happens to everyone. I should probably have stayed at the *Gazette*." She looked up in alarm. She hadn't meant to say that.

Sarah wiped her eyes, and Maureen realized how exhausted her friend looked. Maybe it was just the smeared mascara. Sarah was not the type to complain about work. She usually thrived on challenges. She didn't like the edge in Sarah's voice when she mentioned the *Gazette*, it seemed directed at her.

"So, I just don't know," Sarah said, pressing her mimosa glass to her forehead. She set down the glass and put her hands over her eyes as if the light in the restaurant was burning her face.

"Hey, are you okay?"

"Just tired."

"You have to give the AP some more time," said Maureen. "You've always done well."

"I just don't seem to do anything right there."

Maureen tried to keep her voice calm. "This is just a stage. Things will get better. You will succeed and you will get over Cole."

Sarah looked up quickly, as if a fire alarm went off. "But we haven't broken up. Do you think he's going to leave me?"

"I mean, you know, you deserve all good things," said Maureen, unsure what to say. Sarah gave her a hard stare, then finished off her mimosa.

"What's up with Gabby? How are you two getting along?"

Gabby and Maureen warily circled each other, claws on the ready. Hissing so softly only the other could hear. Gabby now oversaw all features in the paper as well as all of Sunday's copy. All the editors, including Maureen, had to submit story lists to her every week. With great fanfare, Gabby hired a lifestyles columnist who lived in Weston and wrote about the techniques for baking the most delicious biscuits, proper dinner candle placement, and how to freeze raspberries so they wouldn't stick together. Maureen liked to complain about this writer.

"I could not believe her column when she did a piece about food in the movies and went on and on about the delicious-looking Southern biscuits in *The Color Purple*, " Maureen said.

"Didn't she notice the movie was a searing story of misogyny and racism, not Southern cuisine?"

Maureen shrugged.

"You think Gabby is still licking Ken's love pump?"

"Oh, I don't know," said Maureen. "They don't seem so chummy anymore. Maybe I was imagining that. It's a cruel thing to accuse a woman of sleeping her way to the top. Anyway, she's given up smoking and now Ken doesn't smoke in meetings anymore, so that's a relief." She added with a malicious smile, "And she's put on weight."

"How wonderful," said Sarah.

Sarah tried to sip from her empty glass while Maureen carefully picked up the remaining crumbs of the coffee cake with her bright fingernails.

"There's something else," Sarah said, slowly. "I've started writing this book, this sort of fantasy novel. I've been thinking of it for years and finally getting it on paper."

"Oh," said Maureen. "A fantasy. Like a sexual fantasy. You could always sell it to Playboy. They pay big bucks."

"No, no, you dirty minded gal. It's an adventure story set in another world. With magic, not too much magic, and dragons and unicorns, things like that."

"I'm not sure there's a market for that," said Maureen.

"Well, that's not the point," said Sarah, exasperated. "I just want to write it. I always liked sword and sorcery stuff. And now I really love writing on my Macintosh, it was worth the money, really it was. I've been thinking of this story since I was a kid. It feels more like I've lived it than imagined it. I just never wrote it down. My mind would run faster than my pencil or my fingers on a typewriter. But the Mac, I mean, I know people hate the way computers are taking over, but I really love that machine."

"A fantasy novel," said Maureen. "Like the Tolkien stuff you read in college."

"Let's just say it's not a Jane Austen novel. Because," she

added, with a sly grin, "Things actually happen in this book. They don't just have dances and talk and blah blah blah someone gets married. People fight and die. It's life and death."

Maureen could not resist taking up the old challenge.

"It was a life-or-death struggle in Austen's world. If you didn't get married, if you didn't find a husband, you could die in poverty. That's always a theme in 18th and 19th century literature. You love *The House of Mirth*, you know that."

Sarah shook her head. "But all those plots imply marriage is the only goal of women."

"That was just the way it was then. No choice."

"Exactly," roared Sarah. "I want to read about choices. Having adventures. Saving the kingdom. Riding into battle. I want to have choices. I…" She started to cry. Maureen was really alarmed.

"Seriously, what is wrong?" she asked.

"Nothing," said Sarah, with a ragged sob. "Nothing. I don't know. I just want to work on this book. I just don't know if it's any good."

"I'm sure it's fine."

"Look, would you mind reading the first part? I know you don't like fantasy and it's not Austen, but you could tell me what it needs. Just the first bit." Sarah reached into her purse and pulled out a stack of sheets, folded like an accordion. She hadn't yet ripped off the perforated edges.

"Of course," said Maureen, a bit taken back at being asked to read something right then and there. She decided she would try to go lightly on the editing to be supportive.

Maureen read the opening:

> To remember with words is not to remember. To tell you how it began is to distort and twist the truth. At the beginning, I lived without words. My thoughts were images, my needs were felt and never expressed. Hunger, thirst, cold,

damp, fear. Always fear. In the streets of Katunna, there was little mercy for the children of Kakarra, the children, who like the black Kakarra, lingered near the marketplace and snatched what they could. Kakarra, feathers like the night, eyes red like blood, blue talons, green beak. Kakarra, diving out of the sky, and ascending with a piece of fruit or bread or even a chunk of meat. And crying out, somehow, with food in its beak, a note of triumph. Ka-KAARRah. KaKAARRah. That's what they called me. Kakarra. Thief.

Maureen continued to read. She reached the last page, put down the stack, and looked at Sarah who was staring at her mimosa glass as if it would fill itself. "That was not the kind of opening I expected. Who is the narrator? Where is this place?"

Sarah shook her head. "You'll have to see."

"I admit it. I don't know much about fantasy writing, but I kind of want to know what happens next. What is this about?"

"It's about a street urchin in this really tough place called Katunna who wants to escape to the land of Arianna, a place appearing to her in her dreams. The book is the story of her escape and how she proves herself worthy along the way. She ends up rescuing her older, male comrades, and with the help of a unicorn, slays the hideous monsters emerging from her worst fears. She befriends a tiny dragon, who has lost his fire power, and rides the creature known as the Star Horse. She saves both the kingdom of Templar and the land of Arianna."

Maureen nodded. She had tried to read *The Chronicles of Narnia* but only got through one of the books. However, she vaguely knew the myths about King Arthur. "Is this set in the Middle Ages?" she asked.

"Well, pre-industrial, yes. Also, there are five goddesses or deities who help the heroine in her quest to save Arianna. There's the Warrior, strong and bold, but impetuous and self-righteous, you know, a Ripley from *Aliens*. Her sign is the Horse. There is the Dove, the martyr, the self-sacrificing, unworldly maiden. Think Beth in *Little Women*. Cloying at times. The Gardener makes green shoots emerge from the earth and guards the home and the children. She is Mother Wolf. There is the Seductress, voluptuous and sensual, her breasts speak of bounty and pleasure, but beware her bite. Her sign is a snake with diamond eyes that winds around her arm. And then there is the Thief, resourceful, clever, enduring, heartless, and sneaky. She appears as a cat."

"Snakes are scary, not sexy," said Maureen, who was having trouble keeping all these goddesses apart, but was relieved Sarah seemed to be speaking more strongly.

"I pulled the image from a Joni Mitchell song, when she talks about an apple of temptation and a diamond snake around her arm."

"You know she's a heavy smoker. Not a good habit for a singer," Maureen said.

"Maybe you could have Gabby call her about quitting. Anyway, the goddesses have a child together who becomes the queen of Arianna."

"They each have a child?"

"No, they have one together. It's a mystical thing, like the Trinity you Catholics talk about, three in one."

"That isn't exactly how it works."

"Yeah, well, it's a mystical thing. I imagined it as a kid before I understood how things worked."

Maureen noticed Sarah was smiling now. "Look, hang in there at the AP; something will come up. I'm not going to be at the *Gazette* forever, either; at least, I hope not. And you don't have to totally break up with Cole, but you can start looking around, right?"

"I guess," said Sarah. "I'm just tired. At times it feels hopeless.

I think I need to get more rest. All I want to do is work on this book." She dropped her face into her hands again.

"Hey," said Maureen. "Let's get another mimosa."

"Good idea," said Sarah. Maureen flagged down the waiter.

Over the rim of her glass, Maureen watched Sarah, who drank her mimosa a bit too quickly.

CHAPTER
TWENTY-TWO

Maureen to the Rescue

She entered the corridor into which the laboratory door opened, seized the blue jar, tore out the cork, plunged in her hand, and withdrew it full of a white powder, which she began to eat. "Stop!" cried Justin, rushing at her. "Hush! someone will come." He was in despair, and began to call out. "Say nothing, or all the blame will fall on your master."

THE WORDS HAD barely left Emma's tongue when the door flew open, startling her so much her hand flew up, sending white powder flying in small puffs. Mademoiselle O'Malley stood in the open doorway, her hard eyes taking in the sight of the boy and the woman. Stepping forward, with a swift move, she knocked the blue jar to the floor and seized Emma's hands. "Stop, please, take pity," cried Emma, trembling, falling to her knees, her lips white with powder. Mademoiselle O'Malley paid no mind but thrust a wet cloth into Emma's mouth, causing her to gag and throw up bile, tinged with white. Coughing and retching, Emma fell to her side. "Have you no pity! My life is ruined. I have ruined my husband's life."

Justin cried, "Shall I call for Monsieur Bovary?"

"No," said the two women at once. "Leave us, please," commanded Mademoiselle O'Malley. "Now!"

Justin fled. Mademoiselle O'Malley knelt by the weeping Emma and wiped the powder from her lips. "You will be sick, but you will not die," she said, almost tenderly.

"You do not understand, there is no hope," Emma cried, as piteously as a wounded bird.

"There is always hope," Mademoiselle O'Malley said harshly. "You must seek out a banker for a loan. You must tell your husband everything. You must say you deserve more excitement in life and he was wrong to assume otherwise. You are not some pretty caged bird. You are an eagle. You must soar. Come, we will do a fearless inventory of your belongings and sell what we can."

"The debt is beyond reason," Emma said, but there was a sudden lightness in her tone.

"Were you to continue, you would die an exceedingly painful death. Your husband would be even worse off," Mademoiselle O'Malley said. "He will be furious, to be sure, but he will forgive you. You will find work and begin to pay off the debt."

"Work," said Emma, horrified.

"Yes, work. It will give you something to do, something to fulfill your life. Sure, you made a bad choice in marriage, and ran up a huge credit card, er, monetary debt. You have to live with the choices you made. But you can take action to answer the longing created by those romantic novels."

"I have been bad. I have been wicked. I must pay for my sins," Emma said, tearing up anew.

"No, not bad. Just bored. Come," and Mademoiselle O'Malley pulled Emma to her feet. "You cannot give into despair. You must live. You have to forget Cole and go on."

"I can't," whispered Sarah.

"You can," shouted Maureen and woke herself up.

CHAPTER
TWENTY-THREE

Black Monday

A YEAR WAS once a long time. The school year was interminable; summer vacation stretched like a rubber band that never snapped. Days were cut gems, sparkling and distinct. Weekdays were foothills to the high mountains of the weekend. Sarah remembered this. Now days were patches in a quilt, cut from the same pattern and rapidly stitched together. Was the earth turning faster? Was her brain speeded up like something from an episode of *Star Trek*? Which had, incidentally, risen from the television wasteland, with a new captain. Sarah fell hard for Captain Picard. She began to mark her time by Star Dates, not the Julian Calendar.

Sarah was always tired from her shifts and her commute. She drifted into sleep thinking about the story of the street urchin trying to get to Arianna. She dreamed about secret stairs winding through mountains, cities with twisted towers, huts built into trees, and talking animals with snappy comebacks. When she woke, she would write another chapter from what she could remember.

Cole came and went. Sarah would try to withdraw, to not call him, to not pick up when he called, but she would always end up reaching out to him. He would come over as if no time had passed, often with champagne, cocaine or a black negligee. During one of their breaks, she went out with Jacques, an artist who twisted and turned steel into undulating shining towers and plump, shimmering pillows. When he pressed her to spend more time with him, she shrugged and told him he was crowding her; she wondered why he seemed so upset – didn't Cole tell her she was too needy, too demanding? She was giving Jacques his freedom, how could he be unhappy? She stopped answering his messages. And then, Cole called her. They spent a delirious night together with Veuve Clicquot and coke. The next week, after watching *Desperately Seeking Susan* on video, Sarah told him she had a surprise for him and came out of the bathroom with boxer shorts, stockings and garters, a tribute to Madonna's outfit in the film, she said. Cole loved it. So nothing mattered, really. Only getting through the next day until the next night.

On a cool day in October, Sarah took the train for her evening shift and ended up working twenty-four hours straight while AP business reporters attempted to chronicle why the Dow Jones industrial average dropped more than 500 points in a day and if this was a repeat of 1929. Reporters haunted the bars near Wall Street hunting for stories of broken dreams and to collect samples of sardonic humor. "Great quote, but I wish you had a name," Sarah said to the writer who quoted an anonymous observer: "There's just panic at this point. There's blood in the street." She asked another reporter, "Are you sure this is a responsible thing to say?" when the reporter gleefully quoted someone saying, "You watch – people may start jumping out of windows." Black Monday, as it was soon called, would spread to markets around the world.

Cole insisted he wasn't much affected by the market plunge, but he changed the subject quickly when she asked him about it during a brief phone call. Sarah wondered how Sam made out but couldn't reach Elektra.

She found out a week later. At 3 a.m., Elektra knocked, whispering loudly, "Are you up?" Sarah opened the door to a distraught friend.

"I thought it would be different. I thought I was done with bullshit," Elektra sobbed, clutching Carrington as if Sarah's cat could explain what had just happened. "I thought when I gave up men, I gave the lying. The sneaking around. The arguments. The cheating. Been there. Done that. Finito. Ciao, baby."

Sarah stroked Elektra's hand. She was bewildered as well. Sam had seemed so right for Elektra.

"Wall Street," cried Elektra, spitting out the two words as they were the name of her sworn rival. "Wall Street did it."

Elektra buried her face in Carrington's neck. Carrington looked at Sarah, begging for a rescue.

"Tell me what happened," Sarah said gently. Elektra heaved a sigh and Carrington grabbed the moment to slip away.

Sam had pulled out most of her money before the Black Monday crash and while she was looking at losses, she had made out better than most. Turned out she was far more engaged in the market than she had admitted. It was, she confessed to Elektra, really more exciting than theater and, done right, far more lucrative. She was thinking about becoming a stockbroker. She liked the challenge of storming a male citadel. After the crash, she met a friend of a friend of a friend who was also looking to get in the game. Peggy knew she was just as good as any male. Look how they all messed up. Peg and Sam clicked instantly. They would form their own brokerage, Sam would invest in it, and learn the ropes. Then they connected on a deeply personal basis. She would always love Elektra, but Peg was something special. Besides, Elektra should explore her sexuality now, date other women, and find out what the gay lifestyle was all about.

"I don't want a gay lifestyle. I want Sam," Elektra wailed. "I thought I was done with this bullshit. I thought women didn't do this sort of thing. It's all so fucked up. We were doing so well. Sammy and Sugar Pie are heartbroken too, and Eddie is totally desolate."

Sarah doubted the cats really gave a damn, but hugged

her. Weren't men the bastards? She thought of what she said to Jacques. Jacques' voice broke when he finally reached her and she said they would always be friends. She would have been more compassionate, but she was too tired and distracted, thinking about how Cole had promised to spend Saturday with her. Finally! This would be it, she felt it.

She calmed Elektra by getting her to talk about the new articles she had planned.

The next night at a more reasonable time of midnight, Elektra told her she found out from one of Sam's friends Sam had a habit of switching lovers on a dime and Elektra should be happy she lasted this long.

Black Monday had secretly delighted Maureen. The accolades for the Grand Old Man must certainly end now. He was wrong about the economy. And what about Iran-Contra? Now, Wall Street trembled despite his platitudes. Why didn't people see his trickle-down economics were widening the gap between rich and poor? But whenever the Grand Old Man smiled, the country relaxed. He was the benevolent godfather, the Teflon Lord, who said it was morning in America at midnight. Maureen saw herself as the little boy yelling the emperor was naked. She now realized she was the madman at the street corner carrying a "The World is Ending" sign.

To her utter surprise, John agreed with her. John had actually listened to Sam and made some recommendations to his CEO and fellow employees. They took a beating on Black Monday, but John survived. (He actually didn't have much invested.) He was heralded as a financial whiz. He was always in a good mood, and he and Maureen increasingly spent time together. He listened for at least fifteen minutes when she complained about Gabby's latest idiocy and told her repeatedly she was doing an excellent job, just look at how she had helped him. Gabby was a lightweight. Just like his CEO. Maureen was also pleased Gabby's innovations had done nothing to stem the loss in circulation. With Tina, Elektra, Leticia, Jeff, and William all watching her back, Maureen was rebuilding her kingdom.

The energy Tina had once put into dating was now redirected into her writing. She volunteered for every assignment and was now asked to do news coverage as needed. Under Maureen's direction, her writing had sharpened to a bright, hard edge. People often recognized her name when she was introduced with most saying, "I really like that story you wrote," even if most could not remember the exact subject, only the bright glow of the prose.

Tommy always beamed when Tina was recognized. He was utterly engaged in the new technology emerging at IBM, and he told Tina he felt the country was on the verge of some dramatic changes. He and Tina now saw themselves as a team, two people going places together. One of Tommy's buddies called them a "Power Couple." Tina wore the title like the Hermes scarf she impulsively bought while shopping with Maureen. On weeknights, both she and Tommy were too exhausted to do more than talk on the phone; on Friday and Saturday, they went to dinner, shows, and movies. On Sunday, they split time between what they called "Cat Olympics" with their felines and playing "The Legend of Zelda" on Tommy's Nintendo. There were a couple of disparities in their partnership. Tommy seemed to get bonuses or raises every few months, while Tina's salary, despite kudos from the editors, barely budged. Also, Bob and Leo were affectionate to both humans and with each other. They often raced around Tommy's one-bedroom apartment, knocking down books and plates and ending up with a scuffle alternating licking with wrestling. Mindy and Sheena fought to be on Tina's lap and they liked to snuggle with Tommy but otherwise they seemed to merely tolerate each other.

"Why so, do you think?" she asked Tommy.

"I think they are just being females, you know, catty and competitive," he said. "Or not," he added when Tina glared at him.

"Cats can be mercurial and fickle," she retorted. "Like men."

For Thanksgiving dinner, they drove to Tommy's parents' house in New Jersey to stuff themselves and meet assorted relatives. For Christmas, they went to Ohio to meet Tina's parents and assorted relatives. In each case, they were put up in separate bedrooms, which amused them more than anything.

When she heard about Elektra and Sam's breakup, Tina wondered if Elektra might return to men and asked her out to lunch at Mahoney's Pub. Both of them ordered Caesar salads and club sodas with lime and cranberry juice. Elektra said she was getting back to normal. Maureen was keeping her busy with assignments and she was on to something else.

"Here's the deal," said Elektra, who had carefully plucked out all the croutons from her salad to save calories and was now eating them one by one. "I'm thinking, I gotta turn all this bad feeling into something. It has to have a reason, right? Everything happens for a reason. My Nonna always said that. It was horrible, horrible, horrible when my cousin Peter got AIDS but then Nonna demanded to see him and he died knowing she loved him and now even my ma is saying AIDS can't be a punishment from God because Peter turned out to be such a good kid even if he was gay. And no, I haven't told her anything. And I miss Sam so much I think I have to do something with these feelings, right? And I'm looking at Sammy and I see she has found the one spot where the sun comes into the apartment and I'm thinking, that's so cute and I need some sunshine and so I go outside. It was one of those weird warm days, maybe from this hole in the greenhouse gas ozone layer, I don't know. I sat in the sun and I felt better. I mean it was like a warm hug from God." Elektra kissed the cross around her neck. "And I'm thinking this is a great idea and I got it from my cats. And I go back upstairs to thank them and Sugar Pie — I think it was Sugar Pie — had puked right in the sunny spot but she looked like she had gotten something out of her system. So I cleaned it up and threw out the underwear Sam left at my place. So I started writing a kind of Ann Landers thing. "Good Advice From Bad Cats." Of course, I had to make up the questions and I'm thinking, this could be a good column."

"What did Maureen say?"

"Oh she loved it. But frigging Gabby said we already had too many columnists and Martha fucking Stewart from Weston was charging more and more and the paper had no budget. I said, to hell with that, and I went to the Bridgeport paper with the samples of "Good Advice from Bad Cats" and the editor loved it. I think I'm going to get a contract."

"Go for it," said Tina.

"See, more good things are happening. How are things with Tommy?"

"Tommy is fine. I'm starting to understand this whole computer thing more. He helped me buy a Commodore and set it up. Hey, did you know my cats are the only ones in the world who can type? This is so hysterical. They walk across the keyboard. I was wondering how these strange letters appeared on the screen."

"I gotta get one," said Elektra, crushing her last crouton with a spoon. "I tried to hold out against answering machines but sooner or later the machines are gonna get us. That's what Denise says."

"Denise?" asked Tina.

Elektra blushed and shrugged. "She's a copy editor at the Bridgeport paper. We just chatted on the phone a few times."

"Oh," said Tina.

A couple months later, at 3 a.m, Elektra knocked on Sarah's door, mascara making black rivers on her cheeks.

"I thought it would be different. I thought I was done with this," Elektra cried, albeit with a strange note of triumph. "I thought Sam was bullshitting when she said we would always be friends, but now she's telling me she misses me and Peg thinks money is everything and it turns out Peg really likes dogs better. So Sam wants to get back together. What am I going to do? What should I tell Denise?"

This required a Crane Night, the first in months, at Bobby V's. No men, no partners, just French fries, nachos, chardonnay and Sea Breezes, plus a dessert with four forks.

When Sarah fell asleep beside Carrington that night, she found herself in the Mountains of Desperation, scaling the last peak. She now looked over a rolling plain with a sea of long grass, rippling in green waves. Arianna shimmered in the distance, towers peeking from a green forest bordering a rushing white river. She had made it there. She woke up to a hot dawn. It was August 1988.

CHAPTER
TWENTY-FOUR

The Tank

"WHAT A GOOFBALL," said Elektra. "He looked like a mole with a helmet. I never saw anything more ridiculous in my life."

"The pundits are saying this was one of the biggest mistakes in political history," said Sarah. "No one is sure what he was thinking."

"That doesn't bother me so much," said Tina. "But I think he's soft on crime – he let a convicted murderer out on furlough and the guy raped someone. That is really scary."

Maureen couldn't speak. Instead she erupted into a fiery oration. The image of Michael Dukakis taking a ride in a tank was just a photo op gone a bit wrong. George Bush would have looked just as stupid. Tina must see the Willy Horton ads were a technique to scare white voters about Black people. It was propaganda. Dukakis had been a great governor of Massachusetts. Maureen finally stopped her rant. It had been months since the women had gathered all together and she didn't want to ruin the moment.

Sarah's schedule had become worse, if that was possible. While she would come up to Maureen's for a drink (or two or three), she would often say she was too tired to go out. Tina was usually with Tommy. Elektra was hanging out with both Sam and Denise, although not at the same time. Maureen felt she was standing on the edge of a glacier as it calved, the split carrying away the other three as she remained on what she thought was solid ground.

Tina said crack cocaine was turning people into monsters

and the president had to be tough on crime. Elektra insisted Dukakis should have known he would look like an idiot.

"He. Is. Not. An. Idiot," snarled Maureen. "My dad knew him. Dad said he was a good guy, a serious guy. The Duke pushed through the Massachusetts Miracle. And he came to my dad's wake."

The women were silent for a few seconds. "That's a good point," Sarah finally said. "But you know, I don't think there's much difference, nowadays, between Republicans and Democrats. They all seem to say the same thing. They are tough on crime, pushing economic growth, and so on. All politicians are alike."

Maureen opened her mouth for a quick retort, but Elektra broke in to say Sam was voting for Dukakis and they agreed not to talk about politics. Tina said Tommy was trying to make up his mind. Maureen decided to let things go, although she was in a bad temper the rest of the dinner.

When Maureen called John about dinner on Saturday, they had had a fierce argument over the election. John told her she was one of those knee-jerk, growth-stomping liberals and she told him he was a tree-killing capitalist chauvinist. Maureen later left him a message to gloat about how in the vice-presidential debate Democrat Lloyd Benson had totally flattened Republican Dan Quayle, by telling him, "Senator, you're no Jack Kennedy." John called back to agree it was a great zinger and even if Dukakis was a tax-and-spend liberal, he really missed her and they should have dinner soon. She accepted, even while thinking she really needed to try personal ads again.

Still, they both loved a new chic place in Westport, and John told her again she was the sharpest woman he had ever known, even though she let her heart dictate her politics.

Two weeks before the election, the newspaper's editorial team met to discuss the newspaper's presidential endorsement.

Maureen came prepared with information on the Massachusetts Miracle, Dukakis' other initiatives, and his personal integrity. She was, she thought, quite close to convincing the team to endorse the Democrat. Even Gabby supported her points. Then the publisher of the paper, who generally stayed out of day-to-day operations, popped in. "We will endorse George Bush," he said. And that was that. Maureen took it as a personable affront when Dukakis lost.

CHAPTER
TWENTY-FIVE

Cat Fight

NEWSROOMS ARE STRANGE organisms, continually morphing as reporters and editors come and go. An intern might change the balance with verve and spunk; a new copy editor or designer might add to or alter the in-jokes, building on the general architecture of sarcasm. The men in composing added coarse humor and outright hostility when changes were made after deadline. When anyone retired, huge parties were held at a local bar and everyone got drunk and weepy and sworn newsroom enemies bought each other drinks.

Some things didn't change. Like Johnny D., the mailroom stalwart. He walked with a limp and always had a kind word for everyone, even if he repeated it on each encounter. He distributed the mail and grabbed empty soda cans from desks. Some reporters griped he swiped them before they were empty. "Not done," they would say quickly reaching for the can, when he walked by with his cart. "You gotta wait, Johnny D." "No problem, no problem," said Johnny D. The mailroom clerk supplemented his meager salary by returning cans and bottles, storing them in the mailroom until he had a sack full.

New hires were at first startled by Johnny's limp, his mannerisms, and the many crucifixes he wore on chains around his neck. They soon realized Johnny D. was "The Man." "You're THE MAN," the sports editors would say when Johnny limped by, grinning, and gesturing at their soda can, asking, "You done with that?" When the sports desk got stuck on a stat about the Mets or Yankees, they would ask Johnny D. and he usually had the answer. "You're the man, Johnny," they would say and Johnny always smiled.

Maureen saved her cans for Johnny, although she, too, would have to yell, "Not done yet," as Johnny D. came by. When Gabby complained her drinks were disappearing, Maureen reminded her Johnny D. had been there forever and would likely be there when they were gone. Gabby huffed, but this time Ken sided with Maureen. Maureen tried not to smirk.

Generally she and Gabby had reached a détente. Maureen concentrated on filling the daily feature pages and Gabby attended management meetings where she focused on the "Big Picture." Maureen found she could tolerate meetings now that Gabby gave up smoking, even if Gabby began each meeting by declaring how many days she had been smoke free. But there were times when Maureen thought she couldn't bear another day at the *Gazette*, watching Gabby nod vigorously when Ken praised the return to family values and how the newspaper would avoid any liberal bias in its reporting.

Ever since becoming a newspaper woman, Maureen disliked the Christmas holidays. Unlike many other businesses, not everyone got time off. Everything had to be done ahead of time because, by contract, copy editors and others would get overtime and management didn't want to pay. Long-time staffers who had families wanted to be with them and finagled ways to get days off. Which meant more work for others.

On Christmas Eve, Maureen took a quick dinner break and headed back to work to finish editing. She stopped outside the *Gazette's* building for a minute. She could sense snow was ready to fall. Johnny D. had strung holiday lights on the scraggly bushes outside the front door. Maureen felt a surge of unaccountable pleasure, a leftover memory from childhood. Her dad, due to his seniority, usually had Christmas off, and her mother would be in an unusually happy mood. She and James had the job of putting up the Christmas tree and maneuvering it to stand straight in the stand. Once the tree was straight or nearly straight they would push their faces among the branches and breathe deeply. They would unwrap ornaments in fraying tissue paper and hook them on the tree. "Small ones near the top," their mother would always say. "Big ones near the bottom." Sarah and James always argued about which of the dozens of stars collected over the years should go on top. Still, their parents always praised them for a job well done. "This is the best tree ever," their mother would say. Every year.

Maureen stepped inside the *Gazette's* office and waved at the half-dozing security guard. The newsroom was mostly quiet; senior editors had already taken off and the copy editors were working languorously. The half-empty can of Diet Pepsi on her desk had already disappeared. She noticed the managing editor was still in his office on the phone. Gabby was in her cubicle, her face intent on the computer screen, her hair twisted up into a tight bun.

Maureen was soon buried in her own work and was barely aware of a woman walking by her. She registered, somewhere, that it was the wife of the managing editor who often stopped by the office, so she didn't take her eyes from her computer screen. Then she heard a slap, a slight cry, and a scream, "You bitch!" She looked up to see the managing editor's wife and Gabby face to face. She didn't quite understand what was being said, but it wasn't pleasant. The wife grabbed Gabby's necklace and yanked it off, sending beads and a large pendant flying as if from a slingshot. Gabby tried to back away as the wife tugged on a fistful of her dress, which was hard to do without grabbing a bit of Gabby as well. Maureen leaped to her feet and reached the two women as the wife was using her other hand to yank at the shoulder pad. Just behind Maureen was the managing editor. He threw both arms around his wife's waist and pulled her. "Jesus Christ, Marion, what is wrong with you?"

He dragged Marion, still screaming "Bitch," into his office and threw her into a chair and shut the door. Maureen touched Gabby's arm, asking, "Are you okay?" Gabby bent over and held the edge of her desk. "I need to go to the ladies room." She staggered toward the bathroom, and nearly fell. Maureen quickly grabbed her by the shoulder. Angry words continued to emerge from Ken's office. Maureen put her arm around Gabby and helped her into the ladies room. Gabby promptly went into a stall and shut the door.

"Are you all right?" Maureen called out.

"I just need a minute."

Maureen backed out of the bathroom and returned to her desk, scooping up Gabby's pendant. Slowly the other copy editors retreated to their desks and everyone pretended to work.

In a few minutes, Ken and his wife walked out and quickly left the building. Maureen returned to the bathroom.

"Hey Gab, she … he … they're gone now. I have your pendant," she called out.

Gabby emerged, eyes teary, makeup dissolved. Maureen handed her the pendant.

"Are you okay?"

"Yes, I'm fine. Just shaken."

"Good."

"I don't know what she was thinking. Nothing was going on."

"Right, nothing," said Maureen.

"Well maybe some flirtation but that was long over."

"Yes, right," said Maureen

"Oh, God," said Gabby. "This is awful."

"Hey, hey, it's all right. It's a newsroom. Things happened. You should have been here when David on the copy desk threw a desk chair at a reporter."

"She was upset about nothing. Nothing really."

"Of course."

"You don't get it. You're single."

Maureen felt her comforting expression stiffen.

"You don't understand. It's hard to get a job; I took off years to have my kids and then no one wanted to hire me. My husband just isn't making the money he did when we got married. We have kids. My husband doesn't make enough. There was nothing between us!"

"You mean your husband or Ken?"

"I thought Ken really valued what I have to say, what I can contribute to the *Gazette*."

"He did, he does," said Maureen, confusedly.

"What am I going to do? Will they fire me?"

"No," said Maureen. "They're not going to fire you and they won't fire him. It's a newsroom. Besides, there's only a few people here and they won't say anything." Thinking, she might as well lie.

"Should I quit?"

"Well, do you want to leave?"

"No."

"Then you will have to stick it out," said Maureen. "I've learned this."

"He must be sleeping with someone else."

"Makes sense."

"She just went crazy. I'm not her problem. He's her problem."

"Do you want me to walk you to your car?"

Gabby straightened up. She went to the sink and rinsed her face, wiping it with toilet paper because the towel dispensers were empty. From a pocket, she produced lipstick and dabbed a smear of hot pink on her lips. "No. I have work to finish." She turned to leave.

"Hey Gab," Maureen asked softly. "It was you, wasn't it, who complained about that 'love pump' line?"

Gabby halted, her hand on the door. "I, I'm not sure what you're talking about."

"Just don't pull shit like that again," said Maureen, even more softly.

Gabby straightened her back. Head up, she went back to her cubicle, sat down, and started tapping at the keyboard.

"What happened?" the copy editors hissed at Maureen; she just shook her head and went back to her desk. Gabby left after an hour, walking out slowly.

As soon as she left, the remaining copy editors clustered around Maureen. Turns out Gabby's relationship with Ken had long been suspected and a great deal of analysis ensued.

After Christmas, no one in the newsroom spoke of the incident. Openly, that is. There were no memos, no announcements. Gabby continued to work and go to meetings but made it a point not to sit near Ken. Maureen had to admit Gabby was tougher than she thought.

In January, when Johnny D. came up to collect her empty can of Diet Sprite, Maureen noticed he wore a new string of beads, oddly familiar, with a shiny crucifix attached. "You done with that?" he asked, gesturing at the can. "Yes, Johnny, take it," Maureen said. "You're the man."

CHAPTER
TWENTY-SIX

The Breakup

"You said you weren't interested in marriage," said Cole, his voice unperturbed, inscrutable.

"Well no, I'm not. But I really want us to be together more. I think we should spend more time together," said Sarah. She was going to insist this time. She would be strong.

"How much time?"

"I don't know, more nights, more weekends." Her voice was high and squeaky. She hated the sound of it, hated the way her heart was beating.

"I don't know if you've noticed but you're the one who works all these nights during the week. I have my kid on weekends."

"I would really like to know Henry. Maybe we all could spend the day together."

"You will someday. Right now, I don't want to confuse him. The breakup was hard on him. His mother would totally freak out."

"I know but it's been a long time."

"And it might take more time. It might be one more year. Or six months. That's just how it is."

"I just wish we did more together."

"We do a lot together. And I hope to do more of that."

"Oh, you know, besides that."

"What do you want to do?"

"I don't know. See a movie. Go to the beach," Sarah said, trying not to get flustered.

"If you want to go to the beach in this weather, be my guest."

"We never did go back to the Cape."

"And we won't until it gets warmer."

"What about a movie?"

"Sure. Whatever you want. What do you want to see?"

"I don't know. Like *Dangerous Liaisons*?"

"And when do you want to see this liaisons movie?"

"I have Wednesday night off."

"Can't. I have a client dinner. What about Friday?"

"I work Friday nights right now."

"Call in sick."

"No, I can't do that."

"Why not?"

"I just don't do that kind of thing. And I already called in sick once this month. I might get in trouble."

"You won't get in trouble. Everyone else takes off sick days."

"Well, maybe. What about Monday night?"

"I have meetings until eight. I'm not exactly up for a nine o'clock movie. But I can come later."

"Can we go to dinner first?"

"Sure, we can go to dinner. Whatever you want."

"Sushi? At the place you liked?"

"Love sushi. Love that place. Loved the geisha look you have."

"With the robe and high-heeled sandals?"

"Ah yes. Thinking about it now."

"So what will you wear?"

Cole laughed, a hearty laugh. "Nothing at all. Gotta run. I'll see you Monday." And he hung up.

Sarah got to the restaurant early and asked for a table in the corner and a bottle of warm sake. She liked the delicate fragrance of teak wood. She watched the deft hands of the white-jacketed sushi chef. She spied on the tables nearby, a boisterous group which was likely a birthday party, the young men in jeans and button-down shirts, the young women with forests of hair and ruby lips. A couple sat at the table to her right. The woman kept time to her conversation with jangling bracelets, the man nodded, his eyes half closed, his lips half smiling.

She had several cups of sake before Cole showed up. "Well, mademoiselle, you're a sight for sore eyes." He leaned over and kissed her before sitting down and pouring himself a cup. He smiled at her, and she felt a glow, maybe from his expression, maybe from the sake. They ate cucumber and tuna rolls, teri-yaki chicken, and dumplings. Cole kept filling her cup. He listened attentively and stroked her thigh under the table.

After the second bottle of sake, Sarah was tipsy, fevered, loving.

"When we get back to the apartment, I want to show you something."

Cole's bemused eyes fixed on her. "Yes?"

"I mean, I really want you to read something."

"Like what?"

"I've been writing this story, this book maybe. Working out some ideas."

"About what?"

"It's a kind of fantasy story."

"Fantasy?"

"Yes."

"You mean with fairies, elves and unicorns."

"No, no, no, Well, one unicorn."

"Just one?

"Just one."

Cole sipped his sake. "I'm not sure I am the best judge. I never liked that hobbit stuff."

"Well, this is different. Mostly. Tolkien is the master."

"I think the last folks who read *The Lord of the Rings* passed out in the 1960s in a cloud of pot and patchouli."

"I think people still read those kinds of books."

"I don't know what to say. Do you have a dragon in it?

"One."

"One unicorn, one dragon. How about leprechauns, mermaids, trolls, dwarves, wizards, witches?"

"Would you read it? Just one chapter?"

"Why don't you read it to me? Naked."

"Deal."

They stumbled into Sarah's apartment, Carrington meowing. "Just got to feed her," Sarah said as she pulled out a can of tuna. Cole put his arms around her. "Go ahead," he said, as she fumbled with the can opener. One hand cupped her breast and the other slid under her skirt "Go on. Feed your pussy."

"Wait, you promised," she said, laughing. "You promised."

"You have to be naked," he said.

For an answer, Sarah pushed him away. Slowly, deliberately, she took off her clothes, one piece at a time, nearly tripping when she took off her skirt.

Then she picked up the pages, hoping she wouldn't slur her words too much. And she read. Until Cole slipped off hs pants and knelt before her, burying his head in her crotch. "Go ahead, keep reading," he said.

Sarah went on. By now, Cole was gently pushing her toward the bed. Sarah pulled herself back, still reading.

"Wait, wait," Sarah said, pulling herself away. "So what do you think?"

"It's fine," Cole said. "I guess, if you like that sort of thing. How about some naked fairies?"

"No, really."

"Come on," said Cole. "I told you I don't understand this

stuff. What you need is a 12-year-old kid to read it to."

"How about Henry?" Sarah said.

"Don't be rude." Cole stood up. "Maybe I should just go."

Sarah began to shed tears of rage and longing. "No, wait, wait, I'm sorry. I'm sorry."

"I don't know why you are attacking me. I told you I don't get this stuff."

"I just thought…"

"You obviously can write but why focus on something like this?" He began putting on his pants.

Sarah wanted to scream, "Because this is the story I want to tell."

Instead she cried softly, "Don't go. Please don't go. Please." She put her hands under her breasts and stood up, legs spread. "Please."

Cole sat down on the edge of the bed. "I really don't like to be attacked. Not now. The divorce came through a couple of weeks ago. It's over finally. I guess you'd want to know."

Sarah sat next to him. So he was finally divorced? But he didn't tell her immediately. Why had it taken this long? Why couldn't she meet Henry now?

"In the end it was very civilized," Cole said. "Brutally civilized. Everyone smiling with their lips and daggers in their eyes. My lawyer kicked ass."

"You didn't tell me."

Cole shrugged. "It was just the end of the line."

"Why didn't you tell me?"

"Why should I?"

"Because, because, I want to be with you."

"I'm not sure why. You're always unhappy when we get together. You used to be so spirited and now you get on my case whenever you see me. Besides, you are the one who was always saying you wanted to be free, and how you hated marriage."

Sarah felt the room spinning. As a kid she had dared herself to get on the Rotor Ride at the Riverside Amusement park. As it spun, the floor dropped away and you were held to the sides by centrifugal force. She wanted to beg Cole to love her the way she loved him, but she wasn't sure she was standing on anything. The floor was gone and nothing was holding her up.

"I'm sorry," she said, almost gagging on her pathetic words. "I don't know what I want." In response, Cole pulled her to him and kissed her hard on the lips, his hands reaching around her to draw her against him, smiling as he heard her gasp. "I know what you want," he whispered.

A couple of hours later, Cole slipped out of bed, dressed and leaned over Sarah and whispered, "I have to go. I have an early meeting tomorrow."

"Cole," she said. "I think I need some time off. I need some time to think about where this relationship is going. I need you to not call me for a while. Please don't call."

"Whatever you want," Cole said. He kissed her. And left.

CHAPTER
TWENTY-SEVEN

Unfolding

TINA FELT AS if she were sinking deeper into a canyon. The three cranes peering over the edge were transforming into vultures with pitiless green eyes. All she had said, happily, was she and Tommy were starting to look around for a house for them to move in together.

"He is the one," she said.

"How do you know Tommy is the one?" asked Maureen sharply. "How many men have you actually slept with?"

"Four," said Tina promptly. "How many for you?"

"Ah, I don't know. I mean. I think you're a little young to decide 'This is it,' " Maureen said.

Tina said huffily, "Well sometimes you just know. We'll move in together first and then think about marriage."

"Have you talked this over with Tommy?"

"Yes. Sort of. But I just know."

Maureen tried to hide her irritation. She had struggled all week to schedule a get together. Elektra couldn't meet for dinner Thursday; she was going with Sam and a group of her friends to see the film, *I've Heard the Mermaids Singing* and determine if it could really be considered a positive portrayal of gay women. She could make it Wednesday. Tina said on Wednesday she and Tommy were going into New York for dinner and a show because he hadn't seen *Cats*. She could do Thursday. Sarah, once again, was not returning her calls. Maureen finally got Elektra and Tina to agree to Tuesday. Maureen left two messages for Sarah saying they were going back to the Italian place with the white sauce. Sarah never called back, but to Maureen's surprise, she showed up.

The food was not as good as Maureen remembered; her chicken with ziti was cold and the bread was stale. No one wanted to share a tiramisu. Sarah was deep into her third glass of wine, Elektra was holding forth about Sam's financial prowess, and Tina was bubbling like a giddy teenager about Tommy.

Why did she even bother to try to bring everyone together, Maureen wondered.

"Maybe you and Tommy should just get married now," said Elektra, who had turned down dessert but was now smearing a thick layer of butter on a dry piece of bread. "I had so much fun at my sister's first wedding even though I had to wear a hideous fuchsia bridesmaid dress and the marriage busted up in just two years. Everyone got on the dance floor and all the women fought over the bouquet which my skanky cousin grabbed. I think I finally threw out the dress. Or maybe I used it for a cat bed. I'm gonna have my bridesmaids wear black dresses because who needs a fuchsia dress? That's what I would do for my wedding."

"What! Are you going back to men?" said Maureen in what she intended as a mildly sarcastic remark but came out as a full sneer.

"I could marry Sam," Elektra replied.

"As if that could happen."

Elektra nearly leaped up from her chair. "I can't believe how fucking stupid you're being. Why are you always assuming my love for Sam is any different than yours? You guys always act like this is a frigging stage of life and not my life. My life! Sam and I have really been talking about, really talking, about what we want. For the future."

"So what about Denise?" Maureen asked. "You were seeing her, too."

"That is OVER," Elektra snarled. "We talked about it too, I mean, Jesus Christ, we've been talking about feelings so much I think I should become a shrink and charge fifty dollars an hour."

"Hundred dollars an hour. Shrinks charge a lot," said Sarah. "And why should anyone get married at all? You just end up hating each other in the end."

"Well, that might be the case with other people, but I think Tommy and I will be different," Tina said.

"How so?" Maureen asked.

"Because we get along so well. We never have fights and we don't get mad at each other. By the way, are you really done with John this time?"

"I think this is it. I'm not going to waste any more time on him.

"Ha," said Sarah, who was trying to get the waiter's eye for a refill. "You two are like something out of the Cathy comic. Cathy and Irving. On and off again. Over and over. Just when you thought it was safe to read the comics page again. Irving's back. Ack."

"How is Cathy and Irving different from you and Cole?" Maureen returned.

Sarah fell silent. Then, she said slowly, as if wrenching the words like wet clothes from a tangled pile in a laundry basket, "We broke up. For good this time. I asked him not to call me and he hasn't. Not for a month." She shrugged. "And I won't call him. It's over." She cleared her throat.

"Well, thank God," said Tina. They all looked at her.

"Why are you saying that?" Sarah asked sharply.

"I mean, well, you know, you weren't happy," Tina said, who wished she could shade her face from Sarah's fierce stare.

Maureen jumped in. "He didn't treat you right. I told you many times."

"Even Sam thought Cole was an asshole. Remember the time we all had dinner together and he didn't believe her about the stock market and it went and crashed," Elektra said.

"You will meet someone new and better," said Tina.

"This is not like shoe shopping," Sarah said. "You don't just pick out another pair."

"But you were always saying you didn't want to get married and you didn't want to get tied down. So I don't understand," Tina said, her voice rising.

"Yeah, well, yeah," said Sarah. "I say a lot of things. Maybe I'll just end up like Lily Bart."

"Who?" said Tina

"She's the heroine in *The House of Mirth*. Edith Wharton."

"So what happens to Lily Bart?" said Elektra.

"She dies."

"And this is a book called *The House of Mirth*?"

"Lily Bart was a tragic representative of an era. That shit doesn't happen nowadays," said Maureen.

"Maybe it does," said Sarah.

Tina could see Sarah was on the verge of tears. "Remember you were the one who brought Tommy and me together. You said we should go to Bobby V's and where he and I met. You brought us together."

"I did?" said Sarah. "I don't remember. Sorry," she added as Tina looked down at her plate of half-eaten eggplant parmigiana.

"Well, I say everything will all work out," Elektra said. "Things happen for a reason like my Nonna always says. We just gotta keep going on, despite what some people think," and she shot a sideways look at Maureen.

"So are you going to invite Nonna to your wedding?" Maureen asked.

"Oh for god's sake, fucking stop this," Elektra shrieked as

other diners turned to look at her. "What is your fucking problem?"

Maureen was, Tina noticed, actually blushing. "Sorry," the editor muttered. "Sorry."

"Jesus H. Christ," said Elektra. She looked like she was about to leave the table.

"Anyway," said Tina, trying to get the conversation back on track. "Sam was right about real estate falling and now is a good time to buy. That's what Tommy says."

"Well, true," said Maureen, seemingly trying to be more conciliatory. "But how are you bringing together five cats?"

"Four cats," said Tina.

"Wait, Tommy has three."

"Ratso died."

"Awwwwww," the three women exhaled.

"Why didn't you tell us?" said Elektra. "Oh, poor Ratso."

"I didn't have a chance," said Tina. She didn't want to tell the others how when Ratso was getting weaker and weaker, Tommy kept hoping he would get better. Then Tommy called her to say he had just returned from the vet and Ratso was gone. "I didn't want him to suffer any more." Tina started crying. Tommy's voice just got soft. "I'm going to hang by myself for a while. I'll see you tomorrow."

"Tommy is heartbroken," Tina said. "Really, truly."

"I'm so sorry," said Sarah.

"I remember when my first cat died. God, it was awful," said Elektra.

"Tina, I am really sorry," said Maureen. "Poor Tommy."

"Thank you," said Tina, annoyed that her friends were so sympathetic about cats and were really awful about her success with romance. Maybe Cheryl was right. Maybe having cats actually turns women into cats, mercurial, fickle and competitive.

"Why don't we get the check?" Maureen asked.

"Good idea," said Sarah, tossing back the rest of her wine.

"Yes, I promised Tommy I'd meet him later," said Tina.

"Sam's gonna call me about the weekend," said Elektra.

As they waited for the waiter, Tina folded the corners of her napkin as if to start a piece of origami. Four corners turned toward the middle. Then more folds. But the paper was too soft and didn't hold together. She gave up and crumpled it as she got up to leave.

CHAPTER TWENTY-EIGHT

White Nights

She had long since raised the dose to its highest limit, but tonight she
felt she must increase it. She knew she took a slight risk in doing so –
she remembered the chemist's warning. If sleep came at all, it might
be a sleep without waking.
The House of Mirth, Edith Wharton

As SHE RAISED herself from the bed, and reached for the glass
with the extra drops, Lily Bart found her hand being stopped
and grasped by cool fingers, the pressure firm and comforting.
In the dim light of the room, she could discern a young woman, very fashionably dressed, perched on the corner of her bed.

"Miss O'Malley, it would be ever so kind of you to pass me
the glass."

"Perhaps, Miss Bart. But let me hold it while we converse."

Lily Bart sat up in bed now, a hundred questions with mul-
tiple conclusions, beating against her temples; she wondered if
she had finally drifted into blessed sleep. She wanted only for
the questions to dissolve; she longed to gently wash her hands
of consequence.

"Lily, you must not drink this glass. If you do, you will not
wake up."

"And would that be so bad?" Lily murmured. "Would it
not be pleasant to sink into the abyss and leave worry behind?
I have settled my debts. I have carried myself with honor and
now rest offers me relief without any fears of tomorrow."

"Such a pointless death," said the woman, stroking Lily's

cheek. "You are yet so beautiful and clever. Why do you sacrifice yourself on this altar of respectability? You do not know what will happen tomorrow. Someone, an old friend, may come by; if you do not wait, this life which you so carelessly play with, will be wasted. You must wait. Wait until tomorrow. Just tomorrow. Wait." And the woman moved the glass to the far side of the table. "Rest now."

Lily Bart looked into the strange woman's eyes. Now, she did not seem fashionable or attractive but her words were as soothing as the drops. "I will sleep now and wake tomorrow," she said, laying back in the bed and letting her lashes drift toward her pale cheeks. By contrast Maureen woke up, stiff with fear about Sarah.

"WHY DON'T YOU come out with William and me next Saturday?" Maureen asked. "I'm dragging him away from the copy desk for the evening. We're going to go to the Gracie Mansion art gallery. She's got this weird hip show with paintings and couches because people are always trying to pick art that goes with the couch."

"I don't know," said Sarah, staring at her half-full plate. After much cajoling, she agreed to meet Maureen at the brunch place. "I'm exhausted. And I think I have to work Saturday."

"Are you running at all?"

"I'm exhausted. All the time."

"Come out with William and me. You like William. You like the downtown art scene."

"I'm not keen on doing anything now. I'm just so tired."

"What's up at the AP?"

Sarah shrugged. "Same old shit."

"It's Cole, isn't it?"

"Oh, no," said Sarah. "No, that's over; it's been months now. I'm going to put in a personal ad and start dating."

"He was not good enough for you. Really."

"Maybe not."

"No, really. He is just not worth this."

Sarah put her head in her hands and Maureen could see tears falling from behind her fingers.

"Come on," said Maureen. "He was a jerk. He was awful to you."

"I don't know," said Sarah. "I think I really messed up."

"No, no, no," Maureen insisted. "You deserve someone better than him."

Sarah was sobbing now. "You just don't understand."

"Hey," Maureen said. "It's going to be all right. It's going to be okay. He was just another guy and you've had lots of guys. Right?"

"Mo, I loved him. I really did. Heart, body and soul. I'm not sure why, but I loved him. I never told him and he didn't want to know. So I never told him. Somehow I knew he didn't feel the same way. But I tried so hard, I just wanted to make him love me. And I kept hoping and hoping. I told myself it didn't matter. In the end, I had to face it. I loved him. And he didn't love me. That is why I told him to stay away. I had to do it. And why I haven't called him. I had to love him, I couldn't hold back anymore."

"You broke up with him because you loved him?"

"Weird, huh?" said Sarah. "When I was with him, I had to hold back. When I tried to tell him how I felt, he would shrug it off, telling me I was the one who didn't believe in marriage. Once I told him, 'I need a hug' and he grimaced and said, 'That's what my mother used to say.' He didn't like his mother because she was clingy and needy. And I just hated the thought I would appear clingy. But I wanted to be part of his life. He never wanted me to meet his son. He never saw me as a partner. He doesn't love me. Of all the men I've met, he was the one I wanted. And it's over. I failed."

Tears dropped on the pages she had brought, magnifying letters before dissolving them away. Finally, Sarah muttered, "I just need some rest."

"Sure," said Maureen. "You should take some days off. Maybe we could go to Mexico together."

Sarah smiled, a light in her eyes. Then the light was gone. "No, you know I can't take time off. You know I'm way down on the food chain. It's not like the *Gazette*. I should never have left."

"I thought you wanted to move to New York."

"No, that was what you wanted. That's all you ever wanted. I don't know why I let myself get talked into leaving."

"Hey, calm down," Maureen said.

"It was a mistake."

"No, it wasn't."

"It was a total mistake. I shouldn't have done this. I have totally fucked up."

"No, that's not true."

"What do you know? You always come out on top."

The women were silent. Maureen found herself rubbing her forearm where thin scars still lingered.

"Shit," said Sarah.

Maureen felt tears spring into her eyes. She knew Sarah was just overwrought. She knew Cole was a jerk who didn't appreciate her and Sarah was a great editor. What was going on at the AP?

"Look, this thing with Cole is getting you down, that's all."

"No, I don't think so."

Maureen reached over to the next table, fortunately empty, grabbed a napkin and handed it to Sarah, who blew her nose.

"So quit," Maureen said, softly. "You can leave. But I can't hire you back now. We are in a hiring freeze."

"Oh, so you're going to rescue me now? After pushing me to go?"

"That's not fair," Maureen said. "I didn't twist your arm. Come on. I thought you wanted a promotion."

"This isn't a promotion. This is, this, oh God," said Sarah. "I mean, I don't know. Look," she wiped her eyes with the napkin. "I just want to get some sleep. I am just so tired."

"How about," Maureen started to say and stopped. The women sat, looking at their plates.

"I just want to curl up with Carrington. I just want to work on this book," Sarah said. She added, "Of course, Cole hated it."

"He's wrong," Maureen said. "It's good. It's very good. Cole is wrong,"

"Maybe," said Sarah. "Look, I gotta go. I have to take a nap before my shift. Let's get the check."

As Sarah walked away, Maureen wanted to call out, "Cole is just not worth your love." But she was silent.

Maureen waited until late the next morning and called Sarah, leaving a message. She called a few hours later and left another message. She did not leave a message on the third or fourth call after calling through the evening. She gave up and fell asleep after 2 a.m.

Anna felt herself thrown backwards, away from the edge of the platform, as if by a wind from a great storm, a ferocious release of the elements. She found herself on her back, panting as if she had been dancing. Was she dead; had she flown off the platform into another world? A face appeared above her – a woman's face.

"Anna, Anna, can you hear me? Listen to me."

"He must love another – I ..."

Anna felt herself being violently shaken. A voice came to

her. "You are drowning in your own worst fears. You are blaming a blameless man."

Anna felt her hand clutching the bottle being slapped away. "No, you don't need more laudanum. You are going into detox and you and Vronsky are going to couples counseling."

"I do not understand; it is hopeless."

"What about your son? How can you do this to him?"

"Oh my poor boy. He will forget me – it is better to forget such a mother, such a sinful woman. I left him for Vronsky and now Vronsky will leave me"

The woman slapped her face again, slapped the lovely, distraught face. Anna, startled, held up her beautiful white hands with their rings and jewels as if to ward off evil. The woman grabbed Anna's shoulders, shaking her until her dark hair was freed of its pinning and cascaded in soft waves around the face.

"Get a fucking GRIP," Maureen yelled. "He's not leaving you and even if he did, so what! He never appreciated your teaching! He says he gave up so much for you, but what did he give up? Nothing!"

"But what am I without a husband or lover or a family? What shall I do?"

"You will go on," Maureen screamed, shaking Anna until the rings on her beautiful white hands clinked like little bells. "You will write that book. You will get yourself on Prozac."

Anna just looked at Maureen, her lovely eyes shedding rivers of tears. "I cannot. I cannot do this."

Maureen was crying now. "Yes, you can. You can do this."

Anna reached out, her white hands trembling, and gently pushed Maureen away. "I cannot." And Maureen watched as Anna got up and walked back to the edge of the platform, amid the sound of a train coming into the station.

CHAPTER TWENTY-NINE

Making Soup

Elektra stopped by Maureen's desk to pick up a press packet for an upcoming show at the Stamford Center for the Arts. She plopped herself down in a chair and waited for Maureen to get off the phone. Maureen hung up, shuffled through the folders on her desk and handed one to Elektra.

"Here's the package for the revival of *Design for Living* by Noel Coward. You know who he is, right?"

"Yes, I certainly do know who Noel Coward is," said Elektra, grabbing the packet.

"So see how many of the stars you can interview."

"Okay."

"The public relations contact is there."

"As usual." Elektra got up to leave.

Maureen leaned over her desk. "Look, hold on a minute. I have to apologize for how I've been acting about Sam. Particularly at the beginning. Really. I really am sorry."

Elektra regarded her warily. "I just don't get it. You are this total liberal and you don't get what's going on here with gay women. I just don't understand."

Maureen looked down at her desk and shuffled some papers. "I guess I had a bad experience in college."

"With a woman?"

"No, a group of women, these gay activists on campus. Very vocal."

"Sounds like your kind of crowd."

"You'd think. But they staged a sit-in at the *Daily Northwest-*

ern office. We'd run this story by our photographer who went skydiving and got this great picture of himself about to jump and we ran the photo really big with the headline, 'If Man Could Fly.' The women said it was a sexist headline and I suppose it might be, but 'If Person Could Fly,' just didn't have the right ring. And when I tried to explain, this one gal told me I was just a tool of the male chauvinists and I wasn't really a feminist. And they all started shouting at me and the guys in the office all stood around smirking. I think Sarah managed to calm them down. Anyway this all made me feel stupid, like I was back in middle school when all the girls made fun of me. And that gal who was the ringleader continued to bug me the rest of the year and I even let her write her own column, which really pissed off some of the other writers, and not just the male ones, either. Looking back, I think she was right about a lot of things, but sometimes women can get so clannish and catty. When you met Sam, I thought you might not want to hang out with us anymore."

Maureen paused to clear her throat. "I haven't really had a group of women friends before our group. I mean, I had friends like Cheryl and I had boyfriends, but this was different. We were different. I was different. It means a lot to me."

Maureen cleared her throat again. "And also you are becoming such an excellent writer. I mean it."

"Well," said Elektra. "Thanks for explaining. I couldn't figure out what was going on. Because Sam really likes you."

"And I like her," Maureen said. "Only, not in that way."

"So I gotta tell you something," Elektra said. "After you made a crack about my Nonna and the wedding…"

"I really am sorry."

"I know. I started thinking and I thought well, maybe it's time to tell my mother. So I drove out to Jersey and omigawd you could not believe the traffic, it was like a parking lot at the mall at Christmas. I didn't get there until close to dinner time. Ma was running around as she usually does on a Sunday and I say, Ma, I gotta talk to you.

"Ellie, she says, I gotta finish this soup because Rose and her husband – this is her third husband by the way, she keeps trading up – are coming over and Roberto is bringing his new girlfriend and I say, Ma, let me help you.

"So we are chopping up celery, carrots and potatoes, and I say, Ma, I have to tell you something and I don't want you to get all crazy. I have a girlfriend.

"She keeps on cutting and says, you have lots of girlfriends.

"No, I say, I mean a girlfriend girlfriend.

"She stops cutting and looks at me and says, you mean like a girlfriend girlfriend, and I say, yes Ma, and her name is Sam.

"And she goes, is Sam a woman? And I say, yes, Ma, her name is Samantha and we are together.

"So you're like a lesbian, she says.

"Yes, Ma, I say. I'm gay."

"And Ma goes, Are you trying to kill me? I mean, your brother just got fired again, and your cousin Francesca thinks she's pregnant and the wedding is three months away and she's already bought the dress. Your stepfather's ex moved back to Queens and wants more payments from the restaurant. Nonna left the stove burner on again and, God have mercy, we have to decide what we're going to do with her, and this knee is killing me. And you're telling me this now?

"And I say, So, what you're saying is that, considering all that, this isn't so bad.

"She actually laughed. But then she says, I gotta sit down.

"She sits and I keep cutting the vegetables and she says, make the pieces smaller, and I do.

"Finally I say, so what do you think?

"And Ma asks, what about your friends, Tina, Sarah and

STEPHANIE SCHOROW

Maureen. Are they lesbians too?

"No, Ma, they still like men."

"And who is this Sam?

"Just someone I met.

"Is she Greek?

"No."

"Italian?"

"No. Her family came from England, I think."

"What does she do?"

"She does finance and stuff."

"She got money?"

"Yeah, Ma, I say. She's got money."

"Who does the cooking?"

"I roll my eyes, but I say we take turns and we go out to dinner a lot."

"Ma sighs and says, I always thought there was something different about you. But I was hoping for more grandkids."

"Ma, you might get more grandkids, I tell her."

"With two women? That would be a real trick."

"Ma, there are ways, I say.

"And then she was quiet. I keep cutting and cutting and she says, okay, that's enough. Put it all in the pot.

"And then she goes, are you happy?

"Yeah, Ma, I say. I'm happy. Who knows? We might even get married someday.

"Just don't get pregnant before the wedding. Franny is going nuts over whether her dress is gonna fit.

"Ma. I'll be careful.

"And then Ma goes, put some salt in the pot. Not too much. Did I tell you about Mrs. Beratis next door? I can't believe how the neighborhood is changing.

"Ma, I say, the world is changing.

"Yeah,' she says. 'I kinda noticed."

Elekta ran out of breath.

"Thanks for telling me all that," Maureen quickly interjected. "So it sounds like she's okay with all this."

"Well," said Elektra. "Wait until I tell you what happened at dinner."

Maureen said she had to finish up the editing but said she would love to hear all about it the next time they all got together. She thought to herself she didn't know when that might happen.

CHAPTER THIRTY

When Doves Cry

TINA STOPPED BY Maureen's desk on Friday to say she was leaving a bit early for a special dinner with Tommy at this new French restaurant. Tommy was leaving for a week to attend a conference called COMDEX and then go to California for meetings. Tina wanted to thank Maureen again for giving Tommy her brother's number. James worked for Apple and Tommy was interested in meeting him. Maureen was on the phone and gestured for Tina to wait. And wait. Tina was ready to stalk off when Maureen hung up.

"Hey, I'm leaving a bit early. We are going to try out La Bonne Chance."

"Whatever," said Maureen. "Have a fabulous time tonight. Just remember you have to file your weekend feature tomorrow. Don't be late again." And she picked up the phone.

Tina remained angry with Maureen while she got ready for dinner. But really it didn't matter what Maureen thought; she had Tommy now. They were a team, a corporation. Origami had to unfold sooner or later.

Even so, the meal at Bonne Chance, despite its deliciously lavish use of butter and cream, did not entirely shake her sour mood. Tommy was in jovial spirits; he didn't seem to notice that Tina was quieter than usual. He scarfed down his steak and talked about hard drives and CD-ROMs. Tina was completely lost. They stayed at Tommy's apartment that night because he had to leave the next morning.

Tina became restless when Tommy started snoring, thinking about Maureen's harsh tone. Even Bob and Leo nestled between them made her think of Mindy and Sheena alone at home. She drove him to the airport, praying that the Volkswagen wouldn't decide to die on the way, dropped him off, and drove home to feed Sheena and Mindy. The cats flanked her as she leafed through the latest Spy magazine, thinking that William, who had been particularly strict when editing lately, would never let her get away with calling Stamford's prime developer Frank Rich a "short-fingered vulgarian."

It was the first Saturday night in a long time she didn't have plans. She briefly considered calling either Elektra or Sarah; she concluded that one would be out with Sam and the other would be sleeping and anyway, Sarah hadn't been in touch with her. Why bother? She decided to take a walk and enjoy the evening. She checked the mirror – nothing major to report – and stepped out into the late afternoon sun.

Strolling in Stamford wasn't at all like wandering through New York. The air smelled sweeter and she felt safer on the streets. She was different now too; she had a boyfriend, she had a real job. Tommy must have arrived in Vegas by now she thought as she strolled past her old apartment building.

"Hey Tina." She looked up and there was Rick, dark hair slicked back, dressed in tailored jeans and sweater. She caught a whiff of his aftershave, the scent triggering a memory of longing. "Hi Rick," she said.

"How are you? Still writing those great features?"

"Good, yes, how are you?"

"Fighting the good fight," he said, his eyes crinkling. "Oiling the wheels of the American justice system."

"Great," said Tina. They were both silent.

"Good to see you," she said and started to walk past him.

"Hold on for a second, okay? There's something I wanted to tell you. I never got a chance. I really feel bad about what happened between us. I just wanted to explain."

"You mean about Angela."

"Yeah, Angie. Tina, have you ever had something that just grabs you and won't let go? That was Angie and me. She was like this tornado, this raven-haired siren who just swept me up. She was a hit of cocaine, a shot of bourbon. I fell so hard I didn't know what I was doing. I couldn't see anything but her; I just ignored everything else. I couldn't eat or sleep; I just had to be with her. I know it wasn't healthy and I almost lost a case because all I could see was her. That's why I just stopped calling you."

"I know. I saw you two together."

"Tina, man. There was nothing I wouldn't do for her. Nothing. And then she left me, dumped me at the side of the road. She said I was too intense. Heck, I'm a lawyer – intensity is part of the game plan. But she couldn't handle it, I guess. And then she was gone. Out of my life. Tina, have you ever had your heart broken by someone, someone who walks away laughing, as if you didn't matter?"

Tina thought of Greg and nodded. "Rick, I'm so sorry."

"Jesus," said Rick, rubbing his eyes. "I said I was over her. But it still hurts and I think that maybe I wasn't that nice to you. And then you moved away. I felt terrible."

"I have a boyfriend now," said Tina. "And two cats."

"Tina, that's great, that's wonderful. I'm so happy for you. He's a lucky guy. I've thought about you and I'm glad you're happy."

"Thank you," said Tina. "And don't worry, you'll meet someone nice, I'm sure."

Rick sighed. "I hope so. Are you on your way to your boyfriend's now?"

"Actually," said Tina. "I was taking a walk."

"I know I don't deserve it, but could I buy you a drink? We could just go down the street."

Tina thought for a moment. "Why not?" she said.

The rest of the night was a blur of drinks and laughter, and Rick intently asking her about her writing. Nearby, someone played Prince's song, "When Doves Cry," on the jukebox and they both stopped mid-sentence to listen.

"I love this song," said Tina. "So sad but beautiful."

"This is like the story of my mom and dad," Rick said. "They were always fighting and breaking up and getting back together and it was hard on all us kids. Maybe that's why I screwed up with Angela."

Tina reached out and touched Rick's hand, breathing in his aftershave like an elixir, and he ordered another round of drinks. And the rest of the evening was a rush until she woke up in Rick's bed, with his arms around her.

At first, she didn't know where she was. She managed to extricate herself and find a bathroom where she threw up. She splashed water on her face. She tried to piece together the evening, grasping for fragments, pleasure that morphed into pain. Brugger. Bagger. Begone. She got carried away. She had to go home. As quietly as she could, she tried to find her clothes and purse.

"Hey, babe," Rick said from the bed.

"Hey. I'm sorry I have to go home, feed the cats." She hiccupped.

"Sure, sure."

"Bye," she said, stumbling into the morning air.

The cats were apoplectic when she got home. Where were you? We are hungry. We are really hungry. She fed them. And then took a hot shower, as hot as she could manage. She stayed in so long that Sheena started to scratch at the door. She crawled into bed with wet hair and hugged her knees. She caught a whiff of Rick; it came from her sweater crumpled on the bed. Why did she like that smell so much? Both cats jumped up beside her and regarded her nervously. She rocked back and forth. She thought of Tommy's face. She thought of the way he would grasp her hand whenever they walked together. She pushed away the clothes she left on the bed and Rick's scent drifted by her again. What was wrong with her? Was she that drunk? What would Maureen think of her after her bold statements about Tommy? She had cheated on him. She put her face in her hands and sobbed. Mindy and Sheena pressed against her, meowing.

The phone rang, and Tina picked it up quickly, thinking Tommy was calling. It was Rick.

"Hey babe, are you okay? You left pretty quickly this morning."

"Rick, oh god. I don't know what I was doing. I think I had too much to drink last night. I've been thinking and I really think I want to stay with my boyfriend. You are such a great guy and I am so horribly, terribly sorry. Please forgive me."

"That's all right. I understand. I really do. We just had unfinished business."

"I don't want to hurt you like Angela hurt you. I feel terrible."

"Babe, don't worry. You're a nice girl and your boyfriend – what's his name?'

"Tommy."

"He is so lucky to have you. You're a really nice girl."

"Oh, thank you, Rick. Thank you for being so understanding."

"Hey, forget about it."

"I will always be your friend."

"Likewise, babe. Take care."

Tina hung up. Of course, she wanted to stay with Tommy. She loved him. She wanted to be with him. She took another shower. She checked the refrigerator. Her hangover was easing and she was hungry. The cats continued to curl around her legs, meowing.

Her intercom buzzer sounded. Sheena hissed. "Don't be silly, it's just the buzzer," Tina said. She pushed the intercom button, "Yes?" "Flower delivery for Miss Tina," came a voice. "I'll be right down," Tina said, stroking Mindy who had started to yowl. Guilt washed over her again. Tommy had probably sent flowers. He missed her.

She ran downstairs and outside the front door was a bouquet of roses. And Rick. She let him into the lobby.

"Oh you shouldn't have," she said, nervously reaching for the clichéd standby, as he handed her the bouquet. "They are beautiful."

"Just to make sure there are no hard feelings."

"Oh, thank you."

"I just wanted to make sure you were feeling okay."

"Thanks so much."

Tina put her nose into the roses, the usual gesture. They had no smell at all, just a faint whiff of dampness.

"So," Rick said, smiling, his hair tousled like a kid after playing baseball. "No hard feelings."

"No, not at all," she said.

"Let's kiss and seal the deal."

Tina nodded. Rick put his arms around her and kissed her deeply. She could now smell something harsh on his breath, and he wasn't letting go, and his tongue pressed into her mouth. As gently as she could, she pulled away.

"That was nice," said Rick. "You taste so good."

Tina, who had not brushed her teeth that day, couldn't help smiling.

"How about another?" And Rick stepped closer.

Tina dropped her head, shaking it slightly.

"Why don't I come up to your place for a while?"

Tina shook her head. "I'm so sorry."

"I think you want this. I think you want me to come up."

"No, really, no."

"I could feel it in your lips. You want me to come upstairs like last night."

"No, please." Tina tried to step back but Rick now put his hands on her shoulders.

"Come on, babe."

"No, really." And Tina pulled away.

"Okay," and Rick dropped his hands. "I understand. You lead me on and then you just walk away. You know that?"

"No, please, Rick. I am sorry."

"I bet you're sorry. You came on to me like a cat in heat last night and now you're just blowing me off. You really are a devious woman, you know that? Just like all the others."

Tears sprung up in Tina's eyes. "I'm really sorry."

"Come on then," and Rick stepped up to her. She stepped back, the roses slipping from her hand.

"I get it. You are just another little cockteaser playing with my feelings. You know that?"

"No, don't say that."

"Your boyfriend should really know what kind of a girl you really are. Tommy should really know what he's got on his hands. I think I should tell him his girlfriend is a whore."

"Go away," Tina screamed. "Leave me alone."

"Hey, Tina, babe, calm down."

Tina turned and ran for the stairs at the back of the hall. She took the steps two at a time. She burst through the door to the second floor and, thank God, her apartment door was unlocked. She was inside, slamming it, locking it. She thought she heard footsteps in the hallway. The footsteps receded and faded. Then the buzzer sounded. Again. And then again.

She reached for the phone and called 911.

"Stamford Police."

"Can you help me? There's a man trying to bother me."

"What is he doing?"

"He gave me roses and then he tried to kiss me."

The dispatcher's tone seemed to shift. "He did what?"

"He tried to kiss me."

"Honey, this is a line for real emergencies. He gave you roses?"

"I mean he scared me. He, I, and then..."

"Where is he now?"

"I don't know."

"Where are you?"

"In my apartment."

"Is the door locked? Did he hurt you?"

"No, he just, he kept trying to give me the roses."

The dispatcher snorted. "Well, the next time someone else gives you roses, don't call 911." And hung up.

The buzzer sounded again. The cats were both howling now. "Maoow," said Mindy. "Maooow," said Sheena. "Maureen," they said. "She will know what to do."

Tina reached for the phone and dialed. The machine answered. "Maureen," she said. "Maureen, please pick up. Please. Please."

"Yes, what is it?" Maureen's voice was cool. "Maureen..." and Tina started sobbing.

"What's wrong?"

"Something bad happened," was all Tina could say.

"Are you at home? I'm coming down."

Tina breathed long ragged sighs. Maureen would judge her harshly but she needed help. There was a hard knock at the door, "Tina, it's me."

Tina opened the door. Between sobs, she gulped, "I messed up."

Sarah woke up from a hazy dream to a ringing phone. She had been on the border of Arianna as Sir Dragonette led her on the Disappearing Path to the overlook. She was so disoriented she picked up instead of letting the answering machine do it. "Hello," she muttered, unsure if she were talking to a human or dragon.

"Sarah, I'm sorry to wake you up. Get down to Tina's place now."

Maureen's voice reached her through the fog. She sat up, threw on a sweatshirt, and stumbled to the door, hoping that this was a crisis with coffee. She arrived at Tina's door, just as Elektra did.

"Get inside and lock the door."

"Omigawd," said Elektra. She rushed over and hugged a sobbing Tina. Sarah came behind and hugged her too.

The story came out in bits and pieces. "That fucking Rick," said Elektra. "What a fucking bastard."

"I am a horrible person," wailed Tina. "I did a terrible thing. I can't believe I slept with him. And now he is scaring the hell out of me. He's going to tell Tommy."

"Tina," said Sarah. "It's okay."

"Tina, look," Maureen said, almost wearily. "You are lucky something worse didn't happen. It was just a one-night stand. Do you know how many one-night stands I've had and the guy just splits. It happens." All the women nodded

"Like there was this time that I met this guy Jerry, we fucked like bunnies and then, poof, he was gone," said Elektra. "Asshole never called me back."

"And," said Maureen. "You are not owned by Tommy. And you think he is the one? Maybe this tells you something."

"I love Tommy, and now I've messed it all up."

"No, you haven't," said Sarah. "You had a fling. It happens. You had a fling with a jerk. That happens. All the time. I should know."

"I just don't know what to do. What if he tells Tommy?"

"He was just trying to freak you out. He wants to see whose dick is bigger," said Elektra. "All men think about is their dick."

Tina started to answer when the intercom buzzed. The women were silent. It buzzed again. And then again.

"You have to answer," said Maureen.

Tina pressed the intercom. "Yes."

"Hey, you forgot the roses. I'm sorry if I was forward. I just care about us so much. Just come down and get the flowers. Fifty bucks, but you're worth it. I was just hurt, okay? I'm sorry if I came on so strong."

Tina glanced at her friends. Maureen nodded. Tina pressed the button to speak.

"Rick. Thank you. Can you just leave the flowers in the lobby and I'll get them later?"

"Of course, babe. I just wanted to see how you were doing. You got so upset with me."

"I know, Rick. You just scared me. And I feel bad about what happened."

"I know you feel bad about your boyfriend. Tommy, right? Tommy. He's a very lucky man, isn't he? He must be a great guy to put up with you. He must be a super great man to put up with a whore like you. Because you know that's what you are? A heartless little cunt…"

Maureen jumped up and pushed the buzzer. "We will be right down." She turned and said to Tina, "You have to talk to him."

"No," said Tina.

"We will go down together," said Maureen. "You have to confront him. He's a bully and you have to confront a bully."

Sarah wasn't sure if she was asleep, dreaming, or cat dreaming. Her pulse was pounding, but she didn't feel fear. She moved slowly, as if in water. Elektra and Maureen held Tina's arms and walked out the door. Sarah followed. They walked silently down the stairs as the goddesses of Arianna shimmered into view. She could see the Gardener and the Seductress walking alongside them and the Dove of the Martyr resting on Tina's shoulder. A snake with glittering eyes was curled around Elektra's arm. Mama Wolf trotted next to Maureen. The Cat Thief goddess padded behind, cunning and merciless.

Rick was standing in the lobby with the roses and stared as the four women approached.

Tina said, "Rick, I'm sorry, but you have to leave me alone."

Elektra said, "You fucking creep, fuck off."

Maureen said, "We will be getting a restraining order and calling your law firm to tell them one of their attorneys is stalking a woman."

Sarah said, "Rick, you need to get help. You are in deep, personal trouble. You need to see a therapist for anger management."

"You fucking whore. Go fuck yourself, you dyke. Just try it." Rick paused and spat out, "You don't get it. You don't get how cruel you women are. You don't care about how much pain you inflict. You break hearts like it's nothing."

Tina said, slowly and firmly. "Rick, you gotta leave right now and never come back. Just GO! Get help. Go to a doctor. Go to a bar. I don't care. But leave me alone."

"All right! Take the fucking flowers," Rick yelled. He threw the bunch at their feet, turned and walked across the lobby, shoved the front door open, and went out.

An hour later, the women were still gathered in Tina's place. Maureen said it was time for a sleepover. Sarah called in sick and Elektra told Sam she would call her later. They dragged in blankets and pillows while Maureen made popcorn. Maureen looked around the room with satisfaction. Tina had calmed down, Sarah was looking happier than she had in months, and Elektra was in rare form.

"Ya gotta admit," said Elektra, munching popcorn. "He was ready to shit his pants when he saw the four of us approaching. It was like the march of the Amazons. He probably thought we were going to castrate him with a rusty kitchen knife."

"We could have," said Sarah, giggling.

"Tina, how are you feeling?" Maureen asked.

"Okay but," Tina sighed shakily. Mindy was in her lap purring. "What am I going to tell Tommy?"

"Just tell him the whole story and he will understand," said Sarah. "Just be honest."

"Don't tell him a frigging thing," said Elektra. "I mean Sam and I have agreed never to talk about Denise or Peg again."

"Why do you have to tell him anything?" asked Maureen.

"Well, you know," said Tina.

"Did you use a condom?"

"Yes, we did."

"Then you don't have to say anything. Your body is your body. You own it, no one else. Look, say you tell Tommy. Tell him all that happened. I bet he would get angry at Rick, he might try to confront him. And that would be worse. No, this gives you a chance for reflection. Do you really want to stay just with Tommy? If he is the one, then make it official. But do it out of love. Not out of fear. I just hate this idea that a woman does a single wrong thing and wears it like a scarlet letter for life."

"God, you're so fucking wise sometimes," said Sarah, tearing off the wrapper of a Hersey bar. "It's really annoying."

"It's just like that horrible movie *Fatal Attraction*," said Tina. "Only I'm the bad husband and Rick is…."

"Glenn Close!" shouted Elektra. "Omigawd, that's it."

"Here's the thing," said Sarah, who had hashed over the movie at length with Tina when they saw it. "He, Michael

Douglas, I loved him in *Wall Street* incidentally, slept with her twice. First time was a fling but then he did it again. You did what he should have done."

"Glenn Close was so evil," said Elektra. "She boiled a bunny. A poor little bunny! I was rooting for her until then."

"The truth is the audience was rooting for the husband at the end," said Sarah. "Men are allowed to have flings but women aren't."

"Just think about *Tess of the D'Urbervilles*," said Maureen. "One strike and you're out."

"Tess of the whosis?" said Elektra.

"Tess of the DOO BER VILLES. The Thomas Hardy book. It was a movie, too. Called *Tess*."

"Oh that. That was boring," Elektra said.

"Beautifully filmed, however," said Tina.

"So you know Tess married this handsome guy named Clare and he confesses to an affair long ago and she forgives him and then she explains how she was raped –yes, raped – and had a kid and he can't forgive her. I was furious when I read that. She should have kept her mouth shut," Maureen said.

"Oh, come on," said Sarah. "Then there wouldn't have been a book. I think Hardy was trying to show the unfairness of society."

"Well, it always bugged me."

Elektra said, "Nastassja Kinski starred in the movie. Wasn't she the woman in the poster posing with the snake? Naked!"

"She had a bracelet on," Maureen said. "I had a boyfriend who had that poster in his bedroom. I had to stare at it when we had sex."

"See, snakes can be sexy," said Sarah.

They talked until midnight and made plans to see *The Heidi Chronicles* together. They each took home three roses.

Tina braced herself for Tommy's return. She patiently circled the airport for two hours until she saw him at the curb. They went to Tommy's place and ordered Chinese food delivery. Tommy talked nonstop about his meetings in San Francisco; he had gone to lunch with Maureen's brother and he was now reconsidering Apple's future.

Tina nestled against Tommy, breathing in the scent of sweat and detergent from his shirt. Leo was in Tommy's lap. Bob was perched like a gargoyle on the arms of the couch. Tina was thinking the only thing missing was Sheena and Mindy – there was nothing else that she lacked. This was it. This was really it. Tommy kissed the top of her head.

Tina took a deep breath, "I think we should talk."

"You're not mad at me for something," said Tommy. "Are you?"

"I have something to tell you," Tina said. She opened her mouth. Closed it. And opened it again. "I think, I think, we should figure out if we really want to have a commitment to get married. Let's talk."

The night after they looked at engagement rings, they went to Bobby V's. As Tina picked at her salad and Tommy munched a burger, she saw out of the corner of her eye that Rick was walking toward them, wearing a Yankees cap.

"Well, hello, Tina," he said. "This must be Tommy."

Tina could not speak. "Pleased to meet you," said Tommy, his mouth full.

"I want you both to meet my girl Sondra." Sondra was brown-haired and more voluptuous than Angela, wearing a tight azure dress.

"Pleased to meet you," said Sondra, her voice carrying the lilt of an accent.

"Well, have a good night," said Rick, pulling Sondra to his side and starting to walk away. Then he stopped, dropped his arm from Sondra and turned around. He leaned over the table.

"Hey, Tommy, buddy. I hate to tell you this, but I think you got catsup on your shirt."

"Thank you," said Tommy, dabbling at his shirt with a napkin and spreading the sauce into a wide patch.

Rick shot Tina a satisfied look and walked off with one hand tapping Sondra's butt. Tommy continued, "So I'm thinking…" Tina felt her heart gradually slow down. She remained uneasy.

CHAPTER
THIRTY-ONE

The Duel

TINA SUDDENLY DEVELOPED a passion for cleaning her apartment. She scrubbed the kitchen sink with Ajax until she finally eliminated the dark stains that had marked the sink from the day she moved in. She also took off a layer of skin from her fingertips. She vacuumed so much the cats lived in a state of anxiety. She mopped under the bed, bringing out dust balls the size of kittens. Mindy and Sheena found fresh litter in their box both morning and night. When she wasn't writing stories for the *Gazette*, she was cleaning. She did both with such fierce focus that even Ken stopped by her desk to compliment her output, forcing her to smile until her jaw hurt. Maureen casually dropped over to rescue her, just as Ken was asking what her goals were for her future and she could count on him for a recommendation. Tina stopped eating but only for a couple of days and then consumed an entire pint of Ben & Jerry's that Elektra said was much better than that pretentious Haagen Dazs.

Finally, Elektra and Sarah corralled her. "I told you not to tell him," Elektra said.

"I just didn't feel right holding it in. And I was so worried he would find out."

"That fucking Rick," Elektra said.

"Tommy looked so sad," said Tina, welling up. "I tried to say this was a drunken fling, that I was sorry the minute it happened. I told him that I really loved him and I wanted to be with him. He said he wanted to stay together, but he doesn't answer my calls."

Sarah jumped in before Elektra could speak. "Stop blaming yourself. Shit happens." That was now one of Sarah's favorite expressions. She said she learned it from Maureen.

"You didn't have to say anything!" Elektra said.

"Oh, stop saying that!" Tina retorted.

Elektra was unfazed. "My Nonna always told me the truth is overrated. That's how she stuck it out with my grandfather for so many years. 'I spent all the money on groceries, I need another five dollars,' she'd say. And slip me the fiver."

"What's done is done," said Sarah. "Does he want to break up? Do you?"

Tina pondered the questions. "No, I don't, but I'm not sure about him. He said he was hurt, that he'd been dumped before and it was awful. I said I knew how he felt, I really did."

"But you told him you are not dumping him, right?" Elektra asked. Tina nodded.

"You might need to have it out with him. One way or the other," Sarah said. Tina could tell she was thinking of Cole.

"Look," said Tina. "You have to understand. I was happy with Tommy. I don't need anyone else. I was glad that that part of my life was taken care of. No more drama. No more weird dates. I just think you guys might like the drama more than I do."

"I don't think so," said Elektra. "I just don't want to be bored. I mean Sam drives me crazy sometimes, but she's never boring."

"Cole wasn't boring either but." Sarah stopped speaking.

"You haven't called him, right?" Tina said.

Sarah shook her head. "No, not today, not yesterday, not tomorrow."

"Look, why don't you come over to Bobby V's for a drink," said Elektra. "Get your mind off of this."

Tina demurred. She said she really wanted to finish going through her closet. So Sarah and Elektra took off. Tina started sorting the clothes that had migrated to the back. She was definitely not going to wear that Spandex top again or those pre-ripped Calvin Klein jeans. She didn't pick up the phone when it rang, but no one left a message. About a half hour later, she heard the pounding of feet in the hallway and Sarah and Elektra burst in, speaking at once and gasping for breath.

"You will not believe what just happened," Elektra cried. "You will not fucking believe this."

"Tommy and Rick got in a fight," said Sarah.

"Tommy hit Rick and then Rick grabbed Tommy and they were rolling around on the floor. It was fucking insane and people were cheering, because people love a fight and…"

"WHAT!" Tina yelled. "What happened?"

After a few minutes of descriptions, asides, interruptions and "No, you tell it," and "No, you go ahead," Elektra got the story out.

"So we were sitting at the bar and Sarah and I had a white wine, no, I had a red wine, because that's supposed to be good for your health. We saw Tommy over at the other end and we were talking about it, should we go over or not and then suddenly Rick walks in and I'm thinking this is not going to be good. He sees us and kind of sneers and I sing out, 'How ya doing, jerk,' and Sarah punches me in the arm. Tommy turns around and sees Rick. I'm thinking this is really not good and he walks over and starts talking to him…"

"Who started talking to whom?" Tina interrupted.

"Tommy starts talking to Rick and we can't really hear, but Tommy says something like how's your friend Sondra and Rick goes, man, she's history. She was kind of a whore just like your girlfriend. And Tommy goes 'Take that back" and Rick goes 'Fuck off" and Tommy started yelling, 'Take that back.' And

Rick goes 'Make me' or something like that and the whole bar is starting to watch and Tommy is yelling 'Take it back, take it back…' And Rick yells 'Whore' and Tommy just punched him in the face."

"You're kidding me," Tina shrieked.

"I think he hit the jaw, actually," said Sarah.

Elektra continued the story with relish. "Rick jumps at him then they are grabbing each other and wrestling until the bouncer comes running up and says, break it up or take it outside. He pushes them out the door. We follow them out. Rick starts yelling, 'Calm down,' And Tommy goes, 'Take it back' but oh Tina, I think he was crying."

"There were definite tears," Sarah interjected.

Elektra rushed on. "And Rick goes, 'I gotta tell you, Thomas, you have a lotta balls. You know I'm a lawyer, right? I could sue you from now to the next fucking century.'

" 'I don't care,' Tommy says.

"And Rick goes, 'Look, man, I get it. I'm sorry. Women. You know, women. Fucking women.' He is rubbing his face and saying, 'Thomas you pack a mean punch.' And then we hear sirens and Rick goes, 'Later, man,' and he takes off and we are holding on to Tommy and saying, 'Come on, let's get out of here,' and we sort of drag him away and he goes, 'It's okay, gals,' and he takes off."

Tina's eyes filled with tears and she angrily brushed them away. "I have to call him. I have to talk to him," she said.

"Go on," said Sarah and she and Elektra pretended to look over the clothes Tina was throwing out.

Tina kept calling, leaving one message after the other. Finally, Tommy picked up. "Oh, my God, are you all right?" Tina cried.

"I'm fine," said Tommy. "Don't worry about me." He sounded tired, but strangely upbeat.

"What the hell were you thinking?" Tina screamed into the receiver. "You could have been hurt or killed or even sued."

"Tina. It's all right."

Tina was trying to figure out what she was hearing in Tommy's voice. Could he be happy? Triumphant?

"What is up with you?"

"I won. I never won a fight before. But he backed down."

"Are you crazy?"

"A little. But everything is fine."

"Look, I'm very upset. Can I call you tomorrow? Will you take care of yourself?"

"Sure," said Tommy. "I'm going to have a beer."

Tina slammed down the phone and looked around to see Sarah and Elektra trying not to laugh.

"This is not funny. Someone could have been hurt."

"Violence is never the answer," said Elektra, who seemed to be trying to sound like Maureen. Sarah cackled.

"You don't see women fighting like this."

"Oh yeah you do," both Elektra and Sarah said together.

Tina wiped her eyes with the back of her hand. She didn't feel like crying anymore. She felt something like relief. She felt strong. Tommy had won his fight and now she would win him back.

"This is all so weird," Tina said.

"Shit happens," Sarah said.

"By the way," Elektra said. "Your apartment looks really clean. Are you really throwing out that halter top?"

CHAPTER THIRTY-TWO

Finding Mr. Darcy

MAUREEN WAS NOT pleased to hear about the fight between Rick and Tommy. Mostly, she was disappointed she had missed it. She did not hear about it until Elektra dropped something about "the fight" and then she had a talk with Tina, who seemed surprisingly confident that she and Tommy would work things out. She tried to call Sarah but could never reach her. Finally they ran into each other in the hallway. Sarah was coming home from an overnight shift and shivering despite the warm temperatures. She didn't want to talk, she said. Everything was fine, and that she just needed to sleep. Maureen asked her about the fight. Sarah smiled a bit at that and said that maybe it proved Maureen right about Tommy and Tina. Maureen didn't want to hear that now. Maybe she was wrong about a lot of things.

"Have you heard from Cole?"

Sarah shook her head. "I'm not calling him. There's no point."

"Maybe he misses you."

"If he missed me, he would call. There's no point. No point to anything, really."

"Are you working on your book?"

"Sometimes. That seems a bit pointless too. No one is going to publish it."

"Look, get some rest. Let's talk later, all right?"

"Whatever."

That night Maureen dreamed she was leading a group

therapy session. Sylvia Plath was on time as was Diane Arbus. Anne Sexton staggered in, a lit cigarette in one hand, a full pack in the other. When Marilyn Monroe sauntered in wearing a sequin dress like a second skin, Arbus started snapping photos until Maureen had to intervene. Last to arrive was Virginia Woolf, pale and serene in tweed. Maureen insisted she first take the rocks out of her jacket pockets.

"What the hell are you doing here?" Arbus growled at Marilyn. "If I had your looks, all my problems would be solved."

"Don't be silly," Marilyn said in her breathy voice. "If I had your talent, Arthur would still be with me."

Maureen held up her hand. "One at a time. Who wants to share first?"

Sylvia raised her hand. "Have you any idea what it's like to have your husband sleep with another woman?" she asked.

"Yes," said Diane, Anne, and Marilyn.

"To have the man you adore, your soulmate, the father of your children, twist and turn your feelings, to make you believe you are the one who failed," Sylvia continued.

Diane raised her hand. "I was hip. I didn't need marriage, that was for squares. My husband and I had a great relationship until his girlfriend insisted on a divorce. My new boyfriend was married and that was perfectly fine… until" her voice faltered. "It wasn't."

"I could not inflict more pain on my dear Leonard, not when the voices began again," said Virginia.

Maureen jumped in. "Look at you, all you bright, beautiful talented women. You have so much to live for."

"Darling, you just don't understand," said Marilyn, her voice like a fluttering bird.

"Demons bearing demons," said Anne. "The ripples in the pond are not from the wind but what dwells below." She stood and bowed, and the others applauded.

"Not bad," Virginia murmured.

"Is everyone still taking their Prozac?" Maureen demanded, looking around the room at the women whose faces were beginning to blur.

Diane shrugged. Virginia shook her head. "Recipe for a Prozac cocktail," said Anne brightly. "One part fresh cut grass, one part crumpled paper ripped from the typewriter, four parts vodka, one Prozac. And a cherry."

"But you have so much to live for. Why are you giving up?" Maureen shouted.

"You just don't understand. You just don't understand," the women chanted.

Maureen woke up with a start. What didn't she understand?

The newsroom meeting that day was somber. Circulation was continuing to fall. Not a lot, but enough to make the senior editors continue the hiring freeze and consider whether another makeover of the newspaper's layout was required. Frank, the news editor, noted that long-time readers just didn't like change. Remember what happened when they tried to drop Prince Valiant from Sunday's comics? Readers threatened to storm the newsroom like it was an enemy castle. Ken jumped in with a hearty, if rambling, pep talk, saying they had to pull together, that this was a temporary glitch. People were just uneasy about the economy ("Bush's fault," Maureen muttered) and that would change.

The meeting broke up and Maureen hurried to her desk to finish up the features for the next day. The phone rang. "Hello, features desk," Maureen said, hoping to dodge any public relation flaks, the journalists' favorite word for persistent public relations agents, asking for Maureen O'Malley.

"Hey," said John.

Maureen broke in before he could launch into his usual

tirade. "I'm on deadline right now. Can I call you back?"

"Okey-doke," said John, who never said okey-doke. "So sorry to bother you when you're so busy."

"What's wrong?"

"Nothing. Everything is great. Totally great."

"John, what's going on?"

"I got shit canned."

"You got fired?"

"Fucking bunch of motherfuckers. They said, fuck you, but I say fuck you, you fucking fucks."

"John, are you drinking?"

"I pour my fucking heart into their backassward company with a jerk-off CEO and his idiot minions…"

"John. Listen. As soon as I finish, I'll come over. Okay?"

"I love you babe. I don't know what I'd do without you."

"John, I'll be there soon."

Both unnerved and annoyed, Maureen rushed through her work. John had often declared he was on the brink of being fired but this seemed like the real thing. Given what he told her he had said to his boss, she was slightly surprised he hadn't been tossed before. After a few minutes, she decided this could be one of those episodes, even though she could almost smell the bourbon over the phone.

Rush hour had all traffic at a crawl. Maureen found tears welling up in her eyes. Why was she rushing to help John? Why did it always have to be her? When was John going to try to master the art of snaking through congestion to come to her rescue? For that matter, why was she always the one looking out for Sarah, Tina, and Elektra? She tried to hold back a sob.

"My dear Miss O'Malley, you must control yourself lest calamity befall your carriage," said Jane, appearing with her hat and white gloves just as Maureen thought she would break down.

Maureen wiped her eyes with one hand while the other gripped the wheel and breathed deeply. "I'm just so upset."

"Then unburden yourself as undoubtedly there will be adequate opportunities given the state of congestion before us. The discourse may prove calming."

"I'm so sick of helpless men."

"You speak in the plural. However, I deduce that the singular person you are referring to is Mr. John."

"I keep waiting and waiting and waiting for the right guy, the right person to appear."

"Indeed, this is a frequent complaint of many who seek matrimony."

"Oh, I know. But I've waited so long. I want a man with spirit and strength, a guy's guy, who can be tough on the job and tender with a crying child. Someone who would spring to action for me. That's whom I've been waiting for all these years. Don't you get it? I want Darcy. Where is my Mr. Darcy?"

The car was silent, then. The beeping of horns sounded outside.

"Are you quite finished?"

"Yes," said Maureen, wiping her nose on the sleeve of her blouse.

"May I again remind you that Mr. Darcy is a fictional character?"

"I know."

"As is Mr. Knightley, Mr. Tilney, Mr. Wentworth, Willoughby and so many others. Though, perhaps, not Mr. Collins. I am quite sure he was based on a real person. But I would suppose a man such as the pompous Collins would not inspire your romantic yearning."

"No. But Jane, it's just that I'm close to the age that you were when you, you…"

"Expired."

"Yes, and I just can't seem to find the right balance between work, love, professional time and time for myself."

"You know that I never married."

"Yes, and I thought about that a lot. That you could write so well, so passionately about the dance of man and woman and never finish the dance yourself. How hard it must have been, how lonely."

"My dear friend. You have no conception of what it was like."

"I'm sorry," Maureen said, but Jane continued.

"I did, indeed, mourn the lack of male companionship. In particular, I desired a gentleman who would admire my exceedingly sharp wit while in a position to offer me a comfortable situation. My yearnings were quite overwhelming at intervals. Yet, my dear, you cannot imagine how much I would have given to live in this world of yours. How I would have reveled in what you take for granted, in being able to make your own life, neither depending on a husband nor family nor the condescending aid of distant relatives. I could not earn a living by my cleverness, however considerable, nor find employment outside the home."

"But life seemed so much simpler then."

"My dear friend. My writing, the activity most important to me, was never considered more than an amusing distraction by the society in which I resided. The proudest moment of my life was not finishing my first book; it was the day I received a modest sum from my publisher, my first real wages. You, by contrast, have employment, you have your own abode, and own your own carriage. Despite your society's propensity for haste, for fashions that strain credulity, for modes of conversation that are neither wise nor witty, this is where I would have been most happy. My dear, you may endure my same fate. You may die, husbandless, childless, and perhaps that furry creature that you dote upon will be forced to dine on your lifeless corpse as you so often predict. But you can make your own way in the world."

Someone beeped, an extended angry noise. Maureen, pondering what Jane had told her or what she had told herself, had stopped at a green light.

A man in a Mercedes passed her, yelling, "Hey lady, I'm driving here."

Maureen floored it.

When she got to John's place, she was first relieved. It was in its usually orderly state, jazz posters on the wall, neat piles of records and tapes, and a spotless kitchen. John met her at the door with a hug. John had, indeed, been given his walking papers and two weeks' notice. Something about new directions and they would be happy to give him recommendations. It took a while to get all this information given John's ranting about the CEO.

Maureen immediately asked to see his resume and John said had been years since he had done a resume and he didn't trust those lying bastard fucks to give him a good recommendation. Maureen persisted. There were so many jobs in his field, he could say he decided to take a new direction and she had friends she could call and then she stopped because John was sobbing. She had never seen him cry before.

"Maureen, I'm scared all the time. All the time. My father told me I would fuck up. He said I should just go into the insurance business with him. He always told me I would screw up. He was always yelling at me. He never thought I could do anything."

Maureen put her arms around him and he clung to her. She often spent Christmas with him, his father, mother and John's two younger brothers. All the men vied to speak the loudest and longest. When they played Scrabble together, shouting accompanied every turn. It didn't matter if Maureen won, they just wanted the other men to lose.

"John, your father loves you, he wants you to succeed."

"He never tells me that. Maybe he does, but all he ever says is you fucked up again."

Maureen hugged John until his sobs subsided. "Sweetie," she said. "You don't have to tell him. Wait until you get another job. Just wait."

John continued to hold her. "I know I'm a fucking asshole. I know I talk too much. But I don't know what I would do without you. I love you. I really do."

"I know," Maureen said.

"No, seriously. I do love you. I want to be with you. I know I have no right to ask this, but will you stay with me forever? I know I can be a handful. I know I'm messed up but I'm coming back. And I want you to be with me when I do."

"I know you will."

"I will show those fuckers. And I want you with me forever. I have no right to ask, but I adore you, I love you, and besides, of course, I have a big dick."

Maureen pulled back from John, who was grinning maniacally. She burst into laughter that shook her entire body. John was laughing too, tears drying on his face. "You know you love this about me," he said.

Maureen stroked his cheek. "I guess I do." They both knew they weren't talking about sex.

The next morning, Maureen was dressing as John staggered out of bed and headed into the bathroom.

"Hey honey?"

"Yes?"

"Can you put on the coffee before you go? I'm going to jump in the shower. And get the newspaper? It's usually by the door, but the morons often throw it in the bushes."

Maureen set up the coffee maker and listened to the sound of the water running in the bathroom. She was trying to parse her feelings. Did she want a man to rescue her? Or did she want to be the knight in shining armor? Did she really need someone to take care of her or did she thrive on taking care of others?

"John, you're no Mr. Darcy," she called out.

"What?"

"Never mind."

She decided to go home before work; she could allow herself to be late. She had to think everything over.

Hercules was patiently waiting for his breakfast. He ate daintily while she showered and then he jumped beside her in her towel and robe as she read the paper on the couch. Her hair dripped on his fur. He rubbed against her until she put down the paper and put her arms around him. Pet me and I will make you feel better, he said. I am here for you. I am always here for you. She hugged him, her rock, her stalwart, her Mr. Darcy, the male who would always be there for her until death do them part.

CHAPTER THIRTY-THREE

Tina's New Friends

SHE WAS NO longer a wisp of air; she was solid. Each foot struck the ground with purpose. She had coalesced. Yet Tina still liked to wander Manhattan streets with a blank mind, eyes filled with the tumult of faces and patterns of building, her nose attuned to the smell of sausage from street vendors and the hot breath of bus exhaust. She decided to take the train in early on a Friday. She was meeting Maureen and Elektra later for dinner. Sarah might eventually join them. The day was cool but the sun was prying open the clouds and Tina could feel the occasional sweep of heat on her face. She decided she would first wander along her old routes and the vicinity of the long-gone Red Ink.

She had stopped at a storefront to regard the haughty mannequins – when would this Spandex fixation ever end? – when she heard someone call her name.

"Well, is this Tina?"

Tina turned from the window and saw a familiar face, wolfish eyes behind sleek wire-rims, a bald dome, ringed with neatly trimmed, wavy hair.

"Randy?"

Randy was grinning, a well-groomed Randy, no less, in a suit. And was that a tie?

Randy hugged her, another non-Randy gesture. "Tina, I thought that was you. Wow, you're looking good."

"Ahem," came from a woman coming up beside Randy.

"Tina," said Randy. "Let me introduce my wife, Jewel.

Jewel, this is Tina who used to work in the shop."

"Pleased to meet you," said Jewel, sounding anything but.

"Pleased to meet you," said Tina. She was having trouble processing Randy, this new, yuppie Randy, and Jewel, a short, heavy-set woman with so many rings on her hands she looked like she was wearing brass knuckles.

"Tina used to write these great stories for the prop business. She actually got a job at a newspaper because of those," Randy said. "She is a great writer. You're still at the newspaper, right?"

Tina found herself blushing a bit. "Yes. I'm really doing well there. Lots of assignments. So what happened to the shop?"

"Oh well," said Randy. "Right after you left, I hired Jewel, and she immediately realized we could do something else. We sold the shop and started our own public relations firm. We do all kinds of promotional work for great causes."

"And some paying customers," Jewel interjected.

"See, she keeps me in line," said Randy, linking his arm through his wife's, who was now eyeing Tina with hungry eyes.

"You work for the *Gazette*?" Jewel asked. "Because we have some clients in Weston."

Randy shook his head, but he was smiling. "See, Jewel is always working the angles." He reached into his pocket and pulled out a leather wallet with RC embossed on the side. "Here's our card."

Tina looked at the writing: "Red Ink Public Relations: Better Read than Dead."

Turns out Jewel's first husband turned out to be a real schmuck and left her virtually nothing in the divorce so she started working for Randy. She was soon encouraging Randy to parlay his contacts in Hollywood and on Broadway into a full-service promotional business, far beyond the flyers and annual reports he had been printing. "Randy is really a genius at promotion," said Jewel. "He just needed a push in the right direction." Selling the shop gave them the stakes for a new business, she explained rapid-fire, which they now ran out of their co-op.

"We just had a meeting with a new client, hence the monkey suit," Randy said.

"It was a great meeting. I keep telling him how impressive he looks now that he's cut his hair and beard," Jewel said. "We nailed it."

"I can't wait to get out of this tie," said Randy. "Hey, do you want to get a drink with us?"

His wife tugged at his arm.

"Oh, yeah, I forgot, we're meeting your mother. Another time."

"Another time," said Jewel. "I'd love to hear about your newspaper work. Do you have a card?"

"Another time," said Tina, handing over her card.

"See," said Randy, happily. "She keeps me in line."

A few hours later, Tina was sitting in a bar on the West Side waiting for her friends and inwardly conversing with some new friends, Cyndi, Roseanne, and another Tina.

"I'll have a Sea Breeze," Tina said.

"Give me a Jim Beam on the rocks," said Roseanne, stifling a belch.

The other Tina narrowed her eyes at Roseanne, shook her head, and pursed her lips. "I'll pass," she growled and crossed her long legs giving a quick tug at her leather skirt.

Cyndi wrinkled her nose. "I want something with a tiny umbrella in it," she said. "Something not too sweet, not too bitter." She fluttered her eyes at the bartender who seemed dazzled by the mane of shaggy hair and the Kewpie-doll lips.

"Whaddya recommend? What's a fun drink with a kick?"

"I dunno," he stammered.

"Singapore Sling. Yeah, that will do it," Cyndi said. "I can handle that."

She turned to Roseanne who was rolling her eyes. "Don't be such a downer," Cyndi trilled.

"Come on," Roseanne said. "I need a stiff one and that seems like a sissy drink. And Sea Breeze? What the hell is a Sea Breeze?"

"Well," said Tina. "There's vodka, cranberry juice and grapefruit juice, so it's kind of a diet drink."

"Oh, honey, you don't really believe that, do you?" the other Tina said. "Sounds like one of the lines Ike would try out on me."

Roseanne snorted. "If I drink ten of those, I could be a skinny alcoholic. Hey, what are you looking at?"

She was glaring at a couple of young men, in tight jeans, staring at the other Tina and Cyndi, who was peeking at herself in a small compact mirror.

"Are you, are you really…" one of them started to say.

"In da flesh," said Cyndi, shaking an arm jingling with bangles. "Now, beat it guys, I'm here with my gals." She ran a hand through her mane, jumpstarting it to grow a couple inches. "Go on now, shoo, find another private dancer," said the other Tina with an imperious wave.

"Where are those drinks?" Roseanne called out.

Tina happily regarded her forearms, imagining them wrapped with leather, lace and bracelets studded with silver and rhinestones. It was warm in the bar so she draped her leather jacket over her shoulders and stretched her legs, the spiked heels of her shoes reaching to the next stool. She decided her face needed some attention and pulled out her Clinique makeup bag. With the generosity if not the dexterity of Nefertiti, she made ebony strokes above and below her eyes, extending the top line up like a parenthesis. She applied Spectacular Sunset Gloss generously to her mouth.

The bartender set two glasses, both with a rosy color in front of them. "Hey, where's my umbrella?" Cyndi asked. "Ya promised me an umbrella."

The barkeeper returned with a small umbrella and a short glass with amber liquid and ice cubes.

"Cheers," said Tina.

"Chin, chin," said Roseanne and downed her glass in a gulp.

"To happy times," said Cyndi, waving her glass in the air. "To happy things, time after time."

Tina sipped her drink, her tongue searching for the vodka in the sugary juice, her lip gloss leaving a rosy smudge on the rim. The vodka seemed to be hiding in the tart sweetness, but the hint of alcohol was leaving a glow of power and contentment. She thought she would order a different drink for the next round. Maybe a vodka martini. Something not so sweet.

"Well, wouldja look at what the cat dragged in," said Roseanne. "Look who's slumming."

"My, my, my," said Cyndi. "My evil twin."

"Maybe we could, like, accidentally spill a drink on her. Mess up that fine Versace outfit," said the other Tina.

"Oh, she's all right," said Cyndi. "She can't help it; she always was a pushy bitch. She just does what works."

"Well, I'm a domestic goddess, and you won't see me getting all uptown and prissy," said Roseanne. "Well, well, the queen of all things deigns to talk to her subjects. Hiya Maddie, you desperately seeking something here?"

The girl with the streaky blonde hair and rhinestone boots walked up to the four women, hopeful and defiant.

"Hey girls, what are you drinking?"

"Cyndi is on her second Singapore Sling. Maybe you'd like a Shanghai Surprise," Roseanne said nastily, as Cyndi aimed an elbow at her side."

"Ya looking good," said Cyndi.

"Thanks," said the girl. "I have this new personal trainer."

"I got a personal trainer, too," said Roseanne. "We work out horizontally."

The girl shifted from one rhinestone heel to another. Tina felt a pang of guilt. Maybe Madonna didn't hang out downtown anymore but things hadn't gone well for her lately. Maybe the drink was making her generous or maybe she just had really liked the last album, but she thought Madonna needed cheering up.

"Why don't you join us?" Tina asked, and Madonna brightened. "I would like a gin and tonic with lime," she said primly. "To us, girls."

Cyndi pulled out her compact to add another layer of lipstick. Tina realized she hadn't checked the mirror closely this morning. Nor yesterday. Or the day before. There had been no sightings of Nubbies or Pimplets. When was the last time she had a Sweat Bomb? As long as she was sure to clean her face after running, she seemed to have entered a post-pimple era, her mother's words finally coming true. She would have to tell her that on their weekly call.

Her mom always asked about Tommy. Would they get back together? Then about the cats, and then about her work. "Tommy made you happy, didn't he?" she asked. The remark stung her. Maureen was the one to hire her based on her unusual clips. Elektra showed her what fearlessness looked like, and Sarah taught her to run. And when she had been too scared, too guilt-ridden, to confront Rick, they stood behind her and forced her to go downstairs. With the thought of Rick, her hand went to her chin as if to hide a blemish that had erupted with sizzling speed.

"Whatja doing hiding your face?" said Cyndi, setting her glass down.

"Probably something to do with a guy," said Roseanne, burping.

"I just thought about Rick," said Tina.

"He was a bad boy," said Madonna. "I like bad boys."

"And they like you," said Cyndi. Her high voice dropped an octave. "In some ways, Tina, you and Rick are alike."

"Me? You're kidding," said Tina.

"Yeah, you, baby. You both are jealous types, kiddo. But you turn your feelings inward. When Greg and you broke up, you stopped eating, you went numb. Rick took rejection and pushed it outward. He dumped you for Angie, but then he couldn't handle it when you dumped him. Especially after Angie's treatment. He can't handle rejection from women."

"A punch in the face from another guy, however, that he can handle," said Roseanne.

"Guys lash out," said the other Tina. "Women take it on the chin and blame themselves. I sure know this."

"Come on, Tina," said Madonna. "You were even jealous when you thought your cat Mindy dumped you for the new cat Sheena. And then they gave you exactly what you wanted, their undivided love. That made you strong. Besides, aren't you glad you never really got involved with Rick? And aren't you glad you're rid of Greg?"

Tina hadn't thought about her college boyfriend Greg in a while; it was even hard to picture his face. Yet she still remembered the pain of that last phone call, the sudden twists that life can take, the right turn when you were expecting to go left.

"Now, you have given Tommy something to be jealous about," Cyndi said softly. "You hurt him. What will you do about that?"

Tina started to reply when Elektra interrupted. "We're here, we're here. Oh, you got started already. Is that a martini?"

Tina tried to focus on Elektra. She had been so deep into

her imagination that it took a few seconds to realize that it was Elektra, not Cyndi Lauper, settling herself on a barstool and Maureen, not Tina Turner, attempting to get the bartender's attention.

Elektra leaned against the bar and called out, "What's a girl have to do to get a drink around here," rattling her shopping bag.

"How are you?" asked Maureen, thinking Tina was really wearing a lot of eyeliner even though she looked happier than she had been since the Tommy breakup.

"Fine," Tina said. "Just thinking about the assignment. You know," as Elektra looked puzzled, "The new female archetypes, what popular images of women are telling us today. I was imagining hanging out with Cyndi Lauper, Tina Turner, and Madonna."

"Female whatitshoosie?" said Elektra. "Hey, love what you did with your eyes. Did you use a Magic Marker? I think we should order some French fries. I'm starving. Tina, you wouldn't believe what we found at the consignment store. Show her, Maureen. And look at the snake ring with the rhinestone eyes. I got it for Sarah. It's like something out of that weird story she's always talking about."

"Hello, gals," came a familiar voice and there was Cheryl standing beside them, teetering on heels and clutching the arm of a balding man in a rumpled suit, a tie poking out of his pocket. Tina hadn't seen her since the book club had disbanded. How many years ago was that? "We just stopped by for a drink and there you are. I would like you to meet my husband, Roger. Roger, these are the gals from the book club."

"Nice to meet you," said Roger, his eyes passing quickly over the women as if they were on a subway platform and he was in the train rushing by.

"Roger," said Cheryl, her voice pitching up to the notch

she used when showing an East Side co-op with a doorman, parking, and a frantic seller. "These are the gals with the cats."

Roger suddenly focused on the women. "Oh right."

"You see," Cheryl said, her tone even more bright. "We now have a cat."

"Rufus," said Roger.

"Diane – you remember Diane from the book club – found him hanging around her house and we took him in. He really took a shine to Roger."

"Really did. Smartest damn cat you've ever seen," said Roger.

"You just can't believe what a darling he is," said Cheryl.

"He's the man of the house now," said Roger.

"You would not believe how adorable he is."

Maureen said, "Oh, we can, we really can."

"He's smarter than a lot of people we know," said Roger.

"Oh, Roger," said Cheryl.

"I believe it," said Elektra.

"We might even get him a little brother," said Roger. "He would be a good influence."

"Be careful what you wish for," said Tina. "Remember, cats abhor a vacuum."

"So how is Diane?" Elektra asked. "Is she happy with married life?"

Roger let out a huge guffaw as Cheryl pulled his arm. "Well, Diane is single again. Her husband found out about her and her personal trainer, and that was that."

"I'm sorry to hear that," said Elektra who did not sound at all sorry. "Maybe she should try cats."

Roger guffawed again.

After a few more pleasantries and cat talk, Roger and Cheryl went off to meet another couple. Soon, the women were talking about the uproar over *The Satanic Verses*. Tina said she tried to read it but found it really boring. Elektra said she didn't understand why people got all riled up over a novel. In Midtown, Sarah was editing copy from bureaus in Dallas, Boston, and Beijing, hoping she would make it out in time to meet her friends and get a drink. She was trying not to think about Cole. She would not call him. She would not. Not today.

CHAPTER
THIRTY-FOUR

The Last Day

S<small>ARAH MUST HAVE</small> left the door open just for a second.

"Carrie," she called. "Carrrrrieeee." There, yes, a flash of black and gold, sprinting through the hallway. There she was. But no, it was the rug, just a black and gold rug that was bunched up in a lump.

"Carrie!" She sprinted through the apartment into rooms she rarely visited. She ran through a doorway, into another room that linked to the other apartments and then outside. She reached the edge of a cliff.

"Carrie," she screamed, peering down. Wait. Was that a spot of black and gold? At the bottom? She had to get down. Cats could survive long falls. She had to get down there. Carrie was hurt. But here was Cole, walking toward her. He had come back. He was carrying a small, limp body in his arms, and he was laughing.

Sarah opened her eyes and sat up. She called out and Carrington jumped beside her. She reached the right spot behind the ears, and scratched, letting the dream recede like the tide, images breaking up and being carried away bit by bit. She turned to look at her alarm clock, blinking 11:05. Her shift started at three. She slid back on the pillows, pulling Carrington on top of her.

At one o'clock, she lurched to her feet and stumbled to the kitchen; the empty glass and the empty wine bottle were sideways on the counter. She poured out cat food, managing to get most of it in the dish as Carrington wove around her feet. Was there water in the bowl? It was hot today, maybe she should leave out two bowls. Or was it cold? It was summer in the dream; was it summer now? Coffee must be made. She measured out the scoops, one, two, then water, then flipped the switch on Mr. Coffee. She held onto the counter willing the machine to hurry. She drank the coffee hot. She poured out more into the mug, the heat and aroma cutting through the fog, fog like the little thief found in the cave. A mist, a steam, a vapor that spiraled around her legs and her hand holding the small sword and her hand resting on the silken side of the unicorn. She had to go through the cave. She had to save her friends. She couldn't see anything, no monsters, no soldiers, but fear was hissing around her. She set the mug in the sink. She needed to buy dish soap. The dishes were piling up. The figurines on her shelves needed dusting. She could not remember Mexico anymore.

Her body now felt lighter. She ran a shower as scalding as she could stand. She could do this. Maureen said she could do this, Maureen was always strong. But the look on Maureen's face when Sarah wept. The look on Cole's face when she asked him to stay away, as if it were nothing. As if she were nothing.

Cole is not worth this, Maureen had said. He is not worth it. Sarah had no words to explain how she was walking through a landscape of scorched earth and into a cave filled with shadows. He's not worth it. But I needed him to come back. He's not worth it. I needed him to call. He is not worth it. I'm not worth it. I am not worth it.

She had to get to work. She would be late now; she would have to slink in like a wet rat. "Carrington, would you love a rat?" she asked out loud as Carrington licked her paws.

She looked like a rat in the mirror, ragged hair wet from the shower, dark circles under her eyes. One of her cowboy lovers in Texas said to her, seemingly tenderly, sweetly. "You have such sad eyes." He paused and added, "That bothers me." She stared into her eyes in the mirror, seeing no sadness, no pain. Nothing.

The sky was gray outside, drizzle pricked her face. The sky was gray like the skies over Katunna; there was always a drizzle, a musty, damp smell in the streets. The people had gray skin, dull and opaque. The thief had a complexion like burnt wood, but her skin was dull, her hair matted, tangled and grimy with the mud she used to keep vermin at bay.

She was really late. How did that happen? She started her car with trembling hands, drove and parked in the garage, down in the lowest level, where she finally found a space. Her boots thudded on the cement as she headed for the stairs and the long climb to the train platform. It was really cold here, cold like the dungeons of Kazill, where the true king was imprisoned. No one cares about unicorns and dragons, Cole said. No one reads that fantasy crap. Tolkien was popular back in the 1960s with the hippies. Why are you wasting your time trying to write that stuff?

She had thought she was strong. She had held off calling him. First week, second week, third week. Then a month. Then another. "Not today," she would tell herself. "Not this week." She was strong; she could do this. She was with the unicorn, fighting together in the cave, slashing the thick, dark, air, and the horrible visions of fear and ugliness. Strength coursed through her every time she reached out and felt the silky warm skin of the unicorn beside her.

She had been strong for months. Last night she had given in. She had called Cole. Was it the three glasses of wine, the false strength that said she was over this? That she was over him? She just wanted to say hello. She dialed the number, quickly, foolishly, rashly. Just a short hi. Just to see how he was doing. To her surprise, he picked up. And now she had to get to work.

The train was five minutes late, and inside the car, Sarah leaned her forehead against the window, closing her eyes. As she rushed through Grand Central Station, people bumped into her. She had faded. She wasn't really there. She walked toward the AP offices in Rockefeller Center; the fine drizzle beading on her face. When she sat at her desk, she glanced at the row of clocks with time around the world. She was about fifteen minutes late. She logged into the computer and bent over the keyboard. The room was spinning just a bit. "How are you doing?" She looked up to see Alex standing nearby but not too close. She looked into Alex's face. Could she actually be concerned? "Yes, fine, just got a late start. Sorry."

"Well, Peter was asking, and I told him you would be here momentarily."

"I'll catch up," Sarah said, turning to the computer. Alex remained standing there.

"I was certain you would come in any minute because you're not usually this late, just usually ten minutes behind me."

"I know," said Sarah.

"I like to get into place before Peter shows up."

"That's always a good idea," Sarah said.

"Yes, exactly," said Alex with pep. "Because you don't know what will happen. Seriously, is everything all right?"

Sarah looked up, now annoyed, and saw Alex looking at her hands on the keyboard. Was she trembling?

"I'm just fine. Tired, a bit."

"I'm totally exhausted," said Alex. "You weren't here last night when the crackdown began on the Tiananmen Square protesters. I didn't get out until two in the morning. You were lucky you missed that."

Sarah thought about that. Lucky? She liked the nights when major news broke, when Alex, Peter and all of the staff were locked to their computers or on the phone to stringers around the globe.

"You guys did fine, I think. Good coverage," said Sarah, with a stab of pleasure because she was able to say something nice to Alex who was staring at her. Was Alex's face worried? Gleeful? Smug?

When Alex didn't say anything but just kept looking at her, Sarah spoke again, "I'm sorry I missed the excitement. I'm sorry you had to handle it. I wish I could work a bit more efficiently. It's just so hard sometimes. All the time." And stopped, seeing puzzlement, concern, disdain spread across Alex's face.

"Let's talk later," Alex said, turning away.

Sarah felt a rise of anger. What was she supposed to say? What did Alex want? Had she screwed up again? She was always messing up. She seethed, now, against Alex, against Cole. What a bitch. What a loser. What a jerk.

After an hour, she felt a little better. She was into the work, the editing, the copy flow. She could do this. Her fingers had trouble connecting to the keys, but she stared at the screen and realized there was more to do. Wonderful! She could stay busy. She looked at the copy from the Boston bureau, and there was a mistake in the lead. Right in the first paragraph! Should be effect, not affect. Yes, she could fix that, she would change it and she knew the writer, knew the writer would thank her, not like some of the other prima donnas here. Would thank her, like Elektra who always thanked her. Like Maureen, who always said what she thought, not like Alex, not like the others in the office, with their needling, nudges and jockeying for position.

Cole said she was too sensitive. He never doubted himself. He never worried about what other people thought. He was a mountain – a range of mountains. Her body was crying out for that mountain, that bulk, that reassurance, and the tenderness of his touch on her breast and his lips on the soft of her belly. He wanted her but he didn't want her. She was too sensitive. She was wrong. She didn't please him. She was ugly, she was too moody, she was wrong, wrong, wrong.

"What is wrong?" The Boston writer was on the phone.

"Sorry, I think you meant effect, the noun, not affect the verb."

"Oh, shit," came the voice and Sarah heard the sudden anxiety. A mistake for the venerable AP. "I fixed it," she said, her voice neutral, professional.

"Thanks for the catch," came the voice. Sarah hung up vindicated, happy. She was good at her job. She could do this; she could.

At midnight, Sarah said hi to the overnight shift and walked to the train station. The rain was coming down in torrents. It sluiced down the window as she leaned her forehead against the glass. Everything outside was under water, faintly glowing amid a dark murk.

She got off the train and walked into the garage along with a few solitary passengers, heels thudding on the concrete. She didn't bother to avoid the puddles. She got into her car, the shelter momentarily reassuring. Driving home, Sarah skidded a bit, slammed on her brakes, and stopped before hitting the car in front. She had a curious sense of disappointment. What was she going home for? Cole will never be back.

When she called him last night, he did not seem surprised to hear from her; his tone was oddly lighthearted.

"So how are you?" she asked. And he told her his news, something she never expected to hear him say. She could barely speak, but she managed to cough out, "When did this happen?"

"Oh sometime after you told me to stay away." His voice was gleeful.

"That's pretty sudden."

"Things just happen."

"I wish you joy," she said, calmly, in a voice that was not hers and hung up and fell with the landslide, the momentum carrying her down the mountain to the bottle to pour another glass and another glass until the rocks and debris slowed down at the base of the mountain where she could weep. She had such sad eyes. "Shut up," she yelped at the lover whose name she didn't even remember. "Shut up about my eyes."

She had found him, found the lover whom she adored with heart and soul, and she was not enough for him. Eyes, face, breasts, stomach, legs, thighs. She must not be put together right. How could she see the full moon, glowing like pale ivory when she climaxed, and Cole could feel only a spurt of relief? How could he be so far inside her that there was no space, no room between them and not love her? He was a stranger at the other end of the bridge she was trying to cross. Did he like her better when she was glimpsed at a distance? Her eyes were too sad up close.

She couldn't go home, not yet. She aimlessly wove through Stamford's quiet streets toward Merritt Parkway. She took a right on the ramp and headed north. The bridges were ghostly outlines quickly illuminated by her headlines and then lost in shadow. The windshield wipers kept up a steady dirge. She drove on and on, keeping her mind blank. She could do this. She took an exit after New Haven and pulled over to the side. The sky was lighter now, the color of charcoal dust. The rain had eased to a misting. She turned the car around and got back on the parkway, heading south. In the dim light, she could see the more details of the bridges, the cathedral, the castle, and the eagle with its wings pointed skyward. She pressed the gas pedal. She was close to her exit and she was driving fast on pavement that had turned to slick glass. She could feel the pull of a skid. Was something happening? Was she slaying the monster in the cave? She could do this, she could pass over. She was going to get away. She would reach Arianna and lead its people to glory and there she would be recognized. She was the lost daughter of the true King, the scion of the prophecy. She was the savior in the old song. She would be loved, she would be adored. The car was floating now. She would let it go, fall into the darkness, feel the pain, and it would be over.

There was something in the dark, a small face, with lovely, golden eyes. And the eyes were filled with love and there was purring, come home to me, come home, don't leave me, don't leave. "I love you, Carrington," Sarah said. And turned the wheel slightly and hit the buttress broadside, not head on.

As the world went dark, she was running, calling, "Carrie, Carrie, Carrie. Come here. Come back."

CHAPTER
THIRTY-FIVE

Two Phone Calls
June 1989

THE NURSE WAS definitely not happy to see a cat on Sarah's bed when she came in to say visiting hours were over. Maureen calmly said they were just leaving and that they were only following a suggestion from Sarah's therapist, who by the way, would be featured as an exemplary health worker in a future story in the *Gazette*. Elektra scooped up Carrington and sprinted off with Tina as Maureen gave the nurse her card. Back at Studio 54, Elektra deposited a hissing Carrington in Sarah's apartment where the cat promptly went under the bed. Tina put down fresh water and opened a can of cat food. When they walked into Maureen's apartment, she was on the phone with Sarah's mother; Tina could hear Maureen's firm voice telling her Sarah was stable. She asked Mrs. Gold to call as soon as possible if the hospital contacted her about any change in Sarah's condition.

"Got any chamomile?" Elektra asked. She had taken up an herbal tea regime and put water on to boil. Maureen and Tina slumped on the couch. Tina thought the room seemed off-balance without the four of them. Tina hoped Maureen would start talking. Maureen, the planner, the organizer, and the editor of reality. Elektra brought out mugs and tea bags and poured the hot water. Tina watched as Maureen dunked her tea bag twice, three times, in her cup, pinched it between her thumb and finger and deftly deposited it in a saucer. Tina watched her own tea water darken. Hercules quietly rested at

Maureen's feet. They drank the tea in silence.

Then Maureen did what Maureen always did. She took action. Tina and Elektra just watched. Maureen dialed 411 and got Cole's number. She dialed the phone and put on her editor's voice.

"Hi, Cole, this is Maureen? Have you heard? Sarah was in a car accident. She was hurt badly. I know you're sorry she's hurt. Well, it would be nice if you could see her. Yes, I know you guys broke up but maybe you could send flowers or something. No? Why not? What? What do you mean? When did this happen? Did you tell Sarah? When? She called you out of the blue? Was she upset when you told her? No? Are you sure? Okay, okay. Bye. Uh. Congrats."

Maureen slammed down the receiver. "Cole is married again."

"What? When?" Tina shouted.

Elektra shrieked, "That son of a bitch."

"Last month."

Tina cried out, "But they just broke up. He told Sarah he was never getting married again. And he's married?"

"Calm down, El," said Maureen as Elektra continued to rant. "That son of a bitch, that son of a bitch."

"Did she find out? Why didn't she tell us?" Tina asked, trying to calm down.

"Apparently she called him the day before the accident. God knows why she did that. Maybe this is just a coincidence."

"He's a son of a bitch but I know she will get better," said Elektra. "She's a good person. He's a loser. Hey, do you have anything to eat here?"

Maureen dug out celery and a box of cookies stashed on a top shelf. Tina felt a pain of hunger, she had not really eaten since she heard about Sarah. Still cursing Cole, they dug in, Elektra remarking that the celery canceled out the chocolate chips. Maureen had a cookie in her hand and a celery stalk in the other when the phone rang. She dropped both and picked up the receiver.

"Hello," she said calmly. And then fell silent, so silent, that a chill spread from Tina's heart to the tips of her fingers. If Maureen, her editor, her mentor, her friend, panicked, Tina would fall apart. But Maureen's face was stone.

"Thanks for letting us know," Maureen. She slowly hung up the phone and turned toward the other women.

"That was Mrs. Gold. Sarah is awake."

CHAPTER
THIRTY-SIX

The Funeral in the Pretty Place
August 1989

ELEKTRA'S SENSE OF drama carried her forward after the death. For the funeral, she had dragged out a floor-length black evening gown, dark sunglasses, and a wide-brimmed black floppy hat. Sobs broke from her in waves, and she maintained a monologue of lamentation.

Tina kept her arm around her. Maureen held her hand. Both were uttering reassuring words. "I'm so glad you're here," Elektra sobbed. "I couldn't do this without you."

"I know," said Tina, who despite her private vows to stay calm, was tearing up. "I know."

"I did everything I could," Elektra cried.

"We know, we know. You did everything you could. You were the best," Maureen said.

"You stayed right up to the end," Tina said.

"I went out for just a little while and he was gone."

"Look," said Tina. "Here's Sarah."

Sarah was getting out of Tommy's car. She moved slowly and stiffly, but she was walking on her own now. She had told the others she didn't remember much about what had happened; she had been driving; then she was running along a long road that never seemed to end, chasing something with golden fur. Her concussion was treated, her cuts and bruises began to heal, and she was released from the hospital. An accident in the rain, the police concluded. People said she was lucky to survive. Her car was totaled. She was seeing a therapist who prescribed Prozac and made her promise not to drink.

Sarah limped to the group and put her arms around Elektra. "I am so sorry about Eddie."

"He was such a good boy," Elektra sobbed. "He was my good boy."

"I know."

"I stayed with him night and day. I wanted to tell him I loved him. I was just waiting for the right moment to take him to the vet."

"He knew that," Sarah said. "He loved you so much. He couldn't leave while you were there. He did this for you."

Elektra sobbed into her hands.

Tina could see Maureen was rolling her eyes even as she hugged Elektra. And yes, Elektra was, as usual, over the top. But Tina was feeling guilty that she was inwardly so glad Sheena and Mindy were home safe. She realized with sudden clarity the futility of her two-cat backup plan. You can't escape this moment, she thought. We all must face that time of separation when you have to let go.

She looked at Tommy. "Thanks so much for coming."

"You guys go on. I'll keep watch," Tommy said, his eyes on Tina. Then he turned away.

Tina and Maureen grabbed the bags of trowels and rocks. Elektra hugged the body, wrapped in cloth, to her chest and the group set off with Sarah's arm around Elektra.

Elektra had picked the spot in the cemetery. It was the children's section, nestled against the wetlands that bordered the cemetery, shaded by a tangle of maple trees. There were no large tombstones, only little markers. Tina was pretty sure that they weren't allowed to bury pets in here, but Elektra wanted Eddie to be in a pretty spot. Maureen, surprisingly, agreed, and with the cunning of a general, planned the action. They would move in late in the day when it was almost twilight. No large shovels – that would look too obvious. Instead, they would use trowels to dig quickly.

When Maureen went over the plan earlier that day, Tina thought she had never seen a woman so beautiful. She wished John could see and appreciate Maureen's spirit, but John, as Maureen explained with nonchalance, was freaking out over his new job and would be no help at all. Someone would have to act as lookout. John was useless, Sam was working that day, and William said he didn't want to get arrested for what he called "meowfeasance."

"I can ask Tommy," said Tina, slowly as the others nodded. She went to her apartment to call and was leaving a message but Tommy picked up. "Hello, Tina."

"Hi, Tommy. Sorry to bother you, but I wanted to ask a favor for Elektra. It's about her cat, Eddie. Eddie died."

"Ah. Seldom-seen Eddie," said Tommy. "Are you sure?"

"Yes, of course." Tina smiled, despite her nerves.

"Why do you need a favor from me?"

Tina explained the plan. "We need a lookout."

"And you can't get your friend Rick to help?"

Tina almost hung up then, but thought of Elektra.

"I think you've taken care of that. Courtesy of your right hook."

Tommy actually laughed. It was a kind of snort, but it was a laugh. Tina took that as a good sign and rushed on.

"I really am sorry to bother you. I thought you might want to do this for Elektra, she's got her heart set on this," Tina said rapidly. "Maybe in memory of Ratso. And I would really appreciate it. I really…"

Tina wanted to say, "I really miss you." But she couldn't get it out.

"Okay," Tommy replied. "Tell me what to do."

"First, could you pick up Sarah?"

So with Tommy as driver and lookout, the plan was set.

Once in the cemetery, the group walked slowly, both for Sarah and so as not to arouse suspicion. Although, Tina thought, Elektra's spectral black skirt might cause a passerby to think she had sprung from a grave. When they arrived at the spot Elektra picked, Maureen issued commands as if she were on the news desk.

"Put on the gloves," said Maureen. "Now dig." Elektra knelt on the ground in her long skirt, Tina and Sarah beside her, thrusting trowels into the damp ground. Maureen pulled out clumps of grass and scooped out the loosened soil. In a short time they dug an oval hole about a foot wide and three feet deep. Tina looked at it with a sense of comfort, the small size seemed so right for a cat.

"That's good," said Maureen, standing up and taking off her gloves. They all looked at Elektra. Elektra, sniffling, started to unwrap her bundle.

"I want him to lay on the ground. I want him to be in the earth," she said. She gently laid a black and white cat, stiffened into a curled position into the hole. Tina caught Maureen's eye, knowing she was thinking, "So that's what he looks like." Elektra dropped in a toy mouse and sprinkled catnip over the body.

"Oh, my poor Eddie." Elektra was starting to cry again. Maureen reached down and grabbed a handful of dirt and waited. Elektra gave a heaving sigh. She leaned over and with both hands scooped up a mound of earth and let it trickle slowly into the small grave, covering Eddie like a dark blanket. Tina followed with another handful. Then Sarah and finally Maureen. When the small grave was filled, Maureen gathered the trowels and scattered rocks, sticks, leaves and dry grass on the grave until it blended into the rest of the ground. They all took off their gloves.

"Last words?" Maureen asked, reaching for Elektra's hand. Tina held the other. Sarah took Tina's hand.

"He was such a good boy," Elektra began.

"Heads up," Tommy shouted. The women looked over and saw what looked like two groundskeepers in the distance. Tommy waved and he started walking toward the men.

"Plan B," Maureen shouted, tossing the bag with the trowels and gloves over her shoulder. They scattered; Maureen ran with Elektra who almost tripped on her skirt as she dashed into the trees. Tina and Sarah sprinted along a stone fence that marked the edge of the cemetery.

Sarah was stiff, but adrenaline and laughter loosened her joints like a jolt of oil. "Oh God," she gasped as Tina, close to hysteria, pulled her behind a bush.

"We could be charged with kitty littering," Tina gulped.

"A feline infraction!" Sarah managed before they both dissolved in hysterics.

They huddled behind the bush, trying to stifle fits of giggles, then stealthily made their way out of the cemetery.

The plan worked. Tommy had distracted the groundskeeper by asking about where his great-grandfather Thomas O'Donnell might be buried while the women piled into Maureen's car. The women and Tommy reconnected at Bobby V's. Sam joined them and then John; he gave a remarkably moving speech about love. He now had a job as a speechwriter for the CEO of a major bank. Elektra was exuberant about how the funeral was pulled off. Tina said she had never seen such a moving service. They ate an order of nachos, drank margaritas, and made toasts: To Eddie, to Ratso, to Dougie, and to all the cats, dogs and pets of their past.

"So," said Maureen. "Now that we're here. I have an announcement." She took a deep breath. "I've been offered a job on the news desk at the *New York Times*."

After so many years of sending query letters and networking at conferences, the hire came surprisingly quickly. Leticia

A. Frank, yes, Morticia herself, who reviewed theater for subur-ban editions of the *Times*, had told an editor that if the Times wanted the best in the business, they should hire Maureen. Maureen had an interview, a tryout and now she was going to start in three weeks. She had already called Cheryl about find-ing her an apartment on the West Side.

Tina was stunned. Maureen was leaving the *Gazette*! Was this the true unfolding of the origami?

Sarah took a gulp of her club soda as Maureen said, "We can get that apartment in the city now." Sarah gently shook her head. She had finagled a leave of absence from the AP but did not plan to go back; she wasn't even sure she would stay in Connecticut.

"This is what you wanted," Sarah said. "You should be proud of yourself."

"I always told her she was a fucking awesome, kick-ass editor," said John.

"Omigawd," said Elektra. "Omigawd."

Apparently sensing confusion at the table, Maureen raised her empty margarita glass and spoke louder. "What you should know is that I, ahem, strongly recommended that while Wil-liam will likely move up to features editor, Tina should be pro-moted to his assistant, and Elektra should be hired full time."

"Well, isn't that a pisser," said Elektra.

"Wow," said Tina, thinking of the raise.

"Another round," Elektra declared as Sam said, "Hear, hear."

John raised his mug of beer. "Don't let the bastards get you down," he said.

When the none-too-sober group broke up, Maureen and John walked Sarah to Maureen's car. Sam and Elektra man-aged to slip away before Tina could ask for a ride. She was left with Tommy to drive her to Studio 54. When he pulled up to the front door, he turned off the engine.

"Thank you so much," said Tina. "That was so nice of you. I appreciate it so much."

Tommy stared straight ahead.

"You know Mindy and Sheena miss you," Tina said.

Tommy turned to look at her.

"Would you like to come up and say hello? They would love that." Tina said. "Please?"

"Okay," said Tommy. "Guess I could stand to step in some cat puke again."

Maureen made John sit in the back of the car as they drove to Studio 54 and parked in the back alley. "Are you okay?" Maureen asked Sarah as she and John accompanied Sarah to her apartment.

"Yes, for the hundredth time, yes."

"Sleep well."

"You too."

Sarah walked inside and sat down at her kitchen table. Without warning, despair flooded her, a molten gush of bleakness. She thought of her friends, all with their partners. Why didn't Cole want to be a part of this? He never loved her. She was ugly. She was useless. Her career was going nowhere. She was bruised, battered and beaten. It wasn't just Cole. She deserved it for the stupid things she had done.

I will lie down, she thought. Carrington was curled on her side on the bed and shifted when Sarah lay next to her, stretching out her forepaws and inviting Sarah to stroke her. Sarah told Maureen that she didn't care Cole hadn't called after the accident. It was a lie; she still cared. And yet Cole's image did seem to be fading, his formidable self-confidence receding into blind arrogance as if he had turned from a reassuring Reagan to a bumbling George Bush.

Sarah ran her fingers through the soft hair on Carrie's belly. She scratched behind her ears, causing Carrington to tilt her head in pleasure and smile her cat smile.

"I love you," Sarah said, thinking of Eddie, asleep in the ground, and Maureen's determination to stage the funeral. "I love you," she said, thinking of the sound of Tina's choking laughter and Elektra's restored spirits.

She would not be selfish. She would not give in to the seductive pull of the skid. She whispered in her cat's ear, "I will not leave you." In just a few months, a new decade would arrive and maybe that would be a chance to start over. She maneuvered her body around Carrington and rested her head on a pillow, one hand entwined in cat fur. She closed her eyes. Carrington purred. Sarah breathed deeply. She let her thoughts drift, letting go of pointless despair. Soon she was asleep and lost, lost in cat dreaming.

Book Club Questions for Cat Dreaming

1. What do you think "Cat Dreaming" is?

2. Have you ever had an animal companion that was more like a friend than a pet? Do you think cats and dogs can read our minds?

3. Which character do you relate to most: Maureen, Sarah, Tina, or Elektra?

4. If you could experience the 1980s or go back and relive that decade, would you do so? If so, why?

5. Do you think women's lives are much different now than they were in the 1980s?

6. The characters in *Cat Dreaming* worked in a media world that had yet to be transformed by digital technology. Do you think that reading something on paper is a different experience than reading the same content on a screen?

7. In *Cat Dreaming*, the idea of two women marrying was inconceivable to Maureen. What major social changes have you witnessed in your lifetime?

8. What is the significance of Jane Austen's Pride and *Prejudice* to the plot? What is the role of *Tess of the D'Urbervilles* and *The House of Mirth*?

9. What is your favorite dance song from the 1980s? Finish your book discussion by playing it on your mobile phone and everybody dance.

Acknowledgements

First and foremost I have to thank Steve Eisner of When Words Count in Vermont for his unshakeable faith in this work; that kept me going. I owe a huge debt of gratitude to my two writers' groups: the Medford Writing Group and Works in Progress. You guys are the best. I had tough, excellent editing from Carey Adams, many thanks. Also, great editing from Jean Collins. I am grateful for support and encouragement from Tamara Major, Kathy Howlett, Bev Ford, David Chia, Randy Ross, and Anne Stuart. I have to thank my mother, Florence Srmek Schorow, for copyediting this manuscript, including the sex scenes. Gratitude to Melissa Carrigee and Small Town Girl Publishing for taking a chance on a first novel. Thank you to Bernhard Editorial Services for helping to streamline my prose. Thank you to 187 Designs for the totally awesome cover. Everlasting love to my departed fur persons, Ember, Titan, Shino, and Mooshu, and my current fur boys Chadwick and Ginsburg.

About the author

Photo by Renee DeKona

Stephanie Schorow is a journalist, writing instructor, and the author of nine nonfiction books. She has worked as an editor and reporter for the *Boston Herald*, the Associated Press, and newspapers in Connecticut, Idaho and Utah. *Cat Dreaming* is her first novel.